Also by
NATALIE LLOYD

A Snicker of Magic

The Key to Extraordinary

Over the Moon

The Problim Children

Silverswift

HUMMINGBIRD

NATALIE LLOYD

SCHOLASTIC PRESS • NEW YORK

Library of Congress Cataloging-in-Publication Data available

ISBN 978-1-338-65458-5

10 9 8 7 6 5 4 3 2 1   22 23 24 25 26

Printed in Italy   183
First edition, August 2022

Book design by Christopher Stengel

For my uncle Johnny Cotton,
for teaching me how to find magic in books,
blank pages, and John Prine songs.
I love you with all my hobbit heart.

CHAPTER 1
Fragile as a Falling Star

The first thing I remember about that fateful morning is Uncle Dash swerving my family's van into the parking lot of New River Church.

That's our weekly tradition, mine and his. We get breakfast together, then ride to church and catch up on life. The tires screeched when Dash parked.

Late, as usual.

Dolly Parton was howling about "Jolene" on the cassette player, while I sang harmony. (Dolly Parton is my favorite person I've never met. Well, my second favorite. My first favorite is my future BFF!)

Everything felt the Sunday-same until Dash cut the engine.

And went still as a statue.

"Oh shoot," he said. His eyes went wide as quarters. "Oh Lord. We got a problem, Olive."

"What's up?" I asked, even though I had a theory as soon as I saw his pale face. "Listen to me," I said gently. "Breakfast tacos from Big John's are a bad idea before church. I tell you every week."

"It ain't the tacos," Uncle Dash said. His mouth barely moved around the words. He stared out into the crowded parking lot, steering wheel clutched in his tattooed fingers.

I looked straight ahead, too. But it looked the same as always to me: just a gravel-gray lot with an old stone church rising up ahead of us.

Blackbirds perched, shoulder to shoulder, in a long, inky line along the rooftop. Fluffy maples stood guard all around the lot. The trees were leafy-green again, blooms bursting out of twisty limbs. April had barely started, but summer was already close enough to send love notes across the mountain with its warm winds and scatters of wildflowers. Above it all was a sky the same color blue as my favorite skirt. The one I wore last year, on the first day of school. (I'm homeschooled, but I still believe in the power of a first-day outfit.)

That's back when everything was normal.

Back before I knew Hatch Malone existed.

(Aka the good old days. But I'm getting ahead of myself.)

All in all, it seemed like an ordinary day. But it wasn't. Beginnings are sneaky like this.

"I got the flutters, Olive," Uncle Dash said. His voice sounded all drifty and dreamy. "I think change is on the wind."

He'd barely spoken that last word when Luther Frye hobbled past the car wearing his best white shirt and overalls. Luther's pet ferret, Gustav, sat perched on his shoulder, tail fluffed around Luther's neck like a fine scarf. (That's nothing new or change-worthy. Gustav and Luther go everywhere together.)

"Do you want to talk about it?" I asked. I pushed the heart-shaped sunglasses up into my hair. I always wear a heart somewhere on my person. It's my signature symbol.

Uncle Dash used the edge of his necktie to wipe sweat off his forehead. "I thought it was acid reflux at first. But it's been getting worse all morning. Now it's like . . ." His cheeks inflated like a puffer fish. "Like my heart's too full. Something's up today. I'm plumb sick over it. I don't even know if we should go inside."

"Be honest with me, Uncle Dash." I tried to make my voice as gentle as my mama's. "Are you nervous because we're going to church?"

"Partly," he admitted. "You know I only go to church because the Goad wants me there."

To be clear, he said *the Goad*. Not *God*.

Uncle Dash doesn't think God cares if he goes to church or not. But my grandpa Merlin Goad, the most famous birder in the state of Tennessee, is a different story. Back when I was a baby, Dash left town and entered a season my family refers to as "the prodigal years." He came home tattooed, broke, and brokenhearted. Also, he lost his RV in a poker game. So he had nowhere to live.

Grandpa gave him his old room right back, on one condition: that he go to church. It'd help him ease back into the community, Grandpa said. Plus, it'd help Uncle Dash find some peace. Dash agreed to go even though he says church isn't a peaceful place for him. We all see church very differently in my family.

Grandpa likes church because he feels like it's a refuge place—it's the space where his heart finds rest and where it's safe to ask questions. Mama goes, too. But if you ask her why, she'll only say that she's searching. (Which sounds like a beautiful way to live, honestly. As if life is one big treasure hunt.) Mama's new husband, Coach Malone, goes with her because he loves her. And because he leads the choir. As for my dad, Jupiter, his only holy place is the great outdoors. He hikes on trails on Sundays. He says he doesn't like stained glass between him and the sky. And as for me, I attend church for three primary reasons:

1. Because I'm eleven and I don't have much of a choice.

2. Because there's not much else to do in Wildwood, Tennessee.

3. And most of all, because I've been asking
   God for the deepest dream and desire of my
   heart for months now. And if God's going to
   answer my prayer anywhere, I figure it's here
   in his holy house.

My prayer and wish and wildest hope is this: I want to attend Macklemore Middle School.

This dream may not make sense to you. But to be a student there is the deepest desire of my weary soul. Mama says I'm being very dramatic. But I know my heart better than anybody does. My heart aches to be a Macklemore Penguin.

Currently, I attend the School of Mom (aka homeschool). And it's great. Really! I get to help make my schedule and pick the books I want to read. Also, I get to hang out with Mama most days, and she's entirely swanky. But there are a couple of reasons it's time for me to go to Macklemore. I have a feeling that my future BFF is waiting for me there, for one.

Then there's the deep-down heart reason that matters heaps to me. Even if it's a little bit embarrassing to say aloud.

I've told God all about it, though—many, many times. Which is why I got a little excited about Uncle Dash's anxious flutters. He really does have a special sense about him, a way of knowing when change is on the way. And not all change is bad. Sometimes, change is wonderful.

"What if something changes for the good today?" I asked. "Maybe Mrs. Faye made jalapeño lemonade instead of plain. Maybe Gustav takes a running spell and the choir freaks out 'cause they think he's a rat."

"You think that'd be good?" he asked.

"It would be lively!"

Maybe I get to go to the school of my dreams, I thought.

Dash shook his head sadly. "Nah, I'm pretty sure it's something terrible. We might as well get it over with, though." He burst out of the van, both cowboy boots clonking down at the same time in the parking lot. Then he ambled around back so he could unload my wheelchair.

In case you're curious, I have two wheelchairs. They both have names: Dolly and Reba. Dolly's my sparkly, custom-fitted, go-to set of wheels. I hot-glued my name in rhinestones on the back. I maneuver Dolly's wheels myself, and gosh, I love the way she glides. Reba is motorized, with a maroon seat and shiny red rims that sparkle in the sun.

Contrary to popular belief, I don't hate my wheelchairs. They help me do whatever I want. I consider them my fine chariots. So don't feel sorry for me on account of the wheels.

(Feel sorry for me because of my annoyingly perfect stepbrother, Hatch Malone.)

My door swung open and Uncle Dash held the wheelchair steady. "Thanks!" I said as I scooted into my seat.

I'll be able to roll myself once we get inside the church, which is full of wide aisles and faded hardwood floors. But the parking lot is a gravelly catastrophe. It's impossible to navigate solo. So Uncle Dash took Dolly's reins (aka the handles) and we headed off toward Grandpa's favorite holy place.

"Wait here," I said to Dash when he paused inside the foyer. "This is my favorite part. I must prepare."

I pulled my heart glasses back over my eyes. (I think that's the best way to see people, through pink hearts. Try it if you don't believe me!)

Uncle Dash, despite his flutters, smiled just an inch as he flung open the double doors to the sanctuary.

The air whooshed out of the room, cooling my face and stealing my breath for one glory-hallelujah of a second. Even better, tangled in that burst of cool air was a wave of loud, wondrous music.

Music surrounded me like wind. I gave my wheels a solid push down the aisle, stretched my arms out long and pretended I was one of the sandhill cranes down by Cove Lake. Something about church music makes me feel like I can fly. I can't explain it better than that. The music is one

7

reason I'd get up early and come here even if it wasn't a little bit required. Even if I didn't have this one big, urgent request to petition the Lord about.

I stilled the wheels and swerved up beside the pew. Mama stood singing. My stepdad, Coach Malone, stood onstage leading the choir. (In case you're wondering, my stepbrother, Hatch, was still in bed at home. His view of church is that he doesn't want to go. So nobody makes him.)

Dash slumped into the pew beside me. Mama offered him an open hymnbook, but Dash waved it away. So she passed it to me. I barely mumbled over the words, though; I was too busy looking around, waiting for the winds of change to sweep through the room.

"Good morning, friends!" said Pastor Mitra. I knew I'd like that lady the first time I met her last summer. She always wears kindness in her eyes and high-top sneakers under her holy robes. "We got plenty to be excited about today, don't we? The May Day Festival is only a few weeks away! Summer's coming, and the sun is shining! I'm thankful we all get to be here together. Before we begin this morning, would you take some time to greet your neighbor? Shake their hand. Give them a hug. And let them know why you're glad they're here. Miss Melba, would you come play us a fellowship tune while we mingle?"

Melba Marcum leaped out of her seat, her long white hair trailing in a shiny braid down her back. Rumor has it Melba Marcum is the second-oldest person in Wildwood. Her twin sister, Jessie, who was pounding out a twinkly tune on the church piano, is the only person older. They won't tell anybody their actual age, though, just that music keeps them young. I believed it when I watched Melba grab her banjo from behind the piano, step out of her shoes, and pluck a hymn.

The sound of it settled my soul. Every song in the world sounds better with a banjo, I think. Banjo music sounds like sunshine on a string. Like a bumblebee square dance.

That sweet sound echoed around the room as people began to chatter. I tapped Uncle Dash's shoulder. He jumped like a stale piece of bread launching out of a toaster.

"Sorry," I said. "Forgot you were antsy today. Just wanted you to know that I'm grateful for you. Because you love *The Hobbit* and Reese Witherspoon movies and know how to make nachos in the microwave. That's a serious life skill."

"Thanks, Olive," he said, though he was still pale-faced as a ghost in the graveyard.

And that was the extent of my socializing.

Some folks shook hands or hugged one another. A

couple of girls two rows over stood side by side, giggling. I winced at the sharp, sudden ache in my heart seeing them together. I'm not the jealous type. Not usually. I just really, really can't wait to find my own future BFF to sit beside and share secrets with.

But mostly, everybody passing me by just waved or smiled. A little boy with a teddy bear stuffed under his arm hobbled over and reached for me, like he might hug me. I reached back because he was super adorable.

"Careful," I heard his mama say right before she snatched him back against her leg. "That sweet girl is as fragile as a falling star."

My Sunday morning mood flattened, just a little.
This is why the Deep Down Reason
is so important to me.

It's because *fragile* is
how people always describe me.
That, or:
short.

And I wish they'd see other things like
my dark hair or
my heart-shaped sunglasses or
even my dress.
Which is full of mushrooms and garden gnomes;

it's so jazzy!
But what people see
is the fragile part.

It's strange how my bones are inside my body
but they're still,
somehow,
the first thing people see.

Fragile is what I'll always be. I get that.
But I am
a thousand other things, too.

I'm
whole constellations
of wonders and weirdness
and hope.

"I could prove it at Macklemore Middle School," I whispered. I glanced up and imagined my words like birds floating toward the sky. I don't usually pray out loud, because I don't think it's necessary. Mostly when I pray, I picture God holding my heart up very gently to his ear, like it's one of those big, fancy seashells with an ocean sound inside it. I've got a thousand tiny oceans inside me. And I think God listens carefully to every crashing wave, all the fears and hopes. Even if he doesn't answer every single prayer, I think he keeps my heart safe.

Just show me how to get to Macklemore, I begged again, deep inside my seashell-heart.

And that's when prickles tap-danced along the back of my neck. And I had the strange but certain sensation that someone was watching me.

That something wonderful was about to happen.

CHAPTER 2
Like a Skateboard with a Seat

An old lady shuffled toward me down the sunlit aisle of New River Church. She had a wrinkly face and big glasses. She wore a pink dress with purple feathers stuck to the shoulder seams and carried a tiny leopard-print purse around the crook of her arm. I mean, wow, her style was awesome.

But she never took her eyes off me . . . which got a little weird.

And listen, I'm used to people staring. Even if I'm not the one who starts it.

A wheelchair is my normal, but I get that it's not everybody's normal. Maybe some people have never seen a wheelchair in person. Just like some people have never seen a two-headed trundle bird in person. I think a two-headed trundle bird is way cooler, is the thing. Natural wonders are worth staring at. A wheelchair's just a mobility device.

I waved to the lady and smiled. This is what I usually do when people stare. Mama says I don't have to do that, that I don't owe smiles to anybody. But I figure a smile's the easiest thing in the world to give away, and I'm usually glad to share one.

The lady leaned down low to look me in the eye. White hair fuzzed around her hairline like cotton candy.

"Would you like to sit with us?" I asked. "I'm Ol—"

"Listen, little girl," she said. Her eyes were glittery with excitement. "I've got good news for you."

I probably should have stopped her right there and clarified that I was *eleven* and not exactly *little*. I mean, I'm super short for my age. But I'm not a little kid. I didn't say anything, though. For starters, this lady was older and I didn't want to be rude. Also, she was talking so fast there was no place to interject. Plus, I'm always up for some good news. Her voice was booming by the time she declared: "I believe God wants me to say something to you."

"He . . . does?" I asked. I sat up straighter in my wheelchair. I always assumed God would speak to me directly if he had something to say. But maybe that's not how conversation with the divine works.

"Yes, honey! I believe God wants me to tell you that your life will not always look . . . like *this*."

"Makes sense," I said, slinking back against my chair as far as possible. For some reason, I felt smaller on account of the way she looked at me. Or maybe it was the way she was talking to me. My voice came out small, too. So I cleared my throat. "I mean, I'm only eleven. Life's bound to change considerably."

She smiled and said, "I mean, you will not always be in this terrible contraption. Someday you'll walk! You'll jump right out of this chair! I believe God means to heal you."

The volume of her voice rose slowly as she spoke, like mist off rainy pavement. And my arms locked tighter . . . and tighter . . . around my middle. As if I were trying to protect my heart from her words. Which didn't make sense. They weren't bad words. She wasn't making fun of me. But something felt so awkwardly uncomfortable. Like when your sock crumples down in your sneaker and you can't reach it to fix it.

"It's not a terrible contraption," I said.

"What, honey?" She leaned in closer. Too close. Her breath smelled like old books and toothpaste.

"My wheelchair isn't terrible. It's just a wheelchair. It's neutral. It's like a bicycle. Like a plane. Like a skateboard with a seat. Minus the half-pipes." I laughed a little at my own joke. But she didn't.

Instead, her hand rested on my shoulder and she said, loudly, "CAN. I. PRAY. FOR. YOU?"

I glanced beside me for my family's reaction, but they weren't paying attention. Dash's head was nearly between his knees on account of the premonitions. And Mama was two rows down, petting Gustav the ferret. Folks were still talking and the music was still fluttering all around us. Some people, however, were definitely beginning to stare. They'd stopped their mingling just to see what was up.

"Um, okay . . . I guess . . ." I said, keeping my voice gentle and steady. I hoped if I spoke to her quietly that maybe she would pray for me quietly as well.

But she did not.

"LORD!!!" the woman hollered out, as if she had to wake up God from a nap to get his attention. "Would you HEAL this little girl of the TERRIBLE disease that's left her stuck in this CHAIR?"

"OLIVE!" My heart jumped with happiness at this shout, because it was Mama yelling my name. She shuffled down the aisle toward me as fast as her high-heeled boots could haul her.

Mama and Jupiter are always afraid people will hurt me if they get too close. And that's understandable. All it takes is a little fall for me to break a leg. A too-tight squeeze to crack a rib. I was born with brittle bones and that's never gonna change. So it's better to be safe than sorry, they figure. Here's what I know for sure: I really appreciate their overprotectiveness when it comes to weird strangers.

"AMEN," said the lady, looking very satisfied with herself. She patted my arm and hobbled away.

The next thing I saw was Mama's face in mine. Nearly nose-to-nose. "You okay, baby?" she asked.

"Fine," I said. But *fine* is, for sure, the only adjective I could claim.

I'd always believed prayer was a good thing. A sweet thing—like a back porch conversation with Grandpa Goad. Except it's God you're talking to. But that moment—that prayer—had left me feeling as hollow as an acorn hull.

"I should have sat beside you," Mama said. "We're leaving right now."

She reached to unlock my brakes, her dark hair brushing against my face. Then she spun me around and zoomed me out of the church so fast you'd think a herd of vampire buffalo were chasing after us. In reality, only Uncle Dash chased us. "We leaving?" he asked. Then he shouted, "Hallelu—uh . . . Coach Malone is still in the choir."

"Coach knows where we live," Mama said over her shoulder.

I closed my eyes. And instead of whispering a prayer, I made a soul-deep declaration.

I'm changing. Change is coming, and it's me. I am

17

going to Macklemore. I will find my future BFF, and I will prove to absolutely every soul in this place that
> *I'm more*
> *than bones and wheels*
> *and breakable parts.*

Suddenly, the wind was in my face. And we all burst into the foyer and out the front door, leaving the music and the unanswered prayers swirling in the sunlit air behind us.

CHAPTER 3
Candy Bones

Osteogenesis imperfecta.

It sounds like a magic spell
If you don't know what it means.

Like words you'd whisper over muddy sludge
To make the wildflowers bloom.

Like words you'd holler up at the storm
To clear a path for sparkling stars.

It might sound like magic,
But right now,
today,
It feels like a curse.

It's the curse of bones that break easy,
For no reason.

Candy bones,
Glass bones,
OI is the reason I am fragile.

Femur.
Patella.
Socket.
Tibia.
Fibula.

More magic-sounding words that are only bones,
Bones that are built to connect and grow and build a body.

But mine weren't built right.
That's what I believe.
Grandpa Goad says I'm not correct on that account.
That God made us all, and God don't make mistakes.
But I don't understand why God
made me broken.
(I've asked God this question plenty of times.
He hasn't answered me yet.)

"Your bones look like lace on the inside,"
Dr. Kass told me once.

And that's the problem.
If I lived in a novel,
I could have bones made of lace,
or ribbon,
or icy spiderwebs,
or sharp shafts of rainbow light.

But in this world,
a girl needs bones made of concrete.
A heart made of steel.

I'm eleven years old,
but I already know that's true.

CHAPTER 4
The First Feathers Falling

"It's frustrating when people do that," Mama said. She had both hands on the steering wheel, eyes squinty-focused on the mountain road curling up ahead. She told Uncle Dash he could take the other car home because we needed "girl time."

Which meant that Mama felt like she had to do damage control after this morning's prayer meeting. By the looks of things, however, I wasn't nearly as addled by the encounter as she'd been.

"I'm really okay," I promised. And I gulped. "You might want to . . . slow down just a little?"

She tapped the brakes just enough to make us both lurch forward. "I can't believe some random stranger had the audacity to waltz up and pray for you to be healed. As if there's something wrong with you. BACON!"

(Mama's the cussing type, but she's trying to cut back.

So *bacon* is the word she says instead of . . . you know.)

She slammed the brakes and pulled over on the grassy side of the road. Mud slung up over my window, concealing the rippled mountains to my side. I squealed, partially out of fear but a little bit out of excitement, too.

"Look at me, baby," Mama said. She cupped my chin in her soft hand. "There is *nothing* wrong with you, Olive Miracle Martin. I don't take you to church—or anywhere—because there's something wrong with you that I want God to fix. You're a whole person exactly as you are. You know that, don't you?"

"I do," I promised. And I marveled at the gentle determination on my mama's face. Her eyes are beautiful, deep and dark like a tiny universe that's hers alone. Whoever my mama's talking to, her eyes stay starry-focused. And fully kind. I hope I give people that same attention.

She leaned in so close to me I could smell her perfume. It reminded me of freshly cut oranges and vanilla ice cream. "Do you remember why we picked Miracle for your middle name?"

"Yes," I said, reaching out to pat her arm. "You've told me at least four thousand times."

People might assume Mama gave me my middle name, Miracle, because of my bone situation. I was born with a bunch of broken bones and the promise of lots more to come. *Osteogenesis imperfecta* is the actual scientific name of my bone disease. But we call it OI or just *brittle bones* for short.

There's no cure for OI, so I'll have it for the rest of my life. Sometimes this is no big deal to me. Other times I feel like my whole world and everything in it orbits around the fact that I'm fragile.

But Mama didn't name me Miracle because she was hoping for a divine bone transformation.

"I named you Miracle," Mama declared, "because I waited so long for you. You were a dream come true. You still are. Did you know that I yelled out your name for the whole hospital to hear the day you were born? OLIVE MIRACLE MARTIN!"

She rolled down the window and shouted my name across the hills and hollows. Which made me giggle.

"Your name was a hallelujah for the whole world to hear," Mama said. "Because no life should be a whisper. Remember that, okay? You're not a miracle because you have brittle bones or because you use a wheelchair or walker. You're not a miracle if you don't. You're a miracle because you exist. Everybody is."

Fact: The longer my mama talks, the more passionate she gets. She's got steel in her soul; she's a strong woman with a heart the size of a Tennessee sunset. And when she talks about how much she loves her family, she usually gets a little fired up.

I cleared my throat. "Can I ask you a serious question?"

Mama nodded.

"Did you ever pray, or hope, or think—just once, maybe—that God would heal my bones, too? Make them normal?"

"No," she said without the slightest waver in her voice. Her eyes gazed deep into mine. "Your grandpa's more of a praying type than me, anyway. I pray when you get hurt— that your pain will go away. Sometimes I pray that you add beauty and goodness to the world. Or that you see ways to help other people. But I've never prayed for you to have normal bones. I love you exactly this way."

Now, friend: I absolutely believed what Mama said to me. But I must confess that I got a little tangled up in my thoughts at this point.

Because it occurred to me that I've never actually *prayed* for God to heal my bones, either. Lately, I've been focused on way more important things, like finding my future BFF at Macklemore Middle School. Even before that, my bone-prayers were different. When a bone

breaks, it makes me
sick from the start. There's the watery
SNAP
sound somewhere deep inside.
And then all I see
and feel and think about
is how much it hurts. I pray two words:

Help me.

Over and over:
Help me.
I think sometimes I mean it like: "Help
my pain go away."

And sometimes I mean:
Help me
be brave now
so my parents don't see me cry.

I've prayed for straight As and
story ideas and spectacular bird sightings. I prayed
for my granny up north, when she was sick,
and for snow on Christmas morning
so my backyard would look like the Narnia woods.

But I've never prayed for God
to replace my candy bones
with the solid kind.

I guess I assumed the answer was already no, since this
is how he decided to plop me down on the planet. I can't
change the bone-parts.
But I do wish I could change how other people see me.
That's what really gets to me, sometimes.

That is the Deep Down Reason I want to attend Macklemore: to prove to everybody—to people I see, to my parents, to myself, maybe—there is a lot more to me besides the fragile places.

And right there on the side of Highway 101 in Wildwood, Tennessee, a realization flickered through my mind like a holy bolt of lightning.

Mama was fired up because the stylish old lady at church thought something was wrong with me. Which meant that Mama doesn't like that other people only see me as fragile, either. This was the best chance I'd ever had to convince her Macklemore was right for me. For us!

I steadied myself with a deep yoga breath, just like Jupiter taught me. "Mama, this definitely relates to the thing we've been talking about. Don't you think . . . I'm ready?"

"For what?" she asked as she pulled back onto the highway.

"Macklemore!"

"We've talked about this so many times," she said wearily. She turned Dolly Parton back up on the speakers. "It's just too dangerous. There are so many kids who could accidentally knock you down, slick floors you could slip on and break something. A change like that is big. It's so much to think about."

"I have been thinking about it," I said as I turned Dolly down again. As I said, I adore Ms. Parton, but I think she'd want me to speak up for myself right about now. "You see who I actually am. All of what I am, besides just the bone-parts. Macklemore would make other people see it, too."

"Doesn't matter what they see."

"What about what *I* see?" I asked. "Don't you think I deserve a chance at Macklemore to see what I'm capable of? Did you know they have theater there? You know acting is my destiny! They have all kinds of clubs and classes and a four-story library. Probably even my future BFF!"

Mama's only answer was silence.

I sat up straighter. "I'm very encouraged that you didn't just say no. What if I could convince you it was the right place for me?"

She sighed. "How do you plan to do that?"

A zillion ideas flickered through my brain at that moment. But for some reason, the first image that really stuck was . . . Pastor Mitra. I pictured her high-top sneakers and holy robes. I thought about how Grandpa Goad always says there's nothing that calms his heart like a bird-song, a biscuit from Big John's, and a three-point sermon from Pastor Mitra. Maybe this was God's way of helping me out again.

"I'll deliver a three-point sermon," I said.

Mama actually chuckled at this. "You work on that."

She was just joking, I realize. But I took her words very seriously. My heart felt like it sprouted wings, like it was fluttering around inside my cage-bone chest. I would convince Mama and Jupiter today.

Change was *finally* about to happen!

"Yes, ma'am," I said excitedly.

She smirked a little and shook her head. But her smirk soon faded, and her forehead scrunched in confusion. I thought maybe she was pondering Dolly Parton's majestic lyrics. That's one of my favorite pastimes as well.

"Weird," Mama said. "Do you see that?"

My eyes followed the direction of her finger point. At first, I thought I was seeing snowflakes up ahead, the big goose-feather kind that fly in February, that cover the mountain in blankets of white.

But . . . it was too warm to snow.

We were in the middle of of April.

"Whoa" was all I could manage before we were engulfed by a thick cloud of gauzy white.

It looked like we were sitting inside a snow globe. Mama slowed down, turning on the hazards so people would be able to see us. Fluffy white flakes swarmed so thick around the van we could barely see the road ahead. I touched my fingertips to the glass. It wasn't cold, not even a little.

"Those are honest-to-goodness feathers," I said. I didn't need to touch one to know. I'm a birder, like my grandpa. I know a feather when I see it.

"From what?" Mama asked.

I couldn't help her there. I had no clue where the birds were from. Or why they were molting all over the van at exactly the same time.

Each feather looked dipped in sparkle-sugar. They drifted down around the trees and van in a lazy, swirling slow dance. They stuck to the windshield. But only for a breath.

Then they melted . . . same as snow.

Swift as a dream.

"It's sleet," Mama said. "Look! They're melting!"

I shook my head. "Definitely feathers."

The song was only on the third verse when the cloud that engulfed us blew away. We watched it roll off the road and down the mountainside in a blurry ball of white.

"Bacon," Mama said. We both looked around slowly. The feather-snow had all disappeared.

"Huh," I replied. "I'm gonna send Grandpa Goad an SOS immediately. Ask him what kind of bird sheds a million white feathers in April."

"That was some kind of weird weather," Mama said. "Not birds."

"Oh, it was definitely bird business. Grandpa will know."

We turned up the music. Mama got lost in her thoughts. And I began writing a sermon on the empty notebook of my imagination.

What I'd seen was special, don't get me wrong. But

birds do all sorts of marvelous things, all the time, especially in this town. Convincing Mama to send me to Macklemore was priority #1 for me. That's the change I wanted to make happen today.

So all the way home, I plotted and planned.

I didn't pay much attention to how hard the trees were trembling. Or how loudly the birds were singing. I barely even noticed the storm rolling in, slow and steady, stretching over my mountains like a shadow. I didn't listen to the wind whispering through the trees. If I had, I might have heard what all of nature was trying to tell me: Change was on the wind, and it was bigger than any of us knew.

Because the hummingbird was coming.

CHAPTER 5
My Pelican and Me

Most people in town think the Piney Woods are haunted, and they're probably right. Gosh, I hope so. I think it'd be so jazzy to see a ghost. For me, the woods are home and not much ever happens there.

Huckleberry Lane is the actual road where we live. It's twisty and covered in gravel, and it curls off the highway deep into the dark heart of the Piney Woods. A thin layer of mist usually covers the ground like ghostly snow, cuddling close to the tree trunks and rosebushes. All sorts of birds sing their hearts out here, all day and all night. Ravens, in particular. Which is probably what gets people all spun up with their spooky stories. A crow's song doesn't sound as pretty as a sparrow's; it's more like a throaty shout. Grandpa and I think every kind of birdsong is beautiful, but most people don't agree.

My whole family lives within spittin' distance of one another in the woods now. For a while, it was just the two of us in the cottage: Mama and me. Then she married Coach Malone. He moved in, too, as did his perfect, straight-A, king-of-sixth-grade offspring, Hatch Malone.

I'll get to him later.

Grandpa and Dash live in a little house next door, when Grandpa's not away chasing after wild birds.

And then there's Jupiter, who lives about forty-five feet away from our back door in a yurt.

"Looks like he's back from his hike," I said, pointing to the warm light glowing through the windows. "He's probably doing yoga now."

"I'm still not sure why he can't get an apartment," Mama said as she helped me out of the van. "I love that he's close, don't get me wrong. I just think a yurt can't be comfortable long-term."

Mama and Jupiter divorced years ago, way before I was old enough to stitch memories together. But they're still real friends who laugh at each other's jokes and love me fiercely. I think every family's glued together in its own hodgepodge way. But all that matters to me is that we stick together, and we do. Plus, the yurt's kinda cool. And wheelchair accessible.

Sadly, I had zero time to visit him that day.

My mind and heart were already racing, aching to get

inside and craft a sermon that shook my parents to their very core. (In a good way.)

"I asked Jupiter about the yurt the other day," I said quickly as I pushed myself up the ramp to the front door. "He told me that he's on a spiritual journey but has no desire for more physical ones. Also, I have a sermon to write, so I can't help with lunch. Love you! Bye!"

"Olive." Mama grabbed the handle of my wheelchair when I tried to zoom away, bringing me to a quick halt. "You promise you're okay?"

"I'm entirely fabulous," I said truthfully.

She narrowed her eyes at me. "What are you up to?"

"I'm getting started on my sermon," I reminded her. "Don't worry so much about me. I'm fine. I can do hard things."

She smiled at this. Mama loves it when I affirm my toughness and smartness. She turned my wheelchair loose. I heard her yell "One hour till lunch!" as I grabbed a box of frozen fish sticks out of the freezer drawer.

Then I zoomed into my bedroom and shut the door gently.

My heart still felt more like a flutter than a beat, like some kind of wild hope-bird was joy-flapping deep inside me. Today was the day! I could feel it! I pushed myself to the window, flung it wide open, and tossed out a fish stick.

"Hey, Felix," I said. "I can't chat today. Change is on the wind!"

Felix is a pelican who sometimes lives on our roof. Other times, like now, he hangs out in the yard, poking around like a big chicken. This isn't uncommon in my town, just FYI. Wildwood has more bird varieties than anywhere in the world. Sometimes random birds only pass through long enough to visit. Sometimes they settle down here like Felix.

"I've got one chance to articulate the deepest dream of my soul," I told Felix. He cocked his pretty head at me. "I'm going to write it like a sermon."

Felix did not look impressed.

"It'll be stirring," I assured him. "Too bad the Goad's not here, because he'd be good at this. Do birds preach sermons with their songs ever?"

I tossed another fish stick to Felix. He squawked his thanks and probably told me all about how birds don't have to preach. All they have to do is spread their wings and fly. Scrape the skies and sometimes sing. All a bird ever has to be is what it's created to be.

Which gave me an idea! I pushed myself over to my desk and touched my pen to paper.

That's one of my favorite feelings in the world: pen to paper and a page full of words. I could write a thousand things in my lifetime—plays and poems and short stories and songs—and never, ever get sick of the way words feel when they spin out of my soul.

The hour flew by faster than a hungry hawk.

Tiny raindrops turned into a rushing deluge of sound.

Dolly Parton sang to me.

And I wrote—and rewrote—and tried to shape a river of feelings into one fine sermon.

"Change is on the wind, Felix!" I yelled as I flung a final fish stick through the window. I heard him flap his big parachute wings in agreement.

I reached for the framed picture I keep on my desk, a smiley picture of Grandpa Goad and me the time he took me to see the rememory birds. That was my first birding adventure. We camped under the stars and watched comets streak across the night. He told me then that I would do brave and bold things in my life. He was right; this was the beginning.

"LUNCH, OLIVE!" hollered Mama from the kitchen.

I pressed my hand against my chest so I could feel the next deep yoga breath I took. "I feel fireworks inside my soul," I said to Felix. "Like joy and excitement all mixed together, and it's just . . . joy-kabooms. Wish me luck."

Felix squawked. He's such a sweet friend.

I latched the window shut and rolled toward the kitchen with a heart still fluttering full of hope. I barely heard the sound of thunder overhead, rolling low and throaty like a witch's wicked laugh.

CHAPTER 6
The Best Magic Words

If our cottage in the woods were an actual body, with bones and not boards, then our kitchen would be the heartbeat of it all. That's where we laugh the most, where we all end up hanging out even though we have perfectly comfy couches in the living room.

I rounded the corner to some of my favorite Sunday sounds:

splat,

ting,

plop,

sizzle.

Kitchen noises remind me of a banjo sound sometimes. They're happy the same way. Or maybe it was just *me* that was happy right then. Happy, hopeful, and . . . nervous, too. What if Mama and Jupiter say no? What if they keep saying no? What if my life is one big no forever and always and I'm like a tragic princess in a tower who only talks to pelicans?

I couldn't let that happen.

Change is on the wind, I reminded my anxious heart, which was still pounding like joy-kabooms in my chest.

Mama and Uncle Dash were in the kitchen together, cooking up a spaghetti storm. Emmylou Harris was singing about a red dirt road from the record player on the counter. Rain pebbled the big glass windows all around the room, and the trees outside waved easy in the breeze. Little storm-sparrows perched on the outside branches. They only sing when it rains, and today they were so loud I could hear them even inside.

Their song sounded like:

Maybe, baby,
Maybe, baby,
Today's the day it all begins!

Their tune made me so happy that I spun Dolly in two fast circles right in the middle of the room.

"Whatcha dancing about?" Uncle Dash asked from the kitchen.

"Just happy is all," I said, cruising up underneath the table. I pushed away a pile of folded T-shirts. And realized that directly across from me sat my stepbrother, Hatch Malone. He didn't even look in my direction or say hello.

Fact: Even if I'd rolled into the room blindfolded, I could have told you exactly what Hatch would be doing and wearing. Hatch always wears the same blue hoodie, the one with bleach-freckles around the collar from the washing machine. It's faded and frayed at the cuffs. I'm pretty sure the frays exist because he's always rubbing the fabric between his fingers and thumbs. And he usually does this while he's reading the same tattered comic book: *The Adventures of Marvelo the Great and His Fine Dog, Hank.*

Maybe that's not super weird: We've all got quirky habits. I twist my hair around my finger sometimes. My uncle Dash taps his foot. Mama hums. Coach Malone does lunges. Hatch fiddles with his hoodie sleeves and reads a comic book. Every. Single. Day. But here's another bizarre Hatch-fact:

Every single night, my stepbrother goes for a walk in the woods. For as long as he's lived here, in rain or snow or gross humidity, he grabs a flashlight and goes meandering into the darkness. I asked Mama what in the world he does out there. She told me it was none of my actual business. Sometimes the people you live with are the greatest mysteries of all, I guess.

I figured Hatch didn't even see me enter the room, so I focused on the introduction of my sermon. I always pretend not to care that he doesn't notice me. But that's getting more difficult.

For the past year, since we've actually lived under the same roof, Hatch has spoken to me maybe twice. When his friends are here, he's Mr. Personality, talking and laughing and making everybody else laugh so hard they giggle-wheeze.

But when it's just me and him, he never talks much at all. He never laughs at my jokes, even the funny ones. The one way we communicate is through music, but even that's not what you'd call a positive connection. Sometimes when I play music in my room, Hatch plays even louder music in his room. And we go back and forth cranking up our music louder until Mama yells "HEADPHONES, KIDS!"

I get it: Hatch is way cooler than me. This is not a difficult thing to be. But because of this, apparently, he wants nothing to do with me at all.

And yet, I keep trying to figure out how to connect. We live in the same house, after all. We can't be strangers forever.

"Hi, Hatch," I said.

He glanced up at me for a half second and said, "Oh. Hey."

Friend, I don't know if you've ever experienced living under the same roof as someone who pretends you don't exist. It's unsettling. I like existing!

The kitchen door flung open and Jupiter walked into the room barefoot, tall and tan as always. He wore his usual uniform: cargo shorts and a concert T-shirt from a

Dave Matthews show. His long blond hair was pulled back in a ponytail and his arm was full of friendship bracelets that I'd made him over the years.

Jupiter Martin is my dad. But he prefers to be called by his actual name, Jupiter, even by me. Grandpa Goad says this is all on account of Jupiter's "weirdo hippie parenting." I don't mind, though. I love the word *Jupiter* as much as I love the word *dad*. It means the same: that my dad is his own planet, his own shiny universe, and we all orbit around his weird and wonderful light.

I tossed my sermon on the table and stretched both arms toward him. That's like an instinct with my dad, and I don't even care if it makes me look like a little kid. When Jupiter walks into a room, he floods the place with gentle kindness. It makes you want to fly right at him and be hugged. So that's what I did.

"How's my girl?" he asked, wrapping his arms around me. Jupiter smelled like woods and falling rain. He makes me feel safe from the inside out.

"I'm superb," I told him honestly.

He smiled as he stood back up to his full height. "Found this guy wandering in the woods," he said, nodding behind him. Coach Malone walked in next, dripping wet and laughing.

"I'm so sorry!" Mama shouted, running to give him a hug. "I had to get out of that church. I'll tell you about it later."

"No worries," Coach Malone said. "Good way to get in my afternoon run. Hey, Hatch!"

Hatch waved at his dad, never looking away from the comic book.

"Hey, Olive!" Coach Malone said. He jogged toward me, jumped into a squat, and held up both hands for a high five. I high-fived him right back and giggled at his enthusiasm. Then he lunge-walked to the back bedroom for a shower.

Coach Malone is forever jogging or doing jumping jacks or flopping down on the floor to do push-ups. He does this on his way to the fridge or the mailbox or wherever the mood strikes. (The first time I saw him throw himself down on a sidewalk to do push-ups, I thought he'd had a bonafide heart attack.) He's the PE teacher at Macklemore Middle School, my future alma mater. And he's got a cool side hustle: Coach Mo's Mega Bouncers. Those are sneakers he invented with tiny trampolines all over the soles. They make you bounce like a rocket-rabbit, he says. The invention is a work in progress, though. Grandpa Goad tried on a pair once, barely hopped, and put a hole right in the middle of Mama's ceiling with his bald head.

"What's with the pages?" Jupiter asked as he helped me settle back under the table.

"Oh geez," Hatch said, finally looking up from his

comic book at the stack of papers. "Are we doing another family play?"

"It's actually a short sermon," I told him, even though I knew he didn't really care. Hatch never participates in the family plays I write, either.

"About what?" Jupiter asked as he moved the laundry off the table.

"You'll find out," I promised him, and let out a quick squeal of excitement. Hatch just shook his head and looked back at his book.

Plates of spaghetti noodles and bright red sauce were passed along the table. Uncle Dash plopped a basket of bread in the center. Curls of garlic steam rolled off the top. My stomach growled. My heart kaboomed.

Coach Malone lunge-walked into the room and took a seat beside Hatch. Mama and Uncle Dash sat on either side of me. And while there were two extra chairs at the table, Jupiter tossed a pillow on the floor and sat there instead, like always. I could tell he was smiling by the way his eyes crinkled in the corners. My family started talking all at once. But I couldn't focus on a word they said.

Should I launch right into my sermon? Or wait a second?

I could hear the storm-sparrows on the branches singing, "Go, Olive, go!"

My sneaker tapped a restless rhythm on the footrest

43

of my wheelchair. Finally, when the words inside me felt like they might explode, Uncle Dash said:

"Is something on your mind, Olive?"

At last! My cue! "I'm so glad you asked! If I may have your attention, family and Uncle Dash, there is indeed something on my heart. Something it's time to discuss and rethink. As I've mentioned once or twice, I want to go to Macklemore Middle School. Not just go visit. But actually be a student there. A sixth-grade student. I can feel it in my soul: Macklemore is the place where I'll flourish and bloom."

"Oh geez," Hatch said under his breath. His dad kicked him gently under the table. But I don't mind naysayers. I can be persistent in the face of rejection!

"As Mama requested," I continued. I glanced back down at my notes. "I'm going to make today's argument to you like one of Pastor Mitra's sermons. I want to go to Macklemore because I'm fragile. Because I need a BFF. And because it's time to find my wings. I think—"

"Olive." Mama said my name quickly and flatly in her special tone that means *move on*. "You know how I feel about this. You're way less likely to fall and break at home."

"Am I, though?" I asked. "I get it: I'm fragile. And that makes the average day a little more dangerous. But that's exactly why I think it's time for Macklemore. I have *osteogenesis imperfecta* wherever I go. I could fall anywhere, including right here at home, which has happened. I'm going to break bones. That's just the stinko facts of life. I'm not blaming anybody but me."

"Don't blame yourself," Jupiter said quickly. "Your bones are brittle. That's nobody's fault. That's just biology."

"You know what I mean," I said.

"That's what it's called?" Hatch asked. *"Osteo—"*

His dad shot him a look and shook his head no. But, honestly, I don't mind when people ask. Really, it's weirder to me that Hatch has lived in this house a year now and has never asked me anything about my disability. I would rather people ask than stare at me like I'm a two-headed trundle bird. "It's called OI for short," I said. "And yeah, it's why my bones break easy."

"But it doesn't happen every time you walk," Hatch said. "Because I've seen you use a walker sometimes . . ."

"Hatch," his dad whispered.

"No, not every time," I said. "There are lots of different kinds of OI. My type is mild, so when a bone heals enough to start therapy, I'm able to try walking again. Since walking makes my bones stronger. But sometimes they still break. If I fall, they pretty much definitely break."

"Huh," Hatch said, threading his fingers together like we were all in a board meeting. "That's interesting."

"Hatch," Coach Mo said, patting his son's shoulder. "Let Olive finish."

Hatch nodded. "Sorry, Olive. Go on."

My thoughts jumbled together. This was a tangent I hadn't anticipated. Hatch never pays attention to what I say.

"So I might break wherever I go," I continued, trying to jump back in where I left off. "And if that's going to happen anyway, why not . . . see something new? Learn how to adapt and adjust in all kinds of marvelous scenarios? Plus, I'll finally get to meet my future-forever BFF! A girl needs friends, that's my second point. Friends besides just you all. I love you all more than Taco Tuesday, don't get me wrong. But you know how Diana has Anne in the Green Gables books? Or how the girls in the Baby-Sitters Club all have one another? That's what I think is missing in my life. I'd like one true BFF to spend my time with."

I lowered my voice and added, "A friend that's my own age. Especially since no other kids in this town are home-schooled. It's just me, myself, and a pelican named Felix."

"Hatch is your friend," said Coach Malone, and he clapped his hand down on his son's shoulder.

Hatch's eyes flickered up to meet mine. I would describe the look in them as utter and abject fear. "Trust me," he said. "You'd really hate Macklemore."

I should have been mad at Hatch for this weird tangent. But I was mostly just . . . confused. Why was he trying to sabotage my dream? It made no sense.

"I don't know, Ollie," Jupiter said. "It'd be so easy to fall and break there. There are so many kids. Slick hallways."

46

"I'll be in my wheelchair," I reminded him. "Even when I'm allowed to use my walker more here at home, I'll use my wheelchair at school. You realize there are lots of people with OI who go to public school, right?"

"Yes, but what's right for another person might not be the best for you," Jupiter said. "Or us. We can't control a school environment like we can here. And then, if you fall, that's months of hurt and rehab you have to go through. You're on such a great streak right now."

Jupiter was right. It had been almost a year since I'd fallen and broke my right femur bone. And let me just tell you: No bone is fun to break. But breaking a femur—that's the long bone in your thigh—is extra-especially terrible.

Mama nodded sadly. "I just don't think the timing is right. Not yet."

"Then it never will be," I said. Frustration rang out like a soft explosion in my soul. "Something happened inside me at church today, when that lady prayed for me."

"Bacon! I knew it!" Mama's fork made a loud clanging sound when it hit the plate. "I knew that lady got you spun up."

"What lady?" asked Jupiter.

"Tell you later," Mama and I said at the same time.

"Do you know how often I hear people say that I'm fragile?" I asked. "It's a lot. And it's true, I get it. But that's all anybody knows about me: that I was born broken, that I'm fragile, that I'm small, and that I have a great sense of style. Sometimes," I said honestly, "I think even you all get stuck on the fragile part."

"What?" Mama and Jupiter said at the same time. "No!"

"Olive!" Now Mama was saying my name like a hallelujah again. "We think everything about you is wonderful *as you are*! You're smart and kind and so creative."

"You're a natural birder," Jupiter added. "Just like your grandparents."

Hatch's head snapped up suddenly. "Are you really, Olive?" He stared at me with an eager sparkle in his eyes, like I was about to give him a birthday present. Which I wasn't. His birthday's not until December twenty-fifth. (He gets double presents, of course.)

"I'm good at spotting birds," I said with a shrug. "I learned from the best. But I wasn't asking for affirmation. I just want to try out middle school!"

I sat up taller. I took a deep, steadying yoga breath. "Mama. Jupiter. You can't control every environment I'm in. Not forever. I think, if this is my body, I should get a say-so on where it rolls. I think it's time to find my wings. Like, figure out what I'm good at. What inspires me. I think Macklemore is the place that happens."

Uncle Dash nodded. His eyes were shiny with proud-uncle tears. "I agree!"

"I'm really proud of you for saying all this, Olive,"

Jupiter said. "But I'm really terrified about you attending school. It didn't go so well the first time."

"You've tried it before?" Coach Malone asked.

I nodded. "One day of kindergarten. I fell and broke my leg. It was traumatic for all of us. Mama and Jupiter didn't want me to go back."

"I think y'all should let her try again," said Uncle Dash. "Even if it doesn't work out, it'd be good to try."

"Thank you!" I said.

The room settled into an uncomfy silence. But I tried not to let the quiet get me down. At least quiet wasn't a no! Then Mama and Jupiter and Uncle Dash started talking at the same time about public school: Why it was a good idea. Why it wasn't a good idea. Why it was dangerous. Why it was awesome.

Coach Malone clapped his hand on his son's shoulder. "Hatch, would you help Olive if she went to Macklemore?"

Hatch's face scrunched up like he'd just sniffed a bag of rotten potatoes. "Help her . . . how?"

"Just look out for her?" Coach Malone said. "You'd be in the same class. Help her get oriented, maybe."

"I don't know . . ." Hatch said. "I'm kind of busy when I'm at school." And even though he didn't say it in a mean way, my heart sank like a concrete block. Was he that embarrassed to be seen with me? Was it because of the wheelchair? Because I was annoying to him? What was his problem?

Hatch pushed his hand through his thick black hair and said, "I don't get why she's making such a big deal, anyway. Macklemore's just a school."

The sudden urge to fling a handful of spaghetti at Hatch Malone's face overwhelmed me. And I might have done it, if Coach Mo hadn't given Hatch the Look. I thought only Mama gave *me* the Look. But apparently, the Look is something lots of parents occasionally give their offspring. The Look means *stop being rude*. Or *stop talking*. Or just *stop*. The Look says a thousand things even though zero words are spoken.

"Okay, fine," Hatch finally mumbled. "I'll help if she needs it. Whatever."

Coach Malone clapped his hands together. "So there we go. Hatch will be near Olive most of the day. The school will have no problem providing an aide. And I'll be close, too, if she ever needs me."

Mama and Jupiter looked a little stunned by the direction spaghetti Sunday had taken.

I twisted my hands together in front of me to try and keep calm. But I could feel my heartbeat fluttering again beneath my fingertips. I kept looking back and forth between their faces, waiting for another no.

But hoping for a yes.

To my great shock, Mama decreed: "Maybe it's time."

"What?!" Jupiter and I shouted at the same time.

"I really trust Hatch to look out for her," Mama said.

"He's so thoughtful and observant. And he has all his soccer team friends—"

"I'm also president of the Comic Book Club," Hatch said. "It takes up a lot of time."

"I guess with Hatch and Coach Malone there . . ." said Jupiter, his words trailing off into a thoughtful silence. I sat up extra straight. He sounded like he might be changing his mind! "I'd be okay with Olive trying it."

"So it's a yes?" I asked.

Mama looked at Jupiter and nodded. He sighed but nodded right back. "Yes," he said. "If you'll be careful."

In books, there are always magical words, words like *abracadabra* that open locked doors or wake sleeping dragons or turn oceans to ice. But in real life, maybe there's no word more magical than a plain, straightforward, spoken from your parents *Y-E-S*.

"YES!" I shouted.

In an effort to communicate his excitement, Felix slammed into the kitchen window. This is nothing to be concerned about, friend: Felix always crash-lands. He shook his head and bounced around on the grass as usual. But he managed to turn our attention toward the outside world.

Where something was happening.

Something wild and white.

Gusts of white feather-snow swirled past the glass.

"It's really happening," Hatch whispered, rising

slowly out of his seat to stare. The rest of us were too stunned to speak. We watched the feathers land on the window, then tremble for a heartbeat before they faded to dust. In the seconds before they disappeared, they were beautiful: sparkling and icy-white, delicate as butterfly bones on the glass.

CHAPTER 7

Maybe Change Is Coming. (Maybe Change Is Me.)

Over the next few days, feather-flakes gusted through the Piney Woods in fluffy spurts and bundles. Wednesday morning was when they fell the heaviest—hard as rain and silent as snow. But I didn't have time to consider the weather, or the birds that might be causing it, or even my future Academy Award.

I woke up thinking about elastic-waist pants. Because Wednesday was the day I finally got to go to Macklemore.

I'm guessing that elastic-waist pants probably aren't the hottest trend in middle school. But I'd be using my wheelchair, Dolly, all day there, so it made a little more sense. When you sit all day, a button toggle digging in above your belly button gets annoying real fast. On the bright side, my pants looked like real jeans.

On the even brighter side, I was actually headed to my dream school!

Coach Mo got the process started on Monday morning. Then Jupiter and Mama toured the school and figured out my schedule. Then the three of them made me promise to be extra careful at least a billion times. They told me to only use my wheelchair at Macklemore, which I'd already promised to do anyway. And that I'd have an aide named Ms. Pigeon who would "help me out"—whatever that meant.

Here's what mattered to me: Wednesday was here, and so was change!

After I got dressed, I pushed my window open wide and said good morning to Felix. Then I prayed along with the birds who were singing good morning to God.

I prayed that God would help me find my future BFF. That I would feel smart and confident, in a good way. Not a cocky way. I prayed for a big adventure. And then I prayed God would open my eyes to anybody lonely who needed a friend, too. Which is something Grandpa Goad always prays.

Prayers sound extra beautiful wrapped inside my grandpa's deep voice. I wished he was there for my first day. I'd tried calling him for a few days now, but reception is spotty up on Mount LeConte. That's where he was presently searching for birds. I couldn't wait to try again when I got home, though. Telling him about my Macklemore victory was the big reason I needed to chat. But I also wanted his opinion on the feather-flakes.

"Change is on the wind," Uncle Dash said as he helped me load into the van that morning. "What'd I tell ya?"

"Maybe what's changing is me!" I said this a little too loudly. I always talk too much and too loud when I get nervous.

"Maybe," he agreed. He held up his tattooed hand, which I clapped with a double high five.

We'd all decided it was smartest for Uncle Dash to drive me to school. Mama and Jupiter were proud of me, they said, but they were a big bundle of tangled emotions. And while I believe crying is a perfectly fine and natural way to express a person's heart, I didn't really want my parents in tears while I rolled into school. That's an awkward way to make a first impression. And first impressions are a big deal. They're why it took hours for me to decide on my first-day outfit.

"That jacket's so sparkly I'm gonna need my sunglasses," Dash said with a smile in his voice.

"Mama helped me do it," I told him as I buckled my seat belt. I ran my fingers down the flickery sequins of my front lapel. There's no dress code at Macklemore. But every student is given a school jacket they're allowed to personalize however they choose. I decided to make a statement on my first day. So late last night, Mama helped me sew shiny gold sequins all over the arms and down the front. Then Jupiter helped me decide on a seashell necklace and heart-shaped earrings for accessories. That's when I knew my parents really were proud of me, even if they were afraid. If I've learned anything, it's that it's possible to feel both at once.

It's possible to feel a thousand things at once.

I waved to them as we drove away, smiling bright enough for them to see. I wanted them to feel the joy-kabooms in my soul.

"I can't believe they're letting me do this," I said to Dash.

"I can't, either," he admitted.

"I can't remember the last time I was this freaked out. Or excited. I'm freak-cited."

"You'll do great, Olive. You've got a hobbit-heart. You're made for adventure." He said all this like a promise, and I tucked it deep in my heart.

The town of Wildwood is probably the same as most mountain nooks: We've got several little shops, a cupcakery, a town library, and a post office with a spray-tan room in the back. Lampposts flicker on the sidewalks when the sun goes down. Magnolias bloom starry-white in the summer. And all year, in every season, birds of all feathers rest on the rooftops and build their nests in the Lonesome Oak on the town square. It's a peaceful place. A pretty place.

Sometimes, it feels like a magical place.

"Ah!" Dash shouted as the van squealed to a stop at the red light. Now I was the one jumping like a stale piece of bread out of a toaster. Dash never yells about anything. He didn't even yell the time he saw a mouse scamper across the kitchen floor with a Cheeto in its mouth. "I knew something was happening, Olive. Look over there. Do you know who that is?"

At the end of Main Street sat a little restaurant with a copper roof called the Ragged Apple Cafe. It was owned and operated by a fancy baker-lady named Nester Tuberose. Ms. Tuberose was basically a legend all her own at this point. She stayed at her orchard, mostly. If she was at the cafe, she was only there very early baking her famous apple pies. I'd seen her maybe three times in my entire life.

But today she stood outside, staring up into the tree-tops. She wore a long, flowy blue dress covered by a flour-dusted apron. Her hair was piled up on top of her head, poofy to a point like a gray volcano. She had a pinched face and a small pair of glasses perched on her nose. And she kept her fists propped on her hips, like she had business to do with the pines.

"I wonder what she's looking for?" I asked my uncle.

"I bet she can feel change on the wind," he said. "The Tuberose family can tell the future, you know. It's on account of one of their apple trees. The legend says there's an apple tree up on Grave Hill that will tell your future in a single bite."

"That's really cool if it's true," I said to Uncle Dash as we drove away. "She could just be excited, ya know. Some change is good."

"She didn't look excited," he pointed out.

(Admittedly, he was right.)

A voice on the radio snagged my attention.

". . . the feather-flakes are only temporary."

We reached to turn up the volume at the same time, and heard the gravelly voice of our town mayor. "They're nothing to get worked up over. Now, you'll hear all kinds of things about these, uh . . . feather-flakes . . . in the coming days. Everybody loves a legend, don't they? But rest assured, this is just some fancy-pants version of rain or sleet. And yes, I know a blue moon is coming—it's all coincidence! Nobody panic!"

The mayor laughed nervously.

"Why would anybody be afraid?" I asked Dash. "Also, what's a blue moon?"

"Pretty sure it's the second full moon in a calendar month," Uncle Dash explained. "I'm telling you, Olive—people can feel something in the air right now."

"People in this town are also wildly superstitious," I reminded him. "So it could be just that."

"Could be," he said. "Or it could be a whole lot more."

Friend, it was a whole lot more. But I was too focused on my own adventure to even sense it.

The brakes squealed again as Dash stopped the van in front of a tall, rusted gate. The gate was woven with iron roses and a tall golden *M*, matching the *M* on my jacket.

"We're here," I whispered. My heartbeat sounded louder than the words coming out of my mouth. But, as if those two tiny words I'd managed to squeak out were magic, the letter broke in half as the gate swung open. We drove down a long, rain-soaked road twisting over green fields and deep into the far-off woods. Fog looped around the tree trunks there like octopus arms—reaching for me.

Welcoming me.

"You can see the school spires from here," said Uncle Dash. I rolled down the window to get a better look.

I already knew that Macklemore had two spires, just like a castle. The first spire is where the library is located. "What's in the other spire?" I asked.

"Janitor's closet," said Uncle Dash. "Most of your classes will be on the first level. But there is an elevator, now, if you have classes on other floors. And there are ramps, too. I don't think your parents realized how accessible Macklemore is. History is great, but we gotta improve on history. Especially in a school. That's the point, right?"

"Totally," I said with a very slight shake in my voice. My hope-bird heart was fluttering madly.

I heard the wet pavement swish beneath the tires as the van stopped at the front entrance. There, Hatch Malone stood waiting for me. Hatch always goes to school early with his dad so he can have some time alone to shoot hoops in the gym. They offered to bring me along, too, but I wanted some extra time for first-impression preparation.

"He looks thrilled to be here," I joked to Uncle Dash. Really, Hatch looked kinda miserable. His blue hood was popped up over his head, and his hands were shoved deep in the front pockets. There was absolutely zero trace of a smile on his face.

Dash chuckled a little. "Hatch is a good kid, Olive."

A perfect kid, I nearly pointed out. But I decided to focus on the moment at hand instead. The air smelled like roses, like rain, and a little bit like fresh apple pie. That had to be a good sign. If magic had a smell, surely it would be that!

"Ms. Pigeon will meet you in the office," said Uncle Dash as he helped me transfer to Dolly. "She'll help you to your classrooms so you don't have to worry about people knocking into you."

"I could probably do that part myself," I said.

"Well, see how you feel about it after today," Uncle Dash said reasonably. "She'll also help you to the bathroom if you need her."

I nodded quickly. "I remember." I had no desire to talk about the bathroom situation around Hatch. It's not like I needed help in the bathroom. But maybe Ms. Pigeon needed to push me there, for some reason.

"Okay," said Uncle Dash. He stood back and took everything in. "Do you want me to help you through the door or—"

"I can do it myself from here," I said. I adore my family and I'm grateful for their help, but I really can do most things by myself. And while I shouldn't care what people think, a first impression is a big deal. It's why I wore sequins!

"And yes, I'll be careful," I promised Dash, before he could remind me again. "And no, I won't fall. If people get too close, I'll scream, 'I'm fragile! BE GONE!'"

"Great," said Uncle Dash. "Maybe let Hatch push you over the door humps. They're tricky."

He leaned back against the van and shoved his hands into his pockets. Uncle Dash isn't the type to hover, but I knew he'd wait to make sure we got inside okay.

Now it was just me and Hatch, who is still mostly a stranger to me. Who really didn't want me to be there at all.

"Care to push me inside?" I asked. "Past the tricky door humps?"

Hatch's hands gripped my wheelchair handles. "You sure you trust me to push you?"

"Is there a reason I shouldn't?" Even though I was talking to Hatch, it looked like I was just talking to the empty air ahead of me. It's always awkward trying to talk to the person pushing my wheelchair. If I look up, I'm looking up someone's nose. If I speak out in front of me, I look like I'm talking to myself.

"I won't hurt you, right?" he asked. I could have sworn I heard a nervous tremble in his voice, which kinda surprised me. Because if Hatch was nervous, did that mean he cared? Probably not. He probably just had a tickle in his throat.

"You won't hurt me unless you push me off a hill," I said. He made a sound like an almost-sort-of-maybe laugh. Then he began pushing my wheelchair.

At the speed of the slowest snail on earth.

"HATCH!" I hollered.

"What?!" he shouted. My wheelchair came to a jolty stop. "What'd I do?"

"Nothing," I told him. "But school starts at eight a.m. Not five p.m. You can go faster."

"Okay," he said. "Right. Okay."

And he started moving again. Turtle-paced this time. But at least it was an improvement.

A school bus's air brakes hissed against the sidewalk behind us. I heard the the bus door creak open, then dozens of sneaker soles flopping down on the sidewalk. Kids were stepping out of the bus. One of them could be my future BFF! So I sat up straighter. I pushed my hair behind my ears and pulled my heart-shaped sunglasses down over my eyes.

Suddenly, the kids were all around me, walking in herds and whispering things to one another. I only heard snatches of the words they were saying *fear and hope . . . the woods . . . the wish.*

"Did you seeeee the feathers?" one little girl squealed excitedly, running up to her friend and throwing an arm around her shoulder. They giggled and skipped inside the school, pigtails bouncing. I'd never had a friend like that when I was younger. But now, everything was about to change.

I smiled when people passed by.

I even waved, once or twice, when they made eye contact. I felt extra brave.

And bold!

And my jacket was sparkling. This was the moment I'd dreamed of!

But . . . nobody was looking at me at all, really. They weren't staring, which was nice. But nobody smiled back at me, either. Nobody said hi. Every student moved in a wide circle around Hatch and me. Like there was some invisible stink-bubble force field keeping them away. Partly, I knew some people were jazzed up about the feather-flakes.

But there was something else, too. I could feel it in my heart, and it hurt.

"Does this seem weird to you?" I asked Hatch.

He hesitated but answered truthfully. "Yeah . . . the teachers told everybody about you."

"What about me?"

We were so close to the huge double doors now. But Hatch was taking a slow millennium to get there.

"They told everybody that you're new here and that you start today. And that you're . . . fragile. To be careful around you."

"Oh," I said. My heart sank into the vicinity of my sneakers.

"They didn't mean it in a bad way," Hatch said, keeping his voice low. "They didn't want people to avoid you."

"But that's what they're doing," I said, almost whispering. "That's what they'll do." I didn't say this like I was angry. I wasn't. It's just a fact.

"Not for long," he said. "Once they get to know you, they won't."

I appreciated that Hatch was trying to be nice. But even he has no desire to get to know me. Why would anybody else? All morning, my excitement—my hope—had felt like a birthday balloon getting bigger and bigger in my chest as I got closer to Macklemore. But now that floaty feeling inside me was starting to . . . deflate. I knew Macklemore might not be exactly what I imagined. But what if it was *nothing* like I imagined?

I closed my eyes and listened to the birds:

Fragile!
That's what the ravens
in the treetops hollered when they saw me.

Fragile. Fragile. Fragile,
croaked the bullfrogs in the woods,
loud and proud for me to hear.

Fra gile
is even what my heartbeat sounded like.
And in the space between beats, I wondered if I'd made
a bad decision.
But Hatch kept pushing
closer to the door.

There's a place for me here, I told my heart.
There's a friend for me here.
There's magic in these high walls.

These high, beautiful walls. Macklemore School
looked like a place that had fallen out of a fairy tale. From
the foundation to the tall castle spires, the whole building was made of faded brick. Fluffy curtains of green ivy
waved around some of the windows. The border of the
tall double front doors was made of white stone. And deli-
cately carved into that border were . . .

"Hummingbirds," I said.

"Where?!" Hatch shouted. My wheelchair stilled.

"Uh . . . carved around the door."

"Oh. Those." He sighed. "I thought you meant . . . Never mind."

Real hummingbirds are tiny, adorable, and lightning fast. But the birds carved into the stone had wings taller than me, bent in front like they were holding the doors wide open with their strength. They looked mythical and wild.

"Hummingbirds are considered good luck charms in the state of Tennessee," I told Hatch. "Did you know that? My grandpa says if you see a hummingbird, everything can change for the better."

"I believe it," Hatch said. And then more softly, so low I almost didn't hear: "I'm counting on it."

CHAPTER 8
Mr. Watson's Chicken Miracle

I have a feeling very few places in the world actually look as magical up close as they do in someone's imagination. But Macklemore came really close.

The floors were worn and wooden. The hallway walls were brick, same as the outside. And since most students were still unloading from the buses, or grabbing breakfast in the cafeteria, those halls were mostly empty. I had plenty of time to observe every corner of them since Ms. Pigeon pushed even slower than Hatch Malone.

We passed a trophy case, a pencil machine, and a wall devoted to second-grade artists who'd cut their names into the shape of butterflies.

VELMA,

PARMA,

DESHON,

AMIR.

Every name on the wall had wings. That felt so right to me.

I felt butterflies inside me, too.

"This is the beginning of the biggest adventure of my life," I told Ms. Pigeon. "I keep reminding myself that it's okay to be afraid and excited. I call it freak-cited."

"Mm-hmm" was her only answer. I'd tried to make some easy conversation with Ms. Pigeon since we'd met in the office. But she didn't seem to want to talk. Everything Ms. Pigeon said was quick, to the point, and a little trembly sounding. This surprised me, because Ms. Pigeon herself actually looked very fun. She wore a neon-blue T-shirt, jeans, and sneakers. Her gray hair was pulled away from her face into a tight ponytail, like she was ready to have a good time. I imagined her with a smile as bright and bold as the colors she was wearing, but I hadn't actually seen her smile yet. No matter how much I smiled at her.

So I mostly kept my thoughts to myself as we rolled on down the hallway. When my flutters felt too intense, I focused on the truths ahead of me:

My future BFF is here somewhere.

Change happened, and here I am!

"And here we are!" she said, and sighed like she'd been

holding her breath for the past ten minutes. Taped to the door in front of me was a paper sign that read:

MR. JOHN WATSON'S SIXTH-GRADE ADVENTURERS

"You'll like him," Ms. Pigeon said. "Everybody likes him. He's probably the best teacher we've ever had here."

"I can't wait to meet him!" I said, reaching for the doorknob.

"No, no!" she said, reaching over me. "Let me do that."

My shoulders slumped a little, but I managed to hold back my frustrated groan. I figured it would be obvious that I could open a door by myself. I can do most things by myself. I thought Ms. Pigeon would just be there for a little help early on, while I got settled in to Macklemore. But now I wondered if it would feel more like she was babysitting. At the same time, it was really kind of her to help. I didn't want to be rude!

Don't overthink it, Ollie-bird. That's exactly what my grandfather would say to me if he were here and not chasing wild birds in the Smokies. So I smiled and said, "Thanks."

Mr. Watson's room was quiet in a comforting way: The way warm sunshine on a lake is quiet. The way an old library is quiet. The way a hug is quiet. If it's possible for a room to give a hug when you walk into it, Mr. Watson's classroom did that. Since it wasn't time for school to start, there were no students in there yet, besides me. Which was kinda nice, actually. I was thankful I didn't have to make a grand entrance, for one. But it was also nice to meet the room this way. My heart had time to settle in.

"It smells like oranges and crayons," I said. The back wall was one big bookshelf that I couldn't wait to explore. Another wall was full of handwritten poetry and sketched self-portraits. I couldn't wait to add my face to it. Everything looked normal. Except one big box in the front of Mr. Watson's class. Underneath the dry-erase board, nestled beneath a red-glowing heat lamp, were a bunch of chicken eggs.

"I was not anticipating this," I said, leaning over to get a better look.

"I think you should go into every room anticipating two things," said a kind voice behind me. "Anticipate making new friends. And anticipate miracles. That right there is a box full of chicken-egg miracles."

Mr. Watson, leader of the sixth-grade adventurers, was leaning against his desk in the far corner of the room. I hadn't even seen him when we first came in. I'd been too dazzled by bookshelves and an egg box.

"Welcome, Olive!" he said as he ambled toward me. Unlike Ms. Pigeon, his smile came easy. It was as bright and friendly as his yellow sneakers, the kind of smile you feel in your heart as soon as you see it.

"Hello," I said, with a quick wave. "Not to be cheesy or anything, but it's my greatest dream to be a sixth grader here."

"I'm so glad to hear that!" he said. And then he looked at Ms. Pigeon and said, "We can take it from here, Barb."

"You sure?" Ms. Pigeon asked, then whispered, "I'm kind of afraid to let her out of my sight."

I almost laughed because, one, why was she whispering? I could hear her. Also, two, how far did she think I'd be able to get?

"Positive," Mr. Watson assured her. "We'll holler if we need anything."

I heard Ms. Pigeon let out another sigh of relief. Or maybe I was the one who was relieved; who knows?

"I can push myself in here?" I asked once she'd disappeared out the door.

"How about this," said Mr. Watson. "You do whatever you feel comfortable doing. Unless you ask me to help, I won't interfere. Deal?"

"Deal," I said. And then I had to ask, "Why are you hatching chicken eggs in here?"

"As a reminder that miracles are all around us," he said. "We've got chickens about to hatch up front. And back there around the bookshelves there's a cocoon almost ready to split. You won't believe how exciting it is when we're reading a book together one day and *BAM!*

Chickens! Butterflies! It's important to keep an eye out for everyday miracles. Especially right now."

"Why now?"

Mr. Watson sat on the edge of the desk in front of me, clasping his hands in his lap. He lowered his voice and said, "Have you seen the feathers falling all around town?"

"Yes!" I said, wheeling closer to him. "And I'm glad you called them feathers. My mama is convinced they're some kind of sleet, but I'm an amateur expert at birding. I learned the skill from my grandpa. Merlin Goad? You've probably heard of him. He's the most famous person in the state of Tennessee, besides Dolly Parton and Little Debbie. What I'm saying is that I know a feather when I see one."

Mr. Watson nodded as I talked, listening very carefully to me, which I appreciated. "Have you asked your grandfather what these particular feathers mean?"

"He's on an important mission," I said, adjusting my wheels slightly. My sequins were reflecting on Mr. Watson's face and making him squint a little. You should never be afraid to shine, friend. But be prepared to adjust that shine for people who aren't expecting it.

"You might want to get in touch. Because some people think those are more than feathers." Mr. Watson lowered his voice to an almost-whisper: "Some people think there's magic in the air right now."

The tiny hairs on the back of my neck went prickly stiff. "What kind of magic?"

I startled when the bell buzzed through the overhead speaker.

"I'm sure we'll talk about it in class today," Mr. Watson said to me. I don't know if it was something about his voice or his kind smile, but I knew that my heart liked him. And I knew I couldn't wait to hear about this feather-magic, either.

"A quick question, Olive—do you want to introduce yourself today? Or will that make you too nervous?"

"Way too nervous," I verified. I pulled my heart-shades down over my eyes. "I'd kinda like to blend in."

"No problem," he said. "Your desk is up front over there. I've got you surrounded by some really kind students, including your brother."

"Stepbrother," I clarified.

And as if my stepbrother had been summoned from the depths of CoolKid Land, the classroom door flung open. And in he bounced. And I do mean BOUNCED. I knew he was wearing Coach Malone's special sneakers before I even saw his feet on account of how close his head got to the ceiling.

"Everything go okay with Ms. Pigeon?" Hatch asked as he walked alongside me to my desk. Mr. Watson had already pulled out the chair so I could roll underneath it, which was super kind.

"I guess," I said. "I think she's really anxious about pushing me places. Sometimes people hear that I'm fragile and treat me like a stick of dynamite."

Hatch didn't smile. Or laugh. He just nodded and slid into his desk beside me. Then he pulled out his comic book and fidgeted with his hoodie sleeves, the exact same as he does at home. But here's what was weird:

Hatch didn't talk to anybody else who came in the room.

Not the guy who sat behind him.

Not the girl with long braids who carried a zebra-striped backpack.

Nobody. Not a single, sneaker-wearing soul. All the other kids talked to one another. But Hatch didn't say a word.

This surprised me loads considering Macklemore is the place where Hatch Malone is Mr. Popularity. He's in every club, so he says. His friends come to the house all the time. So . . . where were they now?

Then again, this was a weird day for everybody. The feather-snow had folks completely rattled.

Eavesdropping is a skill I'm good at and happen to enjoy greatly. And I kept hearing the same words whispered all around me, tossed out like birdseed for my curious ears: *fear and hope . . . the woods . . . the wish.*

On a gust of banana-perfume wind, a group of girls burst through the classroom door. They were all dressed alike: denim shorts and cropped T-shirts and Macklemore jackets. They wore pink scrunchies around their wrists and laughed almost completely in unison. I felt a familiar little tug down in my heart: I would love to laugh with them. I would love to have friends I could roll into the room with, already knowing some incredible secret.

Hold on and hold tight, I reminded my hopeful heart. *Your future BFF is here somewhere, too.*

And then, just before the late bell buzzed through the speakers, a girl with wings walked through the door.

She wore a T-shirt and denim overalls with a constellation of enamel pins stuck to the front: a rainbow, a taco, a piece of pizza, and a heart (my signature!). She was East Asian with black hair that she wore in a loose braid over her shoulder. She carried her backpack in one hand and a toolbox in the other. And on her back, she wore a pair of wide, glorious cardboard wings. She shrugged out of them easy, as if she'd done it a billion times before, and slid them carefully into the basket underneath her desk.

Which was right beside my desk.

Her notebook made a slapping sound when she tossed it down in front of her. She'd used an eraser to draw her name thick and cloudy across the front.

GRACE ALICE CHO
ENTREPRENEUR

I'd never met anybody gutsy enough to wear wings as part of their everyday outfit, but I knew I wanted to talk to someone who did. I might even want to be friends with someone who did.

"Your wings are dynamite," I said just as she flipped open her notebook to start writing.

She startled like I'd just woken her up from a day-dream. And maybe I had.

"Sorry to bother you," I added quickly. "I just think they're super swanky."

"Thanks!" When she smiled at me, I saw a flash of silver braces. "The wings aren't actually mine, though. I just made them for someone else to wear."

"If you made them, they're yours."

She threaded her fingers together, considering my words as if I'd said something truly profound.

"I like that," she finally said. She pulled an index card out of her notebook and handed it to me. "I'm Grace, by the way."

The card had the same info as her notebook, with a couple of additions:

GRACE ALICE CHO

ENTREPRENEUR

CUSTOM DOGHOUSES FOR YOUR K9 BELOVED
& OTHER ARTISTIC NEEDS

OFFICE LOCATED BACKSTAGE, FOSTER AUDITORIUM

"Wow," I said. "I've never met someone who builds doghouses. Or makes wings."

"The wings are for the school play," Grace informed me.

"A play sounds fun." And it really did—I love theater! Mama always says I'm destined to be an actress, and I agree. Mostly, though, I was just excited to be carrying on a conversation with someone my own age. Felix will be so proud when I tell him. So will Grandpa!

Maybe Grace Cho is my future BFF!

"All right," Mr. Watson said, walking to the front of the classroom. "Everybody dig out a pen and turn to a blank page in your journal. After what happened this weekend, I know you've got a lot to process in your journals. First, I wanted to make sure you know that we have a new friend up front today. Her name is Olive."

The tips of my ears felt prickly and warm. This must be what happens when twenty sixth-grade adventurers stare at the back of your head at the same time.

"We believe three things in this class, Olive," said Mr. Watson. "First, we believe that miracles surround us every day. We take time to notice them. Second, we believe every person deserves respect and kindness. And third, we believe an ink pen is a direct line to a person's heart. Your words are a kind of magic you carry inside you. That's why we write each morning—to turn the magic loose."

I nearly sighed loud enough for the whole class to

hear. I realized he was talking to everyone. But I felt like Mr. Watson was talking to me, specifically. And to know someone besides my parents was already affirming my love for words was incredibly inspiring.

"Every morning, we freewrite," Mr. Watson continued. "I don't look at the pages, unless you want me to. This is just a time to write about whatever happens to be in your heart. So, get going! Pen to paper. Make some magic."

I've never scrambled so quickly for a notebook in my life.

Backpacks unzipped. Papers rustled.

I reached down into the depths of my backpack for a pen. And came up empty.

"Bacon," I said.

"You brought bacon?" Grace asked excitedly.

"No, I forgot a pen." I scrambled through my backpack over and over, as if I could magically make it appear. "I got new folders, a little pencil sharpener shaped like a heart and a set of erasers that smell like fruit. But I forgot a pen. I thought I laid everything out last night!"

"I've got one," said someone behind me. I spun around to say thank you. But the words came to a screeching halt inside my throat. The boy in the desk behind mine probably looked the same as lots of sixth-grade guys all over the world: He was Black, with short, cropped hair and a kind smile. He also wore a shark-tooth necklace. I appreciate a person who knows a good beach souvenir. He pulled a purple pen from behind his ear. "It's a lucky pen. It's yours."

"What makes it lucky?" I asked.

"I decided it is, so it is. And, hi! I'm Ransom McCallister."

"I'm . . ." Now my own name felt stuck inside my mouth. What was wrong with me? I don't get flustered around boys, not even cute ones with shark-tooth necklaces. I'm just Olive. That's all I needed to say: *I'm Olive*. But what came out was, "I'm . . . new. New Olive."

And I swiveled around so fast my ponytail popped him in the face. So much for first impressions.

"If you don't know where to start," Mr. Watson said, "begin with a magical what-if. Someone help me with an example. What if . . ."

"What if the hummingbird is real?" yelled one of the pink-scrunchie girls.

A chorus of sharp gasps filled the room. Then everyone fell totally and immediately silent.

CHAPTER 9

Twig Moody and the Wish-Bird

I was already perplexed by the sixth-grade adventurers. Everybody knows hummingbirds are real. Hummingbirds were migrating toward Tennessee that second. I know loads about them. I didn't volunteer any insight, though. I didn't want to seem like a big-bird-brain know-it-all.

I glanced to my side and saw Grace staring at Mr. Watson as if everything else in the room had disappeared. To my other side, Hatch Malone had actually closed his comic book. He even sat up straighter to listen. So I did, too.

Mr. Watson waited until we were all looking toward the front of the room. Then he smiled like he knew some wonderful, magical secret. "I wondered if somebody might want to discuss the hummingbird after this weekend. Anybody know the old legend? When feathers fly upon the wind . . ."

"The hummingbirds shall soon descend!" the pink-scrunchie girl said dramatically. Everybody laughed like she'd said something truly hilarious. No matter what this girl said, people kept their eyes glued to her when she talked. They watched her like she was a celebrity. "That's the only part I know," she said. "I thought maybe you'd tell us the rest."

"I think I will, Maddie," said Mr. Watson. "Everybody knows Wildwood, Tennessee, is famous for its birds. We've got more varieties than anywhere in the world. So it's not weird to see a stray feather on the wind, or in a ditch, or floating in the fountain by the courthouse. But many years ago—around this same time of year—people swore they saw strange feathers falling over this town like snow."

Mr. Watson began to pace across the front of the room as he spoke. "The first time the feathers fell was 1937—the rainiest year on record for Wildwood. It was a tough time back then. The Great Depression had left most people too poor, and too tired, to do much celebrating. The rain and storms turned gardens into sloppy mudholes; nothing would grow. Even the apple trees withered. Sadness was so thick folks nearly canceled the May Day Festival. Thank goodness the town pressed on. Because on the first day of that festival, as folks walked toward the fairground, dark clouds rolled over the town of Wildwood . . . and strange white feathers began to fall."

"Just like now!" said Grace. She looked excited enough to spring out of her seat.

"Exactly!" said Mr. Watson. "And as those feathers fell, a strange little girl showed up at the May Day Festival carrying an empty birdcage. She was so small she had to stand on a chair for folks to see her. Her name was Twig Moody, she said. And for anybody who believed, she had plenty of magic to share."

Chill bumps freckled both of my arms. Mr. Watson's voice has a low, lovely rumble-sound to it, like a storm in the summer. I would listen to any story he told. But, for some reason, I was especially interested in this.

"People sold all kinds of things at the May Day Festival," he said, leaning back against the whiteboard. "Jars of homemade honey. Poems scribbled on news-paper scraps. Bundles of flowers that were mostly grass and dandelions. Then Twig Moody showed up, offering a wish for free. Nobody knew where she came from. Or who she belonged to. She looked like the other mountain girls. She wore an old, flowery dress and had long black hair that fell in a neat braid over her shoulder. Kind of like yours, Grace."

Mr. Watson startled us when he jumped up onto his

empty chair. "She stood on that chair, waving an empty cage around, promising a wish to anybody who believed. But nobody listened at first. Maybe it's because she was young. Maybe because it sounded too good to be true. But finally, a bunch of kids gathered around her to listen to what she had to say. And that's when Twig Moody began her tale."

"Just a second, please," said Grace. She ripped a full page from her notebook and settled her pen on an empty line. "Okay, I'm ready."

Bacon, I thought. *Should I have been taking notes, too?*

Mr. Watson nodded. "Twig Moody said birds had been drawn to her since she was born. Hummingbirds in particular. Her mama found hummingbirds hovering over Twig's cradle when she was a baby. Whole charms of them followed her to school each day and hovered around her window until she opened her eyes each morning. Then one day, in the midst of the hardest year of mountain sadness, a new kind of hummingbird found Twig crying by a creek in the woods. Twig said this one was different than all the rest, so bright it beamed, shiny as a fallen star, tiny as a baby's fist. Feathers tipped in gold. As soon as she saw that bird, Twig knew it was magic in the feather—magic in the bone—of that brave little creature."

A chill rippled down my spine at those four little words he said: *magic in the bone.*

Mr. Watson stepped off the chair and made his way through the aisles. "Most of those kids wandered away before she was even done talking. All except the Everly sisters."

"The who sisters?" asked Grace.

"Everly," said Mr. Watson, writing the name on the board in beautiful swirly letters. "Two orphaned girls, willowy-thin with sad eyes and frayed ribbons in their hair. They'd come to the festival on a bus with other kids from the Tennessee Home for Children. They listened to the whole story, devoured every word. Most importantly, they believed. And Twig Moody gave them a riddle. 'Solve the riddle,' she said, 'and you'll find a tiny hummingbird who'll grant a mighty wish.'"

"Tell us the riddle!" Maddie begged.

"Tell us!" people said, like an echo, all around the room. All I could do was nod my head—yes—because I wanted to hear it, too!

"Listen closely," Mr. Watson told us.

Grace flipped to a clean piece of paper again. This time, I definitely took notes, too.

"An honest wish won't go unheard . . .
Not for one who seeks the hummingbird.

When bone-white feathers start to fall,
When the blue moon rises tall,
Where fear and wonder both collide,
That is where the creature hides.

Life and death aren't in its grasp,
But if you're brave enough to ask,
There are still wishes,
Yours for keeping,
Find the bird and then,
Start listening!

The words you didn't know were missing
Will drift across your broken heart.
Shout those words into the dark!
Reach for the bird in the blinding light,
Make a wish that's brave and right.

And the bird will leave a golden kiss
On the face of one who gets their wish."

I knew this was probably just a legend, one of a billion folktales that float through this town like fireflies in summer. But the story still took my breath away. It lit my imagination with possibility. What if something so wonderful really existed in this place?

After a few heartbeats, Ransom said, "I bet the Everly sisters made a thousand wishes all at once. That's what I'd do."

"Me too," Mr. Watson said. "But not them. Nobody knew their wish at first, of course. Birthday rules apply to the hummingbird: You can't tell anybody your wish, or it might not come true. So all anybody knew was that the Everly girls brainstormed until they solved the riddle. They ran into the woods . . . and they never came back out."

"Whoa," said Grace, locking her arms around her chest like she was giving herself a hug. "What happened?!"

"The townspeople wanted to know the same thing," said Mr. Watson. "They thought maybe Miss Twig Moody was up to no good, that maybe she was connected to a wild band of outlaws holding those girls for ransom. But Twig insisted she was not. She said the Everly sisters had wished for wings to fly away to a family who loved them, and that was exactly what happened."

This made my heart ache. I'm so lucky to know what it's like to have sweet parents, like Jupiter and Mama. I can't imagine spending years not having them in my life. What a wonderful wish.

"Twig Moody disappeared the next day. All she left behind was a wide-open cage and a sheet of paper with the very same riddle she'd given the Everly sisters."

"The feathers came again, though," said a boy in dark glasses across the room. "My granny said they fell when she was a kid."

"That's right," said Mr. Watson. "The feathers flew again in 1963, if I remember correctly. I think it was a few kids around your same age who claimed they found the bird and made a wish."

I could hardly catch the breaths rising in my chest. This kind of magic seemed too wonderful to be real.

"So I just want to make sure I understand," said Grace Cho. "There's also a blue moon rising this year, too, on the first day of the May Day Festival. And the feathers are falling again."

"That's right," Mr. Watson confirmed.

"It's coming again," Grace said, her voice hovering on a whisper. "Isn't it?"

I glanced back and forth between the two of them. My scalp was tingly with excitement.

"I guess we'll see," said Mr. Watson.

That settled it for me: As soon as I got home, I had to get in touch with the Goad and get some answers about the feather-flakes! And the legend! And the hummingbird! If it's a bird, Grandpa Goad knows about it.

So . . . why hadn't he ever told me before?

"It's all just a story," said Maddie. "I don't know why people are getting so worked up over this."

"Maybe so," Mr. Watson said. "Maybe it is just a story. But maybe stories are everything. Let's get going. Pen to paper, now. Make some magic on the page. And if you don't know what to write about, try this: What if I found the hummingbird? What would I wish for?"

Mr. Watson refused to talk about the hummingbird after that. He went back to his desk, whistling as if it was a totally ordinary Wednesday. But everybody around me began writing, feverishly, like the story of Twig Moody had cracked their imaginations open wide.

That's what it did for me. I scribbled lines like:

What if I had a wish to make?

What if the bird came to me and I could ask for one thing? Just one wonderful thing?

What would I wish for?

My pen stilled. Four words drifted across my imagination as swiftly—and suddenly—as a burst of feathers: *magic in the bone.*

Suddenly, a wild wind howled across the parking lot, flinging open the fire escape door. Whirls of feathers gushed into the room.

Papers flew.

Notebooks fluttered like a thousand paper wings.

People gasped.

"It's just weather, you weirdos!" yelled Maddie.

But some of us weirdos—like me, like Grace, like Hatch Malone—were wonder-struck. I reached for one of the feathers, and it melted in an instant, leaving glitter all over my fingertips.

CHAPTER 10
Three Maddies

Here's a challenge, friend: Try focusing on anything—*anything*—after you find out that there's a magical hummingbird headed for your town.

I knew Macklemore Middle School would be awesome. But a wish-granting bird would be life-changing. Loads of questions were crowding my brain, but these were the biggies: Why hadn't I heard this story before?

And, more importantly, why hadn't I heard it from Grandpa Goad, the most famous birder in the state?

Even Mr. Watson—who was surely the greatest teacher of all time—couldn't completely hold my attention after that. Especially during math. Numbers are my nemesis. I don't like to focus on them even in the best of times. I breathed a little easier when he started talking about decimals. At least I knew about those already.

Then my stomach spiraled into twisty-anxious knots again because I learned decimals in a completely different way. I almost asked for help but didn't. I didn't want people to think I was behind. I'm not, at all. So I took a deep yoga breath, ignored the melting feathers all around my desk, and got to work. I was trying so hard to focus that I didn't say another word to anybody, or even check the time, until Ms. Pigeon walked in the room to show me where the bathroom was at. Leaving early was awkward but I tried to roll with it.

Roll with it. Get it?

That was a joke, but maybe not a good one. Here's the point: My brain felt like a snow globe from the new routine of it all. I felt shook-up over and over, all morning long. Lunch, I hoped, would be better. Maybe I could sit at a table with Grace or Hatch and talk about the feathers and the bird and the wonderful story we'd heard this morning! Maybe I would make friends with everybody else in my class while I was there!

I heard the noisy roar from the cafeteria before we even got to the two double doors. But the sound wasn't pretty, like an ocean roar. It reminded me more of the lion and tiger cages at the zoo in Knoxville.

You got this, Olive Miracle, I told my fluttery heart. I pulled my heart-shaped sunglasses down over my eyes as Ms. Pigeon pushed me into the room.

The Macklemore cafeteria smelled like peanut butter and jelly and glue. And kind of like a trash can before the trash goes out. The feathers in the air had created a buzzy electricity in the place. There was so much happy chatter and laughing. I wanted to laugh, too. But first I had to find a place to sit. I sat up straighter and looked for the three sort-of friends I thought I might be able to connect with. Like Grace Cho, entrepreneur. Or Ransom "Shark Tooth" McCallister. I'd even settle for sitting with Hatch. But I didn't see any of them.

"They all eat lunch in the library," Ms. Pigeon said when I asked her about them.

"That sounds great!" I said. "Maybe I could go there—"

"I already have the perfect spot for you!" said Ms. Pigeon, cutting me off. I knew she was trying to be super thoughtful, so I tried to smoosh down my disappointment.

She pushed me toward the front of the cafeteria, where tall windows framed the faraway fields and woods. Melba Marcum strummed her banjo at the front of the room. She wore one of the green VOLUNTEER vests and paused to wave when she saw me. Her twin sister, Jessie, wore a green volunteer vest, too. She was pushing around a cart of swirly-topped cupcakes with icing as white as her hair. Those looked glorious!

"Those are Tuberose Apple Cupcakes," Ms. Pigeon said. "They're way too sweet, if you ask me." She grimaced when I glanced up at her. "Or they're too sour if Nester Tuberose is in a bad mood when she makes them. She bakes the meanness right inside."

So cupcakes were a no. Lunch with Grace or Ransom or Hatch was a no.

I sighed and looked straight ahead, trying to figure out what to do with my face.

Because Ms. Pigeon pushed me even slower than Hatch Malone. So slow I felt like I was in my own private parade straight down the middle of the Macklemore cafeteria. I almost waved like a parade person, just to be funny. But what if nobody thought I was funny?

"I'm going to put you right up front with the sweetest girls in this school." Finally, Ms. Pigeon settled me at the end of a long table, with the same students who'd sat in the back of Mr. Watson's class. The pink-scrunchie squad! I locked the brakes on my wheelchair.

"Ladies," she said, "this is Olive. Olive, meet the Madelines!"

The three girls around me smiled in perfect unison.

It was a little creepy at first, like a synchronized puppet show. But that thought quickly melted away from my brain as a better thought bloomed in its place:

These could be my new friends. My lunch friends!

One of them might be my future BFF!

I wasn't about to say that, of course. It would sound too creeper-ish.

Just. Be. Awesome, I reminded my heart.

(*You already are,* my heart thumped back. Or maybe it was just my mama's and Jupiter's voices stuck inside me. Sometimes when people say things to you enough, you start to believe them. Maybe it's true for bad things, but I know it's true for good.)

"I'll get your tray for you," Ms. Pigeon said. "The buffet is too tall for you to reach. Mac and cheese, okay?"

"Mac and cheese is superior," I said. Then I looked at the Madelines and smiled. "Hi, y'all."

First Maddie—the class skeptic and class celebrity—said "HI!" and smiled. She had pink braces. Second Maddie said "Hey!" over a mouthful of food. She'd used her pink scrunchie to pile her hair on top of her head in a cool topknot. The third Maddie didn't say anything. She was nose-deep in her Tennessee history book, mumbling over the words, trying to memorize something.

"What grade are you in?" First Maddie asked me.

"Sixth," I answered. "Like . . . you."

We were just in the same class together, I wanted to remind her. Had she not noticed me at all? Had I blended in that well?

"Ooooooh," First Maddie said. "I thought you were a little younger because of all the, ya know . . . sparkle. Like, your wheelchair is very cool. Super unique, the way you did your name in sparkles in the back. My sister did the same thing to her backpack this year. She's in third grade."

"I liked sparkles in third grade, too," said Second Maddie. "I thought the same thing. I don't mean it like it's babyish." She blinked at me. "Just more of a third-grade thing."

"I'm not offended," I said honestly. "Glitter's just my favorite color."

"Aww," said First Maddie. And then they were quiet.

This was not the conversation I'd dreamed of having.

Ms. Pigeon plopped a tray of macaroni down in front of me. The cheese sauce jiggled like Jell-O.

"Thank you," I said. I reached for a milk carton and realized my fingernail polish was glittery, too.

Is there such a thing as too much glitter?

Does glitter make me look immature?

Was it stupid to wear heart-shaped sunglasses and sparkles in middle school? And why did I have to bedazzle my wheelchair in the first place?

The more I thought about it all, the more I realized I actually looked nothing like the Madelines. They were wearing mascara, for one. Mama wears mascara. She'd probably let me wear it, too. But I didn't even think about wearing makeup to school. The Madelines smelled like banana perfume and hair spray. I smelled like coconut deodorant, which I was very thankful Mama had reminded me to wear. They had painted fingernails and matching friendship bracelets. And then of course there's the big difference: They weren't in wheelchairs.

Honestly, that might not be a big deal, either, if Dolly didn't look like a parade float. I'd even put glitter on the wheels before I left the house. What in the actual world?

I pulled off my heart-shaped sunglasses and stuck them in my backpack.

A wad of paper sailed across the lunchroom, popping Third Maddie in the face. It plopped onto her history book. "Ugh," she said, rubbing her forehead where the paper had thumped. Then, "Ooooh. It's a note! Maddies! Scoot!"

The other Maddies slid to the other side of the table, close enough to to read the note for themselves. I couldn't really do that. And I didn't know if they'd want me to. I ate macaroni quietly while they giggled and talked. The pasta tasted like cardboard. It settled like pebbles in my stomach.

The longer I sat there, the less magical the school felt.

Mr. Watson's class had flown by. But lunch seemed never-ending. I didn't want to bother the Maddies or nudge into their conversation. So I pulled my book *Blubber* out of my backpack and started reading instead. I always felt safe in a book. (Judy Blume is my third-favorite person I've never met.)

"What's she doing here?" I heard Second Maddie whisper. "Is she new?"

I was just in class with you is what I wanted to say. But First Maddie spoke up instead, this time in a lower voice than the way she talked to me: "Ms. Pigeon brings the disabled kids to sit here sometimes, remember? So they don't feel left out."

The words in my book all blurred together.

I felt carsick, except I wasn't in a car.

Lonely, even though I was surrounded by other girls.

People have called me disabled before. I call myself disabled. It's not a bad word, and it feels as neutral to me as having brown hair. It's one part of who I am. But her tone made *disabled* feel different, and not in a good way. More like a scratchy-sweater way. I don't want special treatment. I just want to be myself.

My eyes stung. But I refused to cry. Especially here at the table. I couldn't even cry in a bathroom stall, like people do in movies. The only bathroom big enough for my wheelchair was in the office, and only Ms. Pigeon had the special key to get inside.

I had to acknowledge the obvious truth:

Maybe I shouldn't have come here. Maybe the slick floors weren't the real danger at a school like this. Maybe I was just too weird to really belong.

"I'm going to, um, take my tray," I said. "Where does it go again?"

"Up front!" First Maddie said brightly. "Want me to do it for you?"

"I got it," I said. Because how hard could it be to take a tray?

I braced the tray on the tops of my legs, clicked my brakes, and backed up into the aisle.

Where I accidentally—but immediately—knocked into someone.

"Sorry," I said quickly. But Ms. Pigeon saw it happen and came running into the cafeteria shouting, "SHE'S FRAGILE! BE CAREFUL!"

"I'm fine!" I said. And for some reason, I lifted my hands to reassure her. I talk with my hands a lot, like Grandpa does. We're like flutter-bys. That's a bird that flaps its wings any time it tweets, even if it's not trying to fly. This was not a good day to be a hand-flapper, though. I accidentally flipped my sticky-macaroni tray onto the floor, where it clattered as loud as a village bell in a mystery movie.

A terrible quiet settled all over the room.

Miss Melba stopped picking her banjo.

Somebody whistled and clapped from the far-back corner.

"Don't," First Maddie growled in that direction. "She can't help it."

I couldn't help it? What did that mean? Was it worse if they clapped . . . or if they didn't?

"Sorry," I whispered. "Wow, that's embarrassing."

Miss Jessie was suddenly beside me with a sweet smile on her face. "Don't worry about it, darlin'! I drop stuff on the floor all the time."

I wanted to help her clean up my mess. But I knew I could flip my wheelchair if I leaned over that far. So I just said again, "I'm so sorry."

"You need to call me when you need help," said Ms. Pigeon, a little too loudly, as if she were talking to a toddler and not an eleven-year-old. She backed me out of the room extra slowly. I had plenty of time to see my mess and everyone's faces as we left.

This time, I didn't try to smile.

I didn't try to wave.

I mostly watched the laces of my sneakers and the floor floating underneath me.

I wasn't sure if I wanted to blend in or stand out here at Macklemore. Deep down, maybe I wanted a little bit of both. Maybe everybody does. But I knew for sure I didn't want to stand out like this.

"Wait right here," Ms. Pigeon said, parking me away from the cafeteria, in a quiet corner beside a dead plant. "I'm going to go grab some paper towels. After lunch, students get to pick an extracurricular hour. Some kids do band or art or take baking classes. Think about what you're interested in and I'll show you where it is when I get back, okay?"

She scurried away and I realized I was very close to the office.

Maybe I should have zoomed in there, called Mama and Jupiter, and told them that they were right. That I shouldn't have tried this. Not yet. That I wanted to come home.

Home, where my books, my journals, and my pelican were waiting for me. Home, where I could call Grandpa Goad, hear his voice tell me I would be okay, and then talk to him about this fancy feather-weather and the hummingbird legend.

Home, where I was safe.

Except I sometimes think there's more to life than just being safe.

I reached out to touch the brittle brown edge of the plant. "You'd really bloom if somebody'd water you a little," I said. I wiped the dust off the leaf with my finger. Then I dumped the rest of my water bottle into the plant's base.

I closed my eyes.

I was still fragile, even here.

Especially here. That's still how they all saw me.

The ocean inside me roared, reminding me that there is so much in me that people deserve to see. I am a thousand things, a million constellations.

That was the first time a sudden, magical what-if came floating through my mind:

What if . . .
I looked more like them? And moved
like them? Would it be
easier?

I shook that thought out of my imagination.

Help me out, I asked God in my heart instead. *And please not by sending another fashionably strange old woman.*

God didn't answer. But a sudden warm wind blew over the back of my neck. Something tickled my cheek and tapped my nose.

I opened my eyes to see an icy, bone-white feather floating past my face and tumbling down the hallway. I didn't know if I was just imagining it, or if maybe it blew inside when someone opened a door. But this feather felt so different from the others I'd seen. It was the only one, for starters. Like it was sent just for me. I watched until it landed flat against two tall double doors at the end of the hallway.

The feather-snow melted over a plaque inscribed with the words: FOSTER AUDITORIUM

Taped to the other door was a piece of paper I had to wheel closer to read:

AUDITIONS INSIDE FOR THIS YEAR'S MAY DAY PLAY!
HOPE LIKE FEATHERS!
A PLAY ABOUT THE WILD LIFE OF EMILY DICKINSON!

A few other students from Mr. Watson's class walked around me to go inside.

Obviously, this was the theater Grace had mentioned. And this was definitely the extracurricular activity made for me. Maybe this was why I came to Macklemore! If there's any place you can be anything, it's on a stage! If there's one place I could prove I wasn't fragile, it would be up there. Nobody looks fragile in a spotlight unless they want to. I wiped the tears out of my eyes that I didn't even realize I'd been crying.

I didn't wait for Ms. Pigeon to come back. I unlocked my brakes and pushed toward the doors—toward that one mysterious melting feather.

Toward the destiny that was mine.

CHAPTER 11
How to Be a Tree

The Macklemore auditorium door was heavy, so opening it on my own was a chore. Thankfully, somebody saw me trying to wedge it open with my wheelchair and flung it out of my way.

"Thanks," I said without looking up. "Glad you were there—"

Ransom McCallister was looking down at me, a ball cap twisted backward on his handsome head. He smiled and said, "No problem, New Olive. Cool name, by the way. Sounds like a town."

"It's just Olive," I clarified. My heart flip-flopped again even though I could *not* understand why. I smiled back, a little too big. My face felt warm. Thank goodness the room was mostly dark. I did not want to be the kind of girl who freaked out just because a guy was talking to her. Even if he did have great taste in beach souvenirs.

"I figured," he said.

A tall, pretty woman with curly hair was standing onstage, speaking to a small group of students. Foster Auditorium probably wasn't huge, but it felt like a wild, new planet to me. Three red-carpet aisles stretched from the door I'd just rolled through, all the way down front, dividing up three sections of folded seats. An old chandelier with fake, burned-out candles dangled over the audience. The stage was empty today: no sets, no actors, just the pretty theater teacher holding a clipboard. All the stage lights shone down on her, casting her long shadow out into the aisle.

"Is it too late to audition for a part?" I whispered to Ransom.

Ransom looked around and finally found a stack of papers. He presented me with a script.

Hope Like Feathers:
A Play about the Wild Life of Emily Dickinson

"Final tryouts are next week," he said. "So just depends on how fast you can read and memorize it, I guess. I say go for it. Break a leg." As soon as those words came out of his mouth, Ransom's eyes widened. His smile faded. "Oh gosh. Oh shoot. I'm so sorry! I didn't mean that."

"It's fine," I said. "I know you didn't mean it literally.

And hey, I've broken my legs so many times my luck should be through the roof, right?"

His shoulders eased and he smiled. "Need any help getting down the aisle or anything?"

"I got it," I said. "But thank you." My neck still felt warm when I rolled away.

If nobody else had been in the auditorium, I would have let my wheelchair glide a little faster, so I could float like a bird all the way to the front. But I didn't want to interrupt what the teacher was already saying. So I rolled slowly down the center aisle toward the first two rows, where the rest of the students were sitting.

So much had transpired since this morning, when Grace Cho told me about the theater, that I'd pushed this possibility to the way back of my brain. But theater might be the exact answer to my biggest prayer. I love plays: I write them; I convince my family (minus Hatch) to act them out over dinner sometimes. And I love to act them out myself. Acting is one of my big career goals, along with taking care of baby otters. I'm not sure that's even a real career, but I think I'll be great at theater.

And also, theater happens on a stage. People could see that I'm capable of all sorts of awesome things. And I might even make a friend or two.

Since I'd promised Mama and Jupiter I wouldn't stand up any more than necessary, I didn't transfer to a seat in the rows with anybody else. I pulled up to the end of the second row and locked my brakes.

The teacher winked at me. I smiled back and clasped my hands in my lap. Like I mentioned, I flutter my hands when I get excited. I wanted her to see that I could stay calm and take this seriously.

"So as I was saying," she said. "The May Day play is more of a skit. There's a lot going on in town that night. The last day of auditions is Tuesday, then we'll take another week to practice before the big night. Don't forget, after today's meeting, practice happens after school. This is a serious commitment! Carefully consider which part you connect with and want to read for. We'll find a place for everyone. EVERYONE!"

She emphasized the last word and looked at me again. This time I glanced down at my script.

"You might not be ready for a lead yet," she continued. And based on the tone of her voice, I still felt like she was talking to me. "And that's okay. Everybody starts somewhere! We all have a part to play here! So take some time to read aloud to one another, or to yourself, all right? And I'll come around and check on your progress."

I'd barely turned the page when a spiky-haired guy beside me leaned over.

"Good moooooooorning, Macklemore Middle School," he said in a low, lovely voice. "It's play season in Foster

Auditorium and I'm here to interview our new girl . . ."

He stuck the fake mic in my face and waited for an answer.

"Olive," I said with a smile.

"I'm Dylan!" He dropped the paper and reached to shake my hand. "I'm more of a hugger," he said sincerely. "But I don't want to break you."

"You won't break me," I assured him, grateful for his honesty. "I'm really not going to crumble if somebody touches me. My bones are just more brittle than the average person's. I don't mind hugs. And look!" I said, looking down at his hand in mine. "We match!"

Dylan wore the same glittery nail polish I did. I whispered, "The girls at lunch thought it was kind of babyish."

"The Madelines?" Dylan asked, rolling his eyes. "Don't worry about the Madelines. *Babyish* is their new herd word. One of them says something and then the rest of them repeat it and laugh for weeks. They're like parrots. Tomorrow they'll probably all be wearing glitter. I like people who aren't afraid to sparkle. Life's too short to blend in, right? You gotta do you."

"Exactly," I said. "That's exactly why I want to be here. Have you done theater before?"

"Oh yeah," he said. "Tons. I'm going to be on Broadway someday. I've got a gig in Dollywood this summer."

"Oh my gosh," I said, nearly shivering with excitement.

I'd never met a bonafide celebrity before besides my grandpa! "I totally believe you'll be on Broadway. I think some people are born knowing what they're meant to do. Just like birds know they're meant to fly."

"PREACH!" Dylan shouted.

"DYLAN," First Maddie yelled. "You're so loud. Calm down. Leave Olivia alone so she can read."

Dylan rolled his eyes and waved the comment away. "I'll let you get to it," he said. "Holler if you need anything. I know what it's like to be new."

Was Dylan the Actor my future BFF? I didn't know, but there was certainly potential!

My hands trembled with excitement when I opened the first page of my script. Most of the characters in the play were birds: the Bird of Sorrow, the Bird of Joy, the Bird of Darkness, and the Bird of Hope. Apparently, Emily spent almost as much time looking out her window as I did. I imagined one of her birds as a pelican and giggled.

But it was the description of the heroine herself that stirred up a painful longing in my soul.

Emily Dickinson: shy poet, loves to write in her room. Story begins with Emily's sister telling her she will never have ideas worth writing until she leaves her room and sees the world. But Emily has a secret: She already sees wild, magical beauty—and whole new worlds—inside her imagination. As the birds teach Emily how to write those worlds on a page, everything begins to change.

I'd barely read through the line when Mrs. Matheson, the theater teacher, kneeled down beside me. "Hey there, Olive!" she said in a chirpy voice.

"Oh, hi!" I said.

"I am so glad you're here!" She tapped my script. "That's what I wanted to talk to you about. I just wanted to make sure you know that . . . there is some movement in this play. And . . . dancing."

"In a play about . . . Emily Dickinson, the poet?" I asked.

"Right," she said. "Well, sort of. It's one person's interpretation of Emily Dickinson. And I want you to know that we'll find a way to involve you. I don't want you to worry about that. But you might not be able to do the parts that happen on a stage."

I blinked. "What other parts are there in a play? Besides the parts on a stage?"

"Oh, we can get super creative," Mrs. Matheson said with a wink. "The sky is the absolute limit. This is theater! You get to express yourself here! Be anything you want. So we'll find a spot for you down here on the ground." Her eyes brightened with a sudden flash of an idea. "Like a tree, maybe!"

My heart deflated like a sad old birthday balloon. "A tree?"

"Yes!" she said triumphantly. (Mrs. Matheson says everything triumphantly.) "A tree could be perfect for you!"

"So I guess I'm open to that," I said, choosing my words carefully. "I just . . . I'd like to read for a speaking part, if that's okay."

"Hmmm." She patted her hands on her thighs, considering how to ask the next question. "Did you read any plays in homeschool?"

"Frequently," I said. I really hoped Mrs. Matheson wasn't the kind of person who thinks homeschool is inferior just because it's different. I had a hard-core curriculum. My grades were great! Except in math. Because fractions are a beast. But I'm fully prepared to do a play.

"I might even read for Emily," I said. "I really connect with the description. Or maybe one of the birds. I know I might not get a part, but I'd like to try for one."

"Oh, that's so sweet," she said, and she made a little frowny face. "I feel terrible. Listen, we will find a part for you. Okay? We just have the stage issue to think about."

"We could just build a ramp," said a voice I recognized from earlier. Grace Cho was standing in front of us with wings on her back and a toolbox in her hand.

Mrs. Matheson smiled at her, but not exactly in a sweet way. "This is a private conversation, Grace."

"Yeah, I know," said Grace. "But I'm just saying,

ramps are easy to construct. If I had a mentor to help with the saws, we could build it in half an hour."

"Are you actually trying out for a part, Grace?" Mrs. Matheson asked. "I thought you were leading the set team. They meet backstage."

"Yeah, I'm headed that direction." Grace nodded. "A ramp would be part of the set, right? Just a thought."

She scampered backstage, wings wavering.

"We'll talk later, Olive," Mrs. Matheson said. She winked at me as she stood to walk away.

I looked down at my script—a script for a play that I would love to be a part of—feeling absolutely and utterly defeated.

This was a real play.

With props!

An actual audience!

And also, a stage my wheelchair couldn't access.

The same magical what-if from earlier came back again, looping through my mind easy as an eagle over Cove Lake:

What if the hummingbird was real?

I could wish for the stage to have a ramp so anybody could use it. Anytime. So the theater really was for everybody.

Maybe it's super selfish to think that. It would take someone a lot of time and effort to build a ramp. I probably shouldn't expect that kind of accessibility. Or maybe I should. Maybe everybody should. Don't stairs make buildings accessible, too? If the stairs weren't here, students would have to climb on the stage every time they used it. Without them, people would have to scale Macklemore School with ropes and ladders. Those are all good things for everybody. And so is a ramp!

But no matter what, I still wanted to read for Emily. I wasn't worried about moving or dancing. I'm great at moving around in my wheelchair. But there wasn't much I could do if I couldn't even get on the stage.

"You could just read a part so great down here on the ground that she changes her mind," said Dylan as if he'd just read my thoughts. He held out his fist for me to bump, which I did.

Fact: I like theater people.

At the end of the hour, Mrs. Matheson stood center stage alone, again.

"There is no feeling quite like this," she said. "When you are standing in the light. When you are becoming someone else."

Someone flicked the spotlight on, shining it around her in a perfect yellow circle.

"In this light," she said, "you get to become anybody you want. You get to make whatever you want out of these lines and sentences. Some people think theater is like playing make-believe all the time. And maybe it is! But it can help you see your true heart, too."

Class ended. Mrs. Matheson patted my shoulder as

she left, looping her bag around her shoulder. "You don't have to be a tree," she said.

My heart fluttered back awake again. Maybe I'd impressed her already!

"You could always be my assistant director, maybe? Or an honorary member of the theater troupe? Don't worry, is all I'm saying. There are lots of options."

She grinned like she'd just given me the best news of the day. I was speechless. "Stay put, okay? I'll let Ms. Pigeon know you're here."

She walked away, leaving me in the dark auditorium.

I rolled to the front of the room, to the foot of the stage. If I stretched my arm as high as it would go, reaching my fingertips up and up until

I could almost scrape the light from that spotlight.
It was fiery white,
a bright sun so close to me. But still
untouchable.

What if
I could run up the steps easy, like everybody else?
I imagined myself standing on the stage,
not sitting,
spreading my arms in the light.
I'd look like a wild bird in flight,
if I did that.

I imagined my family watching me,
cheering for me.
"Hope is a thing with feathers," I would say.
"That perches in the soul."
That was a line in the play. And I spoke it, like I
was in the play even though I was
alone.

I closed my eyes,
and said another line, then another.
I'm fast at memorizing.
It's like I can write words on my heart sometimes,
especially these.

Maybe I have poetry in my veins,
the same way the hummingbird
has magic in its wings,
magic in the bone.
It was just me and my voice in a dark theater, but it
felt like
church music,
like a rushing river in my soul,
like the first time you see a city skyline sparkle.
Like I'd found something so important there.

Maybe this was my place.
What if I could belong here?

What if the bird could help me?
Something touched my nose,
something fluttery-soft.
I opened my eyes assuming I'd see another lone feather.

A stray piece of magic, hovering on my nose again. But I was wrong.

This time the feathers were all around me. There were hundreds of them, falling like snow all over the auditorium. I could barely breathe at the beauty of it all. There's no way this many feathers got in through an open window or a cracked door.

They had to mean something.

And maybe they meant something for me.

What if
the hummingbird is real?

What if the magic
is for me?

I fluttered my fingers and whispered
Mr. Watson's words,
"Magic in the bone."
And the most dangerous what-if
of all lodged deep into my heart:
What if I found the bird?

What if I
made a wish?

I watched until the last feather fell, floating slowly down.
It turned to dust before it hit the ground.

CHAPTER 12
Grace Cho, Investigator

The feathers disappeared as fast as they'd flown, just like always. I was about to push myself back toward Mr. Watson's class when I heard someone backstage hiss, "Shhh!"

My horrible-wonderful habit of eavesdropping sucked me right in again. I wheeled around the corner to see what was up. The auditorium was connected to the backstage area by a long, dark hallway. I stopped midway, in a shadowy spot beside the janitor's cart, and backed up beside it until a broom-shadow hid me completely.

"Why 'shh'?" Dylan asked someone. "It's not like it's a secret! Everybody's going to be looking for it. Mr. Watson let the cat outta the bag. Er . . . the bird outta the cage. Whatever. Anyway, I can't be your associate, Grace. I have too many auditions to worry about a magical bird."

I should have known he'd be talking to Grace Cho. The

backstage doubles as her office for stage props and fancy doghouses. Apparently, in addition to art, Grace was also interested in finding the hummingbird.

So was I.

"I have no clue what that old riddle means," Dylan said. "I heard a bunch of people are going to the town library to look at old newspapers and get ideas. But that sounds like research to me. Which doesn't sound fun. Life is too short for that."

"Keep your voice down, Dylan!" I peeked around the corner in time to see Grace give him a light shove. "The Madelines are always spying on me."

"Whatever. The Maddies don't believe in the bird. They said it's babyish."

"That's to throw us off track!" Grace said. "They don't actually want to do research of their own for this thing, either. And you know none of them have worthy wishes. They'll probably wish for flat irons and boyfriends. But my wish is serious. It means the world to me. It's already April fifteenth, Dylan! That's a little over two weeks until the blue moon rises and the bird comes out! How am I going to find it in time?"

It felt weirdly empowering to be able to hide in the shadows. I know it shouldn't. I came to Macklemore to get out of the shadows—to make friends and have new experiences. But sometimes my heart needs a little quiet, a little darker place to think. I wonder if other people ever have that weird seesaw feeling in their heart, where sometimes you want so badly to be the one on the stage, in a spotlight, smiling. And some days you so desperately just want to blend in like the periwinkle crayon in a box: needed, awesome in your own way, but not really noticed.

Plus, I was perfectly fine with hiding in the shadows if it meant getting more information about the hummingbird. I was interested in finding it, too. And I was starting to wonder if it wanted to find me.

"You're really not going to help me?" Grace asked. I couldn't see her face, but I heard genuine, heavy sadness in her voice. "You don't want to find a magical bird and see if it grants your wish?"

"No." Dylan's voice was firm but kind. "The honest wish of my heart is to be a beloved Broadway performer. But I already know I can do that. I don't need the hummingbird."

I almost started applauding. Really, I didn't think Dylan would have enough time to be my future BFF. But gosh, I admired his heart.

"I admire your confidence," Grace said grudgingly.

(*Same!* I wanted to shout.)

"You don't need it, either," he told her. His shadow moved closer to hers. "You don't need a wish to make—"

"Stop," she said, spinning around. I ducked farther back in the darkness. "That's nice of you to say. But I have to find it." Grace shrugged out of her wings and propped them in the corner. "I don't even know anything about birds. That would be a good place to start."

My eyebrows floated up my forehead at this revelation. I knew tons about birds.

And I knew someone with even more bird facts, if I could ever get in touch with him: Grandpa Goad. I still couldn't figure out why he hadn't told me about Twig Moody's wish-bird. Surely he knew! But whether he did or didn't, Grace and I could make a great team. *I* could be her associate. Maybe that's exactly what I needed to help me find it! The only problem with that plan was this: Who would get to make a wish if we worked together to find the hummingbird?

Because I might have a real, true, honest-to-goodness wish.

It was just an idea, a silly what-if, but I could feel it, burning like a tiny little flame inside my heart. *Magic in the bone.*

I held my breath, frozen still as a statue, when Grace and Dylan ran by me, late for class. I didn't let the breath out until I heard the heavy doors close.

Until I was alone in Foster Auditorium.

There were no feathers this time.

There was no spotlight.

There was only me and a tiny little wish-flame in my heart that kept growing bigger, brighter.

What if I could make one wish that changed everything?

Something rustled in the cluttered backstage area.

A scrawny shadow darted out from behind a stack of boxes—it was a kid! They zoomed through the back exit door before I could see anything about them at all.

Someone else had been spying on Grace Cho, besides me.

She and I weren't the only ones interested in the hummingbird.

CHAPTER 13

Magic in the Bone

"Home sweet home," Coach Mo declared as he pulled up beside our cottage in the Piney Woods. As soon as he helped me into my wheelchair, he set off for a jog. I was grateful for this. Usually I'm happy to have a conversation with any creature who'll talk to back to me, whether it's a PE coach or a cute pelican. But I had tangles of thoughts in my head. I needed to get a pen to paper and turn them all loose.

Hatch held the door open for me to roll inside. We never made eye contact, though. He kicked off his Bouncers and propped them beside the door for one of his mysterious night walks. Then he raced upstairs. Apparently, he had a lot on his mind, too.

I grabbed a box of fish sticks and zoomed toward my

room when Mama hollered my name from the couch: "Olive! Come in here for a sec!"

I winced. I wanted my parents to think my day was perfect, full of joy-kabooms. For one thing, I can't handle the thought of breaking their hearts even a teeny-tiny bit. And seeing me sad or upset would do that. But also, if they thought I couldn't handle school, would they let me do anything ever? I fixed a big, fake smile on my face and rolled into the living room.

Mama sat on the couch with a box of old pictures in her lap. Jupiter sat on the floor, pretzel-style, with an old scrapbook open in front of him. They were both still, staring at me, eyes wide and hopeful as two baby owls.

"Well," Mama said gently. "Did everything go okay?"

I nodded, my fake smile frozen in place. "Entirely fabulous."

They seemed to relax a little at this admission. The truth is that the day had been more of a seesaw of feelings. I almost cried once. Then I felt like the queen of the world a few minutes later. I loved the spotlight on my face. But I didn't love standing out (and isn't it the same thing?). I liked freewriting and reading but felt a little lonely overall. Then I heard a story about a magical bird. And I couldn't stop thinking about what it meant . . .

"It went better than I thought," I told them.

Mama let out a soft, happy sigh. Jupiter's shoulders

relaxed. He carried on with his picture flipping.

"Taking a walk down memory lane?" I asked, eager to change the subject.

"Yeah, I got a little sentimental this afternoon," Mama said. "I cleaned out the closet and found a box of your baby stuff. Come look at this."

Really, I wanted to get to my room and untangle my brain and feed Felix. But I sincerely love spending time with Mama and Jupiter. I clicked the brakes on my wheelchair and transferred to the couch. Jupiter helped me stand and hobble, easy-does-it, over beside Mama.

It feels both terrifying and delightful when I can put weight on my leg again, even this long after a fracture has healed. Sometimes I ache for solid ground; I think I long for it like a bird wants air. But when my foot hits the ground at first, it always feels so tingly weird, like my body doesn't remember what to do. I know that it should. Walking should come as naturally as snoring or sneezing. But it's like my legs have to be reminded how to do it every time. It's also hard not to think about the future when I take a step. Because there's also the reality, chirping at me in the back corner of my brain that someday, when I least expect it—SNAP. I might fall again.

I probably will fall again.

One step. Then another. That's what Mama and Jupiter tell me: Focus on the step in front of you.

What if I didn't even have to think about taking steps,
though?

What if walking was as natural as breathing?
What if,
what if,
the bird is real?

"Look at this one," Mama said.

My baby pictures are full of wheelchairs
and casts,
and little walkers
and tiny baby-braces made to fit my legs,
to hold them steady
to hold them straight.

My bones are just one part of me,
just a few stars in the constellations
that make me who I am
and I know this, but . . .
what if?

In every picture there is something broken,
and someone who loves me.
I was a lucky,
loved baby.

It would be selfish, to wish for anything besides this awesome life I have.

Wouldn't it?

"Here's a sweet one," Jupiter said. He handed me a photo. It was Mama, holding me in a rocking chair. I had a cast around both legs, which had to make holding me feel very clunky and awkward. But she still cuddled me close. I fit perfectly fine inside her arms. I just want to fit other places, too.

Back in the theater, when I was eavesdropping on Dylan and Grace, I had an idea for a wish. It settled into my mind like a bird in a nest, and it felt so right there. It felt good there.

For just a second, for maybe the space of a breath or a butterfly-clap, I thought . . . *What if I wish for normal bones?*

Is that a bad thing?

It made me so angry when the lady at New River prayed for my legs to be normal. For my bones to be healed. So it's probably terrible for me to want to wish for normal bones, too.

Or is it?

It's not like perfect bones would erase all the hurt we'd had to go through. But it would prevent a lot of pain from happening again.

"Remember these?" Mama asked, holding up a tiny little ruffled sock.

My smile wavered a little. I definitely remembered those. I wore them all the time when I was kid.

I had them on one time when I fell.

There were fractures before my memory started patching time together. I was ten weeks old the first time I broke my leg. It's not like I had some super baby brain and can remember that one.

But the first break I remember was

Easter Sunday.
"Those shoes are too slick," Mama had said.
"Be careful."
I'd just started walking solo again,
without my walker. I should have worn sneakers.
But the leather shoes were shiny-bright,
like Dorothy's shoes in *The Wizard of Oz*.
And the little white socks rippled like ribbons.

I remember:
I was
careful.
But even careful,
just taking a step,
my bone gave out.

POP.
I hit the white, wooden floors and

screamed.
I remember
Grandpa Goad
kneeled beside me,
rested a heavy hand on my shoulder
and prayed.
I couldn't see my mama, but I heard her.
Mama's voice was like a tornado siren.
She was a blur somewhere behind me,
floating around like a caffeinated butterfly.
Talking on the phone,
telling the hospital we're on our way.
Then she let a cuss word slip.

I remember
teardrops and sweat
dried sticky on my face.
"When it hurts," Mama said,
"you don't have to hold it in.
You can roar. Roar like a lion. Roar like
Aslan."
So I did. I learned to
roar. I found
the lion inside my heart.

"Olive?" Mama asked. She and Jupiter were studying my
face. Those two can read me like a book. So I grinned

again. I gave them the biggest, happiest smile I could stick on my face. "I have a little homework to do," I said.

They helped me back into my wheelchair.

And I zoomed toward my room.

Friend, I didn't mention this at first (because I thought it was babyish) but here's a fact: There are lots of fairy tales on my bookshelf.

There are Disney movies stacked on the bottom shelf, too, right beside all my Narnia books. I like princess stories. And stories about superheroes. And hobbits. And warrior girls who swing swords and lead wild armies.

That day, I touched every spine of all those books. And thought, *What if?*

What if the poisoned apple tasted the sweetest? And it transported Snow White to a whole other world?

What if the witch was really good, just misunderstood?

What if Sleeping Beauty woke herself up and found a castle of her own?

What if the story you think you know doesn't end the way you think it does?

What if magic really exists on this mountain and it's looking for me?

I opened the window to toss Felix a fish stick, but he was gone. The stick thumped against the ground. It was just God and me and a deep gray sky. So I opened my notebook to a blank page. Mr. Watson said that our words are like a magic we carry inside us. I used my lucky purple pen and turned my words loose. I wrote the fiery truth burning bright inside me:

I wish for
bones like steel.

Bones that don't break
when they dance,
or fall
or slide in the snow.
Maybe it's selfish,
to hope for that.

Maybe it's okay to be selfish if it's my body.

When the bird grants my wish, I know I'll have a lot to explain to Jupiter and Mama. They might even be sad at first. Because, yes, I know I'm a whole person the way I am right now. But I'll still be me when my bones aren't made of candy.

"Just a less breakable me," I said, whispering the words like a prayer.

Like a declaration.

The night passed like all the others in the cottage in the woods. Around bedtime, I heard the familiar sound of the screen door slapping shut. Hatch was walking into the woods again. Everything was the same outside. But nothing was the same inside me. Because now I knew the hummingbird was close.

On the night of the blue moon, I would find it.

And then I'd make my wish for normal bones.

For a wild and magical life.

I wondered if the butterfly in Mr. Watson's classroom felt exactly the same as me right then: ready to burst. Ready to become something. Does a butterfly realize all it can be before the cocoon finally breaks? I think maybe it does.

CHAPTER 14
The Plan

Uncle Dash had been right: Change was blowing through Wildwood. And I wasn't the only person eager for it. By Thursday morning, Main Street was packed full of folks wandering around, pointing at the treetops and smiling for photos. One family had on headlamps and wore matching purple T-shirts that read HUMMINGBIRD, STOP HERE!

Bacon. This was *not* good.

The May Day Festival was still two weeks away. That's usually when the crowds came. This time, tourists had come to town early, all probably exploring and researching and counting down the days until the blue moon. Kiosks were already being set up outside the Ragged Apple Cafe. They were selling candy apples and pie sticks and also maps of the town and the woods. And people were buying them!

Bacon. Bacon. *Bacon.*

Did all these people know the legend already? Did they know what it meant? Maybe they were just here to see the feathers falling. Still, I felt seriously outnumbered.

It's all good, I reminded my fluttery heart. *I have a plan!*

Somebody was going to find the hummingbird. Or maybe, more accurately, the hummingbird was going to find somebody. And I had a shot at this, too.

First, I had plenty of bird knowledge up my sequined sleeves, thanks to Grandpa Goad. Second, I had an idea for how to figure out what the legend meant. All I needed was an accomplice. A business associate. Someone who could do the literal legwork of helping me. Then we'd just have to *find* the actual bird.

I'd read enough novels to know that any quest like this could be dangerous.

It would be challenging.

And my gosh, I could not wait to get started.

"Oh geez," Hatch said as he met me at the van in front of school. "Did you write another sermon?"

"No," I told him, pulling my stack of papers against my chest. Mama helped me transfer to Dolly. "This is a contract."

"For what?"

"Does it matter?"

"It does," Hatch said. "I like to know things."

"Alas," I said with a dramatic sigh, "this must remain a mystery to you."

"Do y'all need anything before I head out?" Mama asked. Then she cocked her pretty head at me and smiled. "You seem really excited today."

"I'm ecstatic," I said. "I have joy-kabooms inside my soul."

I almost blurted out everything then: about the bird I'd find and the wish I'd make. I probably should give her a heads-up at some point. Wishing for regular concrete bones would be a big life change. But this was a secret quest I couldn't share with my mom. Not yet. She'd be heartbroken if she knew I wanted to change something about myself. So I picked another truth to share. "It's theater. You know it's my life calling. I'm excited about going back today."

"Your grandpa knew his life calling was to be a birder when he was your age. He said sixth grade is when he became absolutely obsessed with birds."

I knew that already, of course. Grandpa Goad had told that story plenty of times. However, he'd neglected to mention a magical hummingbird. "We're a lot alike, me and the Goad. I can't wait for him to get home."

Trying to connect with him up on Mount LeConte still wasn't working out. But if my idea for an accomplice succeeded, it wouldn't even matter. I'd just tell him all about it when he got home in a few weeks.

"Olive!" Mama hollered as Hatch rolled me toward the front door. He spun me around slowly.

"Olive you." Mama mouthed the words. That's just

a silly thing we say to each other sometimes, like a secret handshake with words. I guess she didn't want to embarrass me, so she whispered. But I'm never embarrassed by love-you words. Maybe some people think that's babyish, to tell your parents you love them. But I think love's the best truth in the world. I'd sing it if I were a bird. I'd throw love in lightning bolts if I were a storm. But all I am is me, so I say it when I mean it.

"Olive you right back," I said out loud with a wink. Then, as Hatch slowly spun me back around, I put on my game face. I had business to attend to this morning. I knew Ms. Pigeon would be waiting for me at the office. Which was why I couldn't go there first.

"Sneak me to the auditorium?" I asked Hatch.

"Wait . . . what? *Sneak* you there?"

I nodded. "Sneak me past the office so Ms. Pigeon doesn't know I'm here yet. I need to talk to Grace Cho, and I've got lots of papers in my arms that I don't want to drop."

"Whatever" was Hatch's typical excited response. He pushed me over the door humps. Through the office door, I could see Ms. Pigeon propped against the counter, talking to the school secretary.

"Hunker down, Hatch!" I whispered extra loudly. "Hunker *down*!"

I leaned over so she wouldn't see my head floating past the office window. To my great surprise, Hatch actually lunged down, too, and started pushing me that way.

"This is really awkward for me," he whisper-shouted.

"I'm sorry to put you out," I said honestly. It's really not my goal to embarrass my stepbrother. "I'll never forget this kindness. Getting to the auditorium is life-changing for me."

Hatch mumbled something about how I'm the most dramatic individual he's ever met in his entire life, but I was too anxious to respond.

"Thanks," I told him when he opened the auditorium door for me to roll through. "See you in class!"

He didn't say a word in response, just nodded. I assumed he disappeared into the hallway the same way he disappears into the woods every night, all stealthy quiet and sneaky fast. I never even heard him close the door behind me.

The main stage and auditorium were mostly empty, and very quiet. Ransom wasn't working the spotlight. Dylan wasn't running lines down front. But something had changed: Now the stage lights illuminated a half-painted set. Flat brown houses, boxes of fake flowers, and a tiny desk were center stage. This was Emily's world, slowly coming together. I wished I could get on the stage and roll around and explore, touch every new piece and feel out the space. But there was no time today.

I wasn't there for Emily. I needed the help of sixth grade's most infamous entrepreneur.

As soon as I rolled through the corridor connecting the auditorium to the backstage, I saw a shadow of Grace's wings stretched all across the wall. Four rickety steps were still the only way to access any part of the stage area. So I quietly locked my brakes in front of the first step and waited while she worked.

Should I knock on something? I wondered. I was afraid to just yell out her name. What if she had a saw or something in her hand?

Grace was kneeling down on the ground, her back to me, painting another backdrop. This one was an exact replica of the brown houses onstage. But instead of black and white, these were all vibrant, rainbow-colored houses. They were as multicolored as the wings on her back, which were covered entirely in tacky Christmas bows.

I looked down at the papers in my lap. Was this a stupid thing to do? Was this babyish? What would I do if Grace said no to my big idea? No joke, my heart would be more than a little crushed. My heart would be absolutely pancake-smashed.

As soon as I saw her put down the brush, I shouted, "Um . . . hi!"

"Olive!" she said, jumping a little as she spun to look at me. She said my name like she was genuinely excited to see me. That was a good sign, I hoped. She jogged down to the second step and took a seat facing me so we were at the same level. "What's up—"

I held out my stack of papers, to which I had affixed my own business card.

OLIVE MIRACLE MARTIN

PROFESSIONAL BIRDER

OFFICE = AT MY HOUSE

*BRING FISH STICKS FOR FELIX!

"I can help you," I blurted out. "And I think you can help me. I have an idea for a business transaction that could truly benefit both of us."

Grace's eyebrows scrunched together when she took the paperwork from me. But her face gave nothing away as she read.

"I know you are looking for the hummingbird," I said over the pounding in my heart. "I was eavesdropping yesterday. I shouldn't have been, I realize that. Being nosy is rude and your conversation was private. I'm sorry. Kind of. But I realized we have something big in common: I'm really interested in finding the hummingbird, too. And I've got a real shot; I'm a natural at spotting birds. We could help each other, you and me. And maybe this is cheesy, but I also feel like we have potential to be actual friends. So I drafted a contract. Whoever the bird chooses, it chooses. And we won't be mad about it. We won't let it affect any potential friendship we might have. But I do think we should combine forces."

I waited for the space of a breath, then another. Finally, Grace looked up at me, and just as she was about to say something, the bell buzzed through the speakers. I knew Ms. Pigeon was probably searching for me frantically in the hallways.

"Why don't you take some time to think about it?" I asked, mostly because I was too nervous to hear her answer yet. "I'll be around all day."

I don't know why I said this. Of course I would be around all day. It's a school and I'm a student. But Grace nodded professionally and so did I. And then I zoomed out of the auditorium and toward the Land of Misery.

CHAPTER 15

The Reverse-Cursed Mirror

The Land of Misery, better known as PE class, is the one middle school experience I would have been happy to skip. Contact sports are a big *heck no* because of my brittle bones, so I thought avoiding PE would be easy. But Coach Malone, who is also the PE teacher, thought it would still be a good idea for me to hang out in the locker room with the other girls while they got ready. He said I could make new friends this way.

But I felt as out of place in a locker room as a penguin on a hot beach.

Or as Uncle Dash probably feels when he goes to church. Where are you supposed to even look when a bunch of people all around you are changing clothes? It's completely awkward.

"OH. MY. GOSH," First Maddie yelled. She stood on one of the benches in the corner, waving a ragged piece of notebook paper like a white flag of surrender. "The boys made a list of the hottest girls in sixth grade!"

I groaned—a little louder than I meant to—and backed farther into the corner. I reached around and grabbed my book from my backpack. While First Maddie screeched about the list, I slipped into the pages of *Blubber*. It was hard to focus, though. For one, all I could think about was solving the riddle that would lead me to the hummingbird. How would I do that if Grace said no?

For two, a locker room is so loud. And it's impossible to focus on anything. Even yoga breaths didn't help me concentrate.

Second Maddie and a few others all grabbed at the paper, their squeals echoing sharply in the tiny space. But most girls just rolled their eyes, like I did, and went back to doing their own thing.

"I hate changing clothes for PE," said Third Maddie. She flopped down on the bench closest to me. "That must be nice that you don't have to." She winced. "I hope that didn't sound rude. I'm not being mean—I didn't mean it mean!"

"No, it's fine," I said. "I'm also glad I don't have to change clothes."

Even once I found the bird, made my wish, and got

turbo-bones installed in this body, I didn't think I'd have it in me to be an athlete. The only sport I knew anything about was Quidditch. I had explained all this to Coach Malone, too, who told me I could still be social in here. "Then maybe sit on the sidelines and cheer," he'd said. I told him maybe I could sit on the sidelines and read. He'd rolled his eyes and given up at that point.

"Sorry I didn't say much at lunch yesterday," Third Maddie said. "I have to study a lot harder than the other Maddies do. And even though everybody calls me Third Maddie, I would rather just be Madeline."

"I'll call you whatever you want," I said, closing the book and holding it in my lap.

"Is that a good book?"

"*Blubber*? Gosh, it's one of my heart-books," I told her. "I've read it already, but I love it more every time. It's like a movie in my head. Want to borrow it?"

Third Maddie . . . er . . . Madeline's eyebrows floated up toward her perfectly straight hairline. "For real?"

I nodded quickly, pushing the book into her hands before I could change my mind. It's one thing to give a favorite book to someone who is actually a friend. But giving a book you adore to a complete stranger is a terribly vulnerable feeling. I don't know how librarians do it all day long.

First Maddie startled us both when she jumped up on a bench by Madeline, balancing on one leg like an elegant flamingo.

"Do you want to see the list, Third Maddie?" Then, very loudly, she said, "Hi, Olivia!"

I waved, but I didn't smile.

"I don't care about the list," Madeline said, flipping through the book.

"Are you sure?" First Maddie said, leaning down low. "You're number eight . . ."

"Only number eight?!" Madeline shouted, snatching the paper away. "Why? What happened? I was number two last year—when did I get ugly?"

"I'm number one again," said First Maddie. And she jumped to another bench so effortlessly, like it was a balance beam and this was the Olympics and

I totally lost my focus.
Because when her legs were right in front of me,
my first thought was, *Wow, they're so pretty.*

And I've never in my life thought
a leg was pretty before.
It's just a leg!
Just a body part.
Like an ankle or a toe.

But Maddie's leg was straight and tan
with zero scars. Her leg actually holds her up
without shattering like a Jenga game.

142

This is what pretty looks like,
I realized.
According to the list,
This is #1 Sixth-Grade Gorgeous.
And it's the opposite of
me.

My eyes fluttered back to my lap. I really wished I hadn't given my book away. I know how to hide in a book, how to tuck myself into the story and pretend I'm somewhere else. But now I'm stuck here, in a locker room that smells like sweat and cheese.

And instead of imagining someplace better, I imagined that I looked like a Madeline, wearing shorts and a T-shirt and sneakers and not being self-conscious at all. I'd have braces that sparkle and a pink stripe in my hair. I'd be wearing mascara and my legs would be normal.

Straight.

Strong.

Scarless.

I'd be a normal height, too, so nobody would think I'm a little kid anymore.

I would love to be their kind of normal.

"Let's go, ladies!" Melba Marcum shouted into the locker room. She must have been Coach Mo's assistant that day. Some girls ran out squealing. Most trudged out with heavy-hearted groans. Melba gave gentle hugs to anybody who wanted one, and lots of people did. PE is a really terrible thing to force upon a person.

First Maddie tossed the List of Hotness on the floor behind her. "See you out front, Olivia!"

And then I was alone in the room with the list.

It doesn't matter, I told my heart.

It's so silly. Just ridiculous and stupid.

But I couldn't help it. I looked down.

Hottest Girls in Sixth Grade

I rolled my eyes. But I read the names . . .

1. First Maddie
2. Second Maddie
3. Amy Webber
4. Grace Cho

On and on and on it went. My name wasn't on there. I knew it wouldn't be. I didn't want to be on a stupid list like this . . .

Did I?

My thoughts started scampering around like a wild ostrich stampede inside my head. Ridiculous thoughts like: *Would I be on there if I had legs that were totally straight, like the Madelines? Legs that only have scars from bicycle wrecks and not scars that run from hip to knee where a rod was installed?*

I rolled over to the mirror and looked at myself. I've looked in mirrors tons of times. Sometimes at home, I look at the mirror, hold up a Pringles can, and pretend I'm Reese Witherspoon winning an Academy Award. (I have her whole speech memorized.) But this time was different. And it wasn't just my legs that looked super different.

My whole body looked super different, too. Sometimes, people with OI have a large chest. It's called a barrel-shaped rib cage. I have one of those. The whites of my eyes are a little bit blue, another normal part of OI called blue sclera. Mama and Jupiter tell me it's cool and not even noticeable, and I thought they were right. But today, it was like I could see it more clearly than I ever had before.

I'm shorter. My arms are longer. My shins are bowed, because that's the way my bones grow. My body is so different and it's the kind guys don't find attractive, I guess.

Or maybe it's the kind they don't even see.

Which is no big deal! A body should be the least interesting thing about a person. So I don't know why it hurts a little.

The longer I looked in the locker room mirror,
the more I wondered if it was like
the mirror in *Snow White*.
Magical in a reverse way,

a cursed way.
In a terrible way.

I'd never seen my body
like this,
like my bones were a cage holding the real me captive.
Suddenly, I could find
constellations of things I
didn't like
about myself.
Is that why I like to be alone sometimes?
Is that why the shadows feel so right,
because that's where I fit?

Listen, I'm eleven.
I've got a lot of life ahead of me: Someday
I'll vote and serve jury duty
and maybe even chew on hard candy
without Mama staring at me afraid I'll choke.
And while I don't plan on getting married
until I'm old, I still want to.
I've always figured marriage is like
having a best friend around all the time,
somebody you get to play Nintendo with
and watch movies with and hold hands with.
What if I'm never ever attractive

to someone else
just because of this body I happen to be stuck inside of?
And why am I even thinking about
how I'll never ever get married in sixth-grade PE?!

Some what-ifs are magical,
like Mr. Watson says.
And some are like vultures,
circling around your imagination
and looking for a broken place to bite.

What if
I'm not the kind of girl
who falls in love
or does amazing things
or gets to have a monstrously big life?

"I will be," I promised the girl in the mirror.
I don't break promises to myself.
Thank goodness for the
hummingbird.
Thank goodness for a wish.

Where fear and wonder both collide,
That is where the creature hides.
I just had to find that place.

"Olive?" I heard Coach Malone shout from the gym. "Where you at?"

"En route," I said, pushing away from the cursed mirror.

Then a sudden shadow appeared in the center of the door ahead, stretched all across it like a giant ink stain, narrowing to wing-shadows it got closer to me.

"Okay, Olive Martin," said Grace. I turned around and saw the contract rolled up in the front pocket of her overalls. "Let's talk."

CHAPTER 16

The Dagger, the Dodgeball, the Butterfly

Grace Cho was wearing a glorious set of wicker wings full of tiny holes that let the light shine through. She also wore a very sparkly smile, which made me nervous, honestly. I didn't know if that meant she actually wanted to be my partner or if she was gearing up to kindly tell me "no, thanks."

"I've been running around in these to test the weight," she said. "They're for the Bird of Summer. I made them from an old chair on my grandma's porch."

"They're incredible," I said. "I'd love to be one of the birds in the play. I'd really love to be Emily, actually. But a bird would be cool, too. Speaking of birds . . ." My voice faded into silent hope.

"Let's do it," she said. I could have sworn her eyes sparkled, but maybe I was just seeing things. "And I think finding it together is an awesome idea."

"Yeah?" At that moment, if I'd actually had wings like Twig's magical bird, I would have flown right out of my chair and hugged her. Instead, I rolled close enough to be covered by a woven wing-shadow.

"Why not?" Grace beamed again, silver-sparkly. She propped her hands on her hips. "It's nice to know that it matters this much to somebody else. Some wishes are just wishes, but sometimes they can—"

"Change everything," I said, finishing her sentence. She nodded, and her eyes fluttered down for just a second. Just long enough to make me wonder what was so special to her, what wish was she carrying deep in her heart. I hoped she would tell me someday. I really wanted to know.

"Plus," she said, looking back at me, "how silly would it be if I said no to help from a legit birder?"

"And I need the help of a brilliant builder-artist," I said. "And if we actually see it out somewhere and you find it, and I can't run after it, you can."

"Totally," Grace said. "But you should probably know . . . I'm not a fast runner."

"I don't think you need to be. I have some ideas. But first, to commemorate this amazing occasion, I brought—"

"LADIES!" Coach Malone yelled from the gym. "You are missing a riveting game of dodgeball!"

Grace groaned. "Wanna sit together out there? Or I could sit beside you, I mean. I don't do PE, either. I have asthma."

"OH! Awesome!" I squealed. "Wait, not the asthma part. That's not awesome. But it'll be nice to have somebody to sit with."

Grace pushed the door open to the loud sounds of screeching sneakers and high-pitched screams. The rest of the sixth grade was divided in two on either side of the gym. They were taking turns hurling a dodgeball at one another.

It was exactly as un-fun as it sounds.

"Watch my FACE, First Maddie!" Dylan shouted. "I have auditions in Dollywood!"

"Watch *my* face!" Maddie shouted back.

I scanned the class for my stepbrother but I didn't see him. I did see Ransom McCallister, though. He laughed at something Dylan said as he picked up a dodgeball. Then he swung the dodgeball around his back, gently clipping a boy named Thomas.

"Out!" yelled Coach Mo. The whistle blew.

I watched Thomas jog over to the bleacher with the rest of the "outs." Hatch Malone wasn't there, either.

He was sitting on one of the high bleachers, away from absolutely everybody, reading his comic book. Just like always. A sloth in a green vest had its arms hooked around his neck.

I stilled my wheels. Squeezed my eyes shut tight. Then I looked again.

Hatch still had an acutal *sloth* hooked around his neck. I hadn't imagined it!

"It's one of the therapy animals," Grace said. "Isn't he cute? You can hold him whenever you feel anxious. I always hold him when I take spelling tests."

"That's fantastic!" I said. And then I wondered, *What is Hatch Malone anxious about?*

I watched Hatch fidget with the frayed edges of his hoodie sleeve, exactly like he does at home.

"Why doesn't Hatch play?" I asked. "I thought he was an athlete?"

Grace shook her head. "I don't know him very well, honestly. He keeps to himself a lot. The librarian—Miss Rosie Snow—says he's a nice guy. I've said hi a few times, but he doesn't hear me. He's reading or drawing in his comic book. But he just kind of disappears. Are y'all close?"

"Not really," I admitted. "I've tried to be his friend. Kinda. But he just doesn't seem interested. Maybe it's because we're stepsiblings?"

"I don't know," said Grace. She sat down on the lowest bleacher and turned toward me. "I have two siblings, not even the step-kind, who also pretend I don't exist."

"So maybe that's just a sibling thing," I said.

"Friend thing, too," Grace said. "Sometimes, anyway. I used to be friends with the Maddies. Like, best friends. But this year has been different. We're just not into the same things anymore, ya know?"

I nodded, even though I didn't know. My best friends until now had been my parents and my pelican.

"They're missing out," I said honestly. "I think you're dynamite. And I love your personal style. Which reminds me! I brought you something to commemorate this partnership. I was going to show you right before Coach Mo told us to come out here."

I pulled my backpack into my lap, fishing through it until I found the sealed pencil pouch I'd stuffed inside this morning.

"Did you know hummingbirds like people?" I asked. "Not just the magical bird. But even regular hummingbirds. They're infatuated with humans. They can memorize certain faces. And it's possible to train a hummingbird to eat out of your hand."

"What do they even eat?" Grace asked. "Teeny-tiny worms?"

"Nectar," I said, pulling the pencil pouch free. Inside, I'd packed a handful of plastic rings with giant flowers in the center. "These are nectar rings. My grandpa made them. You put the nectar in the flower part and, eventually, a hummingbird will learn to trust you."

Grace reached for a hot-pink ring. I was secretly delighted; I wanted the yellow one.

"You think the magical bird will eat out of our hands?" Grace asked.

"Maybe. It's worth a try! Also, I feel like it's just nice to offer it some food."

Grace nodded. "I love snacks."

"Same!" This was a wonderful revelation and further proof we could be BFFs! Snacks are a great thing to have in common! "Even a bird with magical powers has got to have some of the same qualities. Now, I also have ideas on how to figure out what the riddle means, so we can find the bird. I'm not trying to brag, but my ideas are really good."

"Maybe tell me right after this class?" Grace said, lowering her voice to a whisper. "I don't want to risk anybody hearing."

The whistle blew again and Coach Mo hollered, "OUT!" Followed by, "Hey, girls. I love that you're socializing, but maybe you could cheer on your classmates, too?"

Grace clapped slowly. "Woo," she said.

I giggled.

"Even if this doesn't catch a hummingbird," she said, "it's kind of a cool ring."

"Do you think a flower is your signature symbol?" I asked.

"I've never thought about it. Do you have one?"

"A heart," I said, pointing to the tiny golden hearts in my ears. They were a birthday present from Uncle Dash.

She considered this. "Maybe mine is a butterfly. Or a dagger. Or a butterfly holding a dagger? Something that looks soft but is super tough."

"I get that," I said. "I want to be seen that way, too, sometimes. Like a butterfly holding a dagger in one hand. And a Judy Blume book in the other."

Grace slapped her hands down on her thighs. "I *love* Judy Blume."

My eyes widened. This was an even bigger revelation than snacks! Not only did Grace have potential to be my BFF, she might also be my BBF—my best book friend! "Same," I said, pressing my hands over my heart.

"I was thinking we should have a name for our squad. What about the BlumeBird Society?"

Now I was speechless. Our squad? That sounded even better than a partnership. That sounded like friend-classification! "I like it!"

And then Grace Cho held up a hand for a high five.

I high-fived her right back. The clap of our hands together wasn't very loud, not with the sound of sneakers squeaking all over the gym. But it felt like a lightning bolt inside my soul. Like a perfectly wonderful summer storm.

Storms mean change is coming, Grandpa Goad always says. And this kind of change felt really nice.

PE might have lasted fifteen more minutes or fifty. I

can't remember. I just know it all flew by because of her. We were birds of a feather, Grace and I. And we were all set to find the bird that could change our lives.

When the bell buzzed through the speakers, Grace looked down at her nectar ring. Then she scooted closer to me. "What's the breakdown?" she whispered while students ran past us. "The quick version of your plan?"

I nodded and leaned close, bracing my hand around my mouth so nobody else could even see my lips move. "We need to figure out the riddle. So step one is we figure out who found the hummingbird when it flew through again in 1963. Then we can track those people down and ask what they remember. They can help us with the parts in the riddle that don't make sense!"

Grace nodded. "Where do we look for them, though? Maybe an old newspaper?"

"Maybe," I agreed. "I heard Dylan say other people were already looking at those, though. So what about a yearbook? Mr. Watson said it was kids like us who found the bird the last time it came to town. Surely, that kind of thing would make a yearbook page, right? I mean, if somebody had a wish granted, that'd be a big highlight! Wait—yearbooks are real, aren't they? Not just in movies? Did they exist back then?"

"Totally real. And there are highlights in the yearbook for sure. I don't know if we can find exactly who saw the bird, but it's worth a shot. So we find someone who saw it and—"

"They help us solve the riddle!" I finished for her. "The bird is in the place where fear and wonder both collide. Where the heck is that? And the legend says the missing words rise up in your soul. Somebody knows what those missing words are. We just have to find them."

"And then we find the bird," said Grace. She flashed her silver smile. "Let's do lunch in the library, Olive Martin. We need Rosie Snow."

CHAPTER 17
Finch Whistles

Ms. Pigeon waited directly outside the gym to push me to the cafeteria. She was tapping her gray sneaker against the floor when I zoomed toward her. Grace stood beside me in solidarity.

"Grace asked me to eat lunch in the library today," I told Ms. Pigeon. "Don't worry," I assured her, "I can get myself to the library easy-breezy. There's no foot traffic that way since most people are headed to the lunchroom. And I brought my lunch today. So you don't even have to get me a tray."

Ms. Pigeon looked concerned about this, glancing back and forth between us. She was a rule follower, I could tell. Sometimes I am, too. But when a magical hummingbird is floating around somewhere nearby, rules can't matter.

"That's fine, but be careful," she insisted.

"Want to push me?" I asked Grace.

Her eyes sparkled again. "Really?"

In a blink, Grace's hands locked around the handles and we zoomed down the hallway.

"Slow down!" Ms. Pigeon shouted.

"Go faster," I said, laughing as we rounded the corner.

"Out of the way!" Grace hollered as we flew down the hall. People parted like a curtain in front of us. They were laughing, but not in a bad way. Not like I'd dropped my tray in front of the whole lunchroom. This was the good kind of laughing—the kind when somebody else's happiness makes you happy, too. Joy-kabooms are contagious.

"I'll take it from here," I told Grace when we'd wheeled past the last stampeding herd of hungry students. I followed her down an empty sunlit corridor, where pictures of construction-paper sunsets were plastered to the walls.

"Library is at the end of the elementary hallway," Grace said as we rolled down a ramp into the oldest part of the school. "Isn't it a little weird that we've never heard about the bird until now? There are people who've seen the bird, but they don't talk about it."

"I've been thinking the same thing," I said to Grace. "I'd never even heard about the feathers falling until they happened."

"Isn't your grandpa a famous bird-dude?"

"Yes! Part of my heart thinks he didn't tell me so I

would discover all this myself. But I also wonder if, maybe, he thinks it's not real."

Or knows it's not real, I thought to myself. I'm not a class skeptic, like First Maddie, but I grew up hearing all sorts of stories and legends that weren't exactly true.

As if she could read my mind, Grace jumped around in front of me. I stilled my wheels just before I ran into her shins.

"Olive," Grace said very seriously. She stretched out her pinkie toward me. "The magic is real. We've got to believe that. BlumeBird Society Rule Number One: No matter how old or boring we get, we will never, ever stop looking for magic together. Especially not if the hummingbird is concerned."

I locked my pinkie in hers and nodded. I was so excited about the idea of having a friend to look for magic with that I forgot one very important fact. Promises are a lot like bones: Sometimes they break, no matter how hard you try to keep them safe.

The entrance to the library tower was at the far end of the hallway. The arched door was wide and wooden with a large knocker shaped like a fox's head right in the center.

"This is like a cottage in a fairy tale where a wonderful witch lives," I said.

"Miss Snow's not a witch," said Grace. "Or if she is, she's the best kind."

When she pushed the door open, it made the most

delightful screeching scream of a sound. I wheeled inside and spun around, and looked up . . . up . . . and up.

There were four stories of bookshelves, all accessible by a swirling ramp that led to the top floor. Skylights in the tower revealed storm-patched skies.

"This used to be the school aviary," Grace said. "Years ago, when the school first started, they kept all sorts of birds here. Which is how some people think all the birds came to Wildwood."

"Whoa!" I squealed suddenly as a large black shadow swooped down over me. A red-tailed hawk perched on the shelf of new releases.

"How'd you get in here?" I asked it. But Grace was the one who answered, "He lives in here. This is where all the therapy animals hang out. Wait till you see the rest of this place!"

I followed Grace up the swirling ramp, all the way to the top of the library tower: past the mystery floor, the biography floor, and an entire floor for graphic novels. Shelves spiraled all around the walls with rolling ladders steadied against them. And perched happily on the ladders, I noticed several birds: a tiny sparrow, a cockatoo, a hawk, and a cardinal. Long tables and funky couches were scattered around each level for students.

I know I said that most places don't look as wonderful as you imagine them. But libraries are different. Libraries are always better. And this one was the best.

When we got to the top floor, a parrot leaped from a top shelf, spread its shiny green wings, and soared through the room. A few canaries perched on an empty table, sharing a scatter of birdseed. Two crows sat on a book stand. One scanned lines while the other used its beak to turn pages.

The next thing I heard was a voice that sounded like winter wind and tinkling chimes. "Hello, ladies. I bet I know what you're looking for."

CHAPTER 18
Rosie Snow (and Edna)

Listen, friend. I don't know if you've spent much time imagining how a mountain fairy would actually look, but I have. Maybe it's because I live in a cottage in the woods. Or in a mountain town full of folktales. So here's the truth: I wouldn't be surprised if the lady standing in front of me had fairy wings hidden beneath her purple cardigan.

She was a Black woman wearing a kind smile and a fluffy yellow skirt. Her long hair shimmered pink at the edges. And a tiny diamond stud sparkled on her nose like a fallen star. She stood beside a gray book cart, filled with thick novels my hands were aching to hold. And, most magically of all, sitting in the middle of the cart was a sloth wearing a green volunteer vest.

"This is Rosie Snow, the librarian," said Grace. "The

lady, I mean. Not the sloth. The sloth's name is Bon Jovi. Miss Snow, this is my friend Olive."

I'm pretty sure my heart exploded into confetti bursts of sunshine. Grace had called me her friend!

"You look like a fairy," I told Miss Snow. "In a good way."

"That's so kind!" said Miss Snow. "Sadly, the only thing magical about me is book-picking. I can help you find a story that makes your heart spin. Or a story that scares you out of your wits. And if I can't, Mrs. Fitch can."

"Is she your assistant?" I asked.

Miss Snow leaned down and whispered, "She's the ghost of the library. She's worked here for over one hundred years—as long as Macklemore has existed. She knows where everything is but still doesn't think graphic novels count as actual novels." Miss Snow rolled her eyes. "So come to me for that. Otherwise, she's a great help."

I wasn't sure if Miss Snow was serious or joking, so I laughed nervously. But Grace nodded along like this was common knowledge.

What kind of school *was* this?

"Olive and I need a nook for research. We're looking for yearbooks." Grace lowered her voice. "We're trying to figure out who saw the you-know-what last time it was here."

"Mr. Watson said some students our age saw the bird," I added eagerly. "So I thought we'd start with the yearbooks from 1963, paying special attention to the sixth-grade class to get some clues."

"Smart idea," Miss Snow said approvingly. She passed a novel to Bon Jovi and he climbed a shelf to house it for her.

"There's competition out there," Grace said. "The blue moon rises in about two weeks. Sixteen days! So everybody's trying to crack this riddle and figure out where it's going to be. But it really, really matters to us."

"You don't think it matters to other people, too?" Miss Snow asked gently. "I think everybody's got a wish. A wish is hope with a little magic sprinkled on it, ya know? And when you hope for a thing for too long . . . it can hurt when it doesn't happen."

"Do you have a wish?" I asked her.

"Of course," she said. "I don't have time to go look for the hummingbird. But if I did, I'd wish for my family to be closer. Or for a friend here I love like family. I've been here a year now, but I'm still homesick. And yes, Grace, you all are my friends. But I need friends my own age, too."

"I get that," I said softly. "That's one of the reasons I came here."

"So it should make sense then," said Miss Snow. "Everybody's got a wish. Don't forget that, okay?"

"We take finding the hummingbird very seriously," I assured her.

When I said the full word—*hummingbird*—a strange hush settled over the room.

Every bird in the library stopped singing and swooping.

Grace stared at me wide-eyed like I'd just said BACON for the whole room to hear. "Maybe we should whisper when we talk about it, Olive. That got a little weird."

"Mm-hmm," Miss Snow said. She stacked some returned library books on her cart like she wasn't all that worried. "It'll get weirder than that. Watch and see. Every bird in the sky is in awe of that glorious creature. Animals always know when magic is close by."

Bon Jovi the sloth stretched his arms toward me.

"Can I . . . hold him?" I asked.

"Absolutely!" Miss Snow said. "That's why the animals are here!"

When Bon Jovi wrapped his arms around me and smiled up into my face, my heart grew wings for the billionth time that day. He smelled like books and clean laundry. I loved him instantly, and I loved that he loved me.

"I think you and Grace will make a fine team," said Miss Snow. "Yearbooks are on this floor, over in Edna's corner. Use the computer to find the section, okay? I'll check on you in a bit and see if you need my help."

Miss Snow smiled at us, then turned down an aisle of candy-colored spines to store some nonfiction titles. Something about the way she spun made me stare. She looked like a sophisticated ballerina shelving books, swirling, spinning, skirt floating around her like a pale yellow cloud. That's when I realized she had something in common with Grace, something beyond just a cool sense of style.

They both had an easy kind of confidence, the kind that fits even better than floaty skirts or wicker wings. Neither of them seemed like the type to talk over another person, but they also didn't mind taking up space in the world however they were supposed to. I wondered if I would feel that way once I could shove my wheelchairs and walkers in storage. I wouldn't have to worry anymore if I was in somebody's way, or if I could get my wheelchair through a door, even. I could just move in my own body. Move as myself.

Gosh, I couldn't wait to find the hummingbird.

"Olive?" Grace asked. "You okay?"

"Oh yeah," I said. "I just get a little daydreamy sometimes. Who is Edna?"

"Probably the coolest lady in this school besides Miss Snow," Grace said, bouncing up on her toes. She hadn't mentioned anyone named Edna helping us find the bird. But I was always up for more friends! I'd even brought extra nectar rings just in case!

"Want me to push you?" Grace asked. "I know you can do it. But if you wanna keep holding Bon Jovi?"

"Actually," I said, "that'd be great. If you don't mind."

"I got you," she said. And we zoomed toward the computers, toward the yearbooks, and hopefully, toward a magical bird.

True fact, friend:

Edna is a llama.

A fuzzy, golden llama, with hair as thick as an old carpet. She wore a special green vest just like the other volunteers, minus the generic name tag. Edna's name was embroidered in rainbow pom-poms on the side of her vest.

"I like to read to her sometimes," Grace said, moving a chair for me so I could slide under the computer table. Bon Jovi climbed out of my lap and onto the top of the computer monitor to take a nap.

"Is it okay to get close to Edna?" I asked.

"Of course!" Grace said. "She's a *therapy llama*, Olive."

She said this as if it was the most obvious thing in the world. As if everybody knew therapy llamas didn't bite.

"Does she spit, though?"

"That's a camel," Grace said, reaching for Edna's fuzzy snout.

I knew Grace wouldn't lie, so I reached for Edna, too. The library-llama kneeled down quietly on the floor and rested her soft head in my lap. When I rested my hand on her fuzzy head, a warm, blissful peace overwhelmed me. Some people need mountains or oceans to feel peace. Some people prefer big adventures or favorite blankets. All I need is an animal close by. I've always wanted a dog, but Mama and Jupiter say we don't have time to train one. And until we do, it might knock me over accidentally.

I smiled as I petted Edna's head. As soon as my wish was granted, I could get a dog!

"Okay." Grace pointed at the computer. "This says old yearbooks are located on the top-top shelf of Section A."

"What's a top-top shelf?" I asked.

"No clue. Let's go find out."

I unlocked my brakes and followed Grace to the far shelves on the highest floor. The top shelf stopped about two feet below the ceiling. But it held zero yearbooks.

Grace propped her hands on her hips, scanning the shelves like she was reading the lines of a book. "I still don't understand what a top-top shelf is. How can it not be the one we see? This is so perplexing!"

"Truly!" I agreed. "I mean, unless it's invisible, there's no higher place than the top. Let me ponder this for a second."

I squeezed my eyes shut tight and tried to think of good advice I'd been given about problem-solving. I get my best advice from Grandpa Goad and Dolly Parton. My favorite gem from Dolly is this: "Find out who you are and do it on purpose." But this time, it was the Goad's advice that won out. He would say, "Olive, listen to your heart. And listen to the birds."

I'd seen a pretty yellow finch when we climbed the library ramp. I always see them; that's one of the first birds the Goad taught me to spot, besides rememory birds.

"We should see how high the birds can go." I wheeled closer to the the shelf, then unleashed my finch whistle. Finches are the first birdsong I tried to mimic, and I realized I was pretty good at doing it.

"I don't know where you learned that," Grace said. "But it's cool." The finch came bobbing around the shelves, blue wings flapping. A quick flutter around our heads and then the bird darted vertically up the shelf. For a few heartbeats, the finch hovered above the top shelf we could see.

And then it seemed to perch on the air.

"Could the shelf be invisible?" I asked.

"No, look, there's a doorknob!" Grace said with a happy squeal. "I didn't even notice it! There are cabinets up there, but they're all the same color as the wall."

She ran for one of the ladders, steadied it against the books, and began to climb. "I hope we found this before the Maddies. They're trying to solve the riddle, too. Dylan found out for sure."

Bacon, I thought as I tried to push down the panic in my heart. First Maddie, in particular, seemed like the kind of person who would always be lucky.

"It's locked," Grace called down from the ladder,

jiggling the cabinet door. But she didn't sound frustrated. "It's weird that they're so well hidden, right? Why not just put them on normal shelves?"

"Maybe Miss Snow put them somewhere safer since they're so historic?" I said. "Or maybe she was just out of room. Want me to find her and ask if she has a key?"

"Nope," Grace said, stretching out her fingers. "It's a pin-cylinder. Those are easy to pick." She began to fiddle, and a moment later, the cabinet door creaked open, and I applauded.

"Give me just a sec," Grace said, waving billows of dust out of her face. "There are lots of yearbooks up here. I have to find the right one."

"Take your time," I said. I rolled around the area we were in, scanning spines and whispering the titles of books. My heart fluttered when a familiar name caught my eye. I reached as high as I could and pulled a gray book from the shelf: *The Collected Poems of Emily Dickinson*. Perfect! There was no better way to get in character for play auditions than reading her actual work. It's like it was meant for me to find it there!

"Jackpot!" Grace shouted as she wiggled out of the cabinet and stood on top of the ladder. She tossed down a thick book that clattered onto the carpet beside me. A plume of dust rose all around it.

The little blue finch flapped around it for a second

before lighting right on top and singing the sweetest song I'd ever heard.

"Nineteen sixty-three," I said. The numbers sounded like a wonderful spell when they rolled off my tongue. "Now, let's see if there's a bird in there."

Grace and I settled into a tiny table near one of the windows. She scoped out the area first, just to make sure we were alone, then scooted close beside me. I opened the crackly cover and scanned the pages slowly. We saw pictures of the school, the basketball team, the giant pumpkin grown by the third-grade class, and then—

"Olive!" Grace shouted out my hallelujah-name and slammed her hand down on the page. The photo in front of us was black and white, a two-page spread of school buses parked in front of Macklemore. Speckled spots that looked like snow drifted all across the scene.

"The feathers," Grace breathed.

"Yes!" I whisper-shouted. She clapped her hand against mine in a silent high five. I traced my finger underneath the lines of the caption as I read it aloud. "October brought the first blue moon in years to the Cumberland Plateau. And with it came swirls of strange white feathery sleet."

I heard the crackle of a chip bag as Grace opened it. "Sorry," she said. "I get hungry when I get excited like this."

"I get hungry most of the time," I told her.

She passed me her chip bag to share and leaned over

to flip through more pages of the yearbook. All the while, I kept glancing around to make sure we were alone. We knew the Maddies wanted the hummingbird. But who else was after it? And what if they'd thought of looking in the yearbooks, too? Hopefully, the deluge of dust meant this idea was ours alone.

"Mr. Watson was right on the year," Grace said, "and good news—it looks like each class has a Top News page. So if somebody saw the bird that year, it will be there. I hope."

"Yes!" I shouted, jabbing my pointer finger into a page as she turned it. I read it aloud: "Three students in the sixth-grade class of Macklemore Middle School claim to have found the legendary Wildwood hummingbird. Among them, pictured here, are M. Frye and N. Tuberose." I looked up at Grace. "The apple lady. I just saw her yesterday morning. My uncle said she knew change was on the wind."

"Talking to her won't be easy," Grace said, chewing her lip. "Nester doesn't like to talk to anybody. Trust me, I know. Maybe we should start with this other person. Any idea who this might be? M. Frye?"

In the picture, M. Frye was a blurry boy in overalls. But! He had some kind of animal . . . maybe a squirrel? . . . perched on his shoulder. I flipped back to the names of all the sixth-grade students, scanning the *F* section.

"Marvin Frye," I said. "What if that's the same as

Luther Frye? Like, maybe one of those names is his middle name? Luther would have been a kid back then. Plus, he's got a thing for rodents. I go to church with him. But I don't know him well. Is it weird if we just go ask him?"

The fact that Luther Frye might somehow be connected to the hummingbird really threw me for a loop. Sometimes it's hard for me to remember that older people had whole lives before I met them. That they were kids who had big adventures—and deep, special wishes—they were desperate to see come true.

"Oh!" Grace said. "I know Luther. I know where he lives, too. His house isn't far from here. I deliver his groceries sometimes. He's the guy with the ferret, right? He's the grouchiest man in Wildwood."

"Why's he grouchy?"

"I don't know that he's grouchy," said Miss Snow. She came around the corner pushing a cart full of books. "Maybe he's just got a lot on his mind. He's a kind man once you get to know him."

"We really need to talk to him about the . . . you know what," I said.

Miss Snow nodded slowly, like she was thinking through something important. "I can help with that. What if I give Luther a call and tell him I've got two girls stopping by today? To ask him a few questions for a school project?"

"You're a lifesaver," Grace said. "And a wish-saver. So this is all good, Olive. We're off to a good start!"

"We can't get cocky about it," I warned her. Because I remembered the crowds in town that morning and realized everybody else seeking the bird might be off to a good start, too. They might have discovered even more than we did. They might already know what the riddle means!

Just as panic started to pound in my chest, Bon Jovi climbed on the table. He opened up his arms and looked at me. I picked him up gently and held him close. He settled like a soft, warm blanket, heavy over my heart.

"Why don't you read the legend again," I asked Grace. "Make sure we're on the right track."

As Grace began to read the words aloud, I said them quietly to myself. I'd already memorized Twig Moody's legend.

An honest wish won't go unheard . . .
Not for one who seeks the hummingbird.

When bone-white feathers start to fall,
When the blue moon rises tall,
Where fear and wonder both collide,
That is where the creature hides.

Life and death aren't in its grasp,
But if you're brave enough to ask,

There are still wishes,
Yours for keeping,
Find the bird and then,
Start listening!

The words you didn't know were missing
Will drift across your broken heart.
Shout those words into the dark!
Reach for the bird in the blinding light,
Make a wish that's brave and right.

And the bird will leave a golden kiss
On the face of one who gets their wish.

"So as long as Luther tells us the missing words and the magic place . . ." I began.

Grace nodded eagerly. "And as long as the blue moon rises in two weeks, we'll find our wish-bird!"

But Miss Rosie Snow was shaking her head slowly, again. "Careful, careful, friends. Magic like this is tricky. It's never as easy to find as you think."

Out of the corner of my eye, so fast I nearly missed it, a shadow darted around the bookshelf and down the ramp. *Bacon! The Maddies!*

"What's wrong?" Grace whispered.

"Someone's spying on us," I said. "Somebody heard everything."

CHAPTER 19

Leaving the Nest

Every true birder knows that each flock has a family name.

A flock of pigeons, for example, is called a kit.

A group of peacocks is called a muster.

My favorite family group belongs to starlings; they're called a murmuration when they fly all together. I think the name fits them perfectly. They look like ink in water, moving in their floaty, fluid pattern. They're marvelous to see.

I don't know if there's a word for a flock of moms, but there should be. Because the moms at Macklemore were huddled up all together on the sidewalk, chattering like chickens. They were all looking in the same direction. They even matched—kind of like the Maddies do—with long ponytails, yoga pants, hoodies, and giant sunglasses.

And they were all looking at the same thing: my family's van. Specifically, the top of it.

"Oh wow," said Grace. "There's a dude on that van."

"That's my dad!" I said when my eyes settled on the sight that held us all enraptured. "That's Jupiter."

Best I could tell, Jupiter had shown up a little early to pick me up from school and decided to squeeze in a yoga session. He'd climbed atop the van, spread out a mat, and was now moving from downward dog to his *ommmm* pose.

Grace glanced down at me. Then up at him. "Are you gonna say hi to him?"

"He's almost done," I told her. I pulled my heart shades down over my eyes and waited as patiently as possible, despite my impending quest. Sometimes I do yoga right along with Jupiter. I really like how it makes me feel: like my heart takes a deep breath. It probably would have been wise to do it before I went to pester Luther Frye, but alas. Time was of the essence.

Finally, he looked up and realized he had an audience.

"Oh." He waved. "Hey, y'all."

"Oh my," said a mama I knew belonged to Second Maddie. They were basically twins. "That is one handsome man."

It's kind of a bizarre thing, to hear someone talk about your dad this way. Like, yes he's handsome in a *dad* way. But he's still a dad, you know?

"Hey, Jupiter!" I said, squinting up into the sunshine when I waved.

"Hey, baby!" He climbed down the side of the van and my arms opened, like a reflex.

"That's so cute," I heard First Maddie say as she passed by. I rolled my eyes.

"Jupiter," I said, "this is my first actual friend at Macklemore. Grace Cho, Entrepreneuer. And we have a question. We were wondering if it's okay if I go with Grace to Luther Frye's house? I know this is a big step. Er, roll. I know you just got up the nerve to let me come here. As you can see, I'm doing swanky-fine. And I think it'd be cool to hang out."

"Remind me who Luther Frye is?" Jupiter kneeled down to be at eye level with me.

"Grouchiest man in town," Grace said. "Hasn't smiled in twenty-two years."

"I don't know if that makes him grouchy," I said. "I see him every week in church. Maybe he just doesn't care to share a smile. It's his face. Who knows? Either way, we'd like to visit him."

Jupiter nodded slowly, but the confusion was evident on his face. "You want to visit a grouchy old man because . . . why?"

"We're on a mission," I told him. Grace slowly shook her head at me. *Noooo,* is what she was trying to say. But Grace doesn't get it: I have to trust the adults in my life. I have to ask my parents for help, probably more than most people want to. That's just how it is. Lucky for me, they're pretty open-minded. Also lucky for me: I would be able to help myself in every way very, very soon.

"Grace and I are gonna"—I leaned close and whispered—"find the magical hummingbird. The one everybody's talking about. It's real and we're going to find it and it's going to grant a wish. To Grace."

So I didn't tell the full truth there. I still wasn't quite ready to disclose my own wish to Mama and Jupiter. And, anyway, he still looked confused.

"We think Mr. Frye might have found it back in the day," I explained. "Or he might remember it, at least. Either way, maybe he can help us out. Basically, this is magic disguised as an oral history project."

Jupiter's eyes glimmered at this description, just like I knew they would. He believes the very best thing about being Appalachian is that you get to take part in so many passed-down stories. Apple pie is the second-best part.

"That would be fascinating." Jupiter seemed to think this was reasonable. "Do you think you two should call before you just go knock on his door?"

"Miss Snow called him for us," I said, twisting my ring around and around on my finger. Grace kept glancing at her watch. "He's expecting us now."

"I'm going to run inside and call my mom," Grace said, skipping back toward the school. "Let her know we're going."

"I didn't say yes yet," Jupiter said as Grace scampered away.

"He lives on Main Street," I said quickly. "That's so close. His house has a ramp already, Grace knows. She delivers his groceries sometimes. So . . . I can go? If I'm careful? I won't stand up or get out of my chair at Luther's. Plus, I trust Grace if I need help."

Help, help, help. If I were a sparrow, it'd be one of my most common chirps. That's something the hummingbird would remedy hugely for me. I wouldn't have to ask for help so much. Maybe ever!

"OLIVE!" Dylan ran past me wearing a set of wings made of clothes hangers. "Look at me! I'm a laundromat bird!"

Third Maddie ran after him shouting, "Give me my wings, DYLAN!"

I giggled as I watched them run, then looked back at Jupiter.

Who was looking right at me, with a glimmer of tears in his eyes. This is not uncommon; Jupiter is a man in touch with his emotions. But these came on pretty fast.

"What's wrong?" I asked.

"It's good to see you so happy," he said.

"I'm happy a lot!" I told him. "Wait . . . do you feel like I'm not happy at home?"

"That's not what I mean. You like it here, though. I can see it on your face." He gently tapped the freckle on my nose. All this was tough for Mama and Jupiter. Whether you're a bird or a dad, it's got to be tough to watch your baby flutter out of the nest for the first time. It's a really special thing to have people in your life who love you enough to let you try.

"You can go with Grace," he finally said. "If you'll be careful."

I threw my arms around Jupiter's strong shoulders again and squeezed.

"But I'm still following along beside you," he added quickly. "Just to see how it goes."

And, friend, that is exactly what he did.

Grace walked, I rolled, and Jupiter crept along beside us in the van all the way through the gates and onto Main Street.

About fifteen minutes into our walk Grace finally asked, "He's really going to follow us the whole time?"

I nodded. "Yep."

Jupiter blared his Bob Marley music, singing along. If we happened to look over, he'd wave like this was perfectly normal, while all the cars backed up behind him honked like a gaggle of geese.

"Y'all are doing fine," Jupiter finally yelled. "So I'll stop hovering and let you have some fun. I'll pick you up in front of Luther's house in one hour, okay?"

"You got it!" I yelled back.

Jupiter waved, and let out a deep sigh. I watched as the van puttered down the road.

It must have been hard for Jupiter. To ride away and not stick right with me, not watch my every move and breath. But he kept on driving, blond hair blowing in the breeze.

Sometimes my dad reminds me of a rock song on the radio. Everything about him is like the best song you've ever heard. Maybe it's because he makes everybody around him feel good. Maybe it's because his eyes always reflect the sky and see nothing but potential there.

CHAPTER 20
How the Frye Boys Met the Bird

The loudest thing on Main Street, Wildwood, is usually the river. It runs in a lazy parallel to the two-lane road. There are a couple of restaurants, then a big statue of Dolly Parton right in front of the courthouse. She passed through town once on her way to Nashville and bought a Moon Pie at Big John's. That's the legend, at least. It was my favorite legend until I heard about the hummingbird.

Wildwood is a peaceful-easy place.

Usually.

But when Grace pushed me out of the Macklemore gates and onto the Main Street sidewalk, there was a pulsing energy in the air. Main Street was even more crowded than it had been that morning. And the whole street felt like a party, like May Day was already here even though it was two weeks away!

Melba Marcum strummed her banjo on the street corner. She was singing "Hotel California," one of Jupiter's favorite songs, while the canary perched on her guitar tweeted along. People were dancing all around her: little kids and big kids and an elderly couple in matching T-shirts. Pastor Mitra was dancing, too, snapping her fingers and shuffling around in a pair of purple Bouncers.

Bright balloons were tied to the lampposts. Cafe workers pushed around carts full of fresh cupcakes, candy apples, and fudge.

"Here ya go, young ladies," said Jessie Marcum from behind us. We turned around to see her holding out two tiny pies on a stick. I hadn't realized Miss Jessie worked in the cafeteria and at the Ragged Apple Cafe. Age certainly didn't keep her down. "They're free today!"

"Oh heck yes," said Grace. "I'm starving."

I bit into the sticky-sweet crust just as a gentle breeze blew down the street and across my face. I'd eaten a zillion pie sticks in my lifetime. I'd been to May Day Festivals before. But it was never like this. Now it felt like the whole town was coming alive.

Or maybe, I realized, I was coming alive.

A news van was parked beneath the Lonesome Oak.

"We might be on TV!" Grace said, pushing my wheelchair toward a news camera set up in front of the Ragged Apple Cafe.

"Let me put on my heart-shaped sunglasses!" I said. We giggled the whole way there.

The mayor stood in front of the mic again. A bow tie is for sure his signature symbol, and the one he wore today had blue polka dots.

"Mayor Matheson," the newscaster said, "we've met families coming from all over Tennessee today just to catch a glimpse of a legendary hummingbird. What would you like to say to all the new visitors here?"

"It's back!" yelled an old man in a yellow T-shirt. He ran down the sidewalk full speed, pumping his hands in the air.

"It's never like this out here," I said to Grace.

"Not in sixty years at least," she agreed.

When I was little, Mama and I did a science project about static electricity. I rubbed a balloon all over the crown of my head and then picked it up and felt it, that invisible force that tethered me to a balloon. That's how Wildwood felt right now, too—as if some strange, invisible force was in the air all around us. The mountains had never looked taller. The flowers had never been bigger—not even in the summer months. The birds sang loud. The river rushed wild.

And I got to be right in the middle of it all.

"Let's keep moving," I said to Grace. "There's a lot of people interested now."

Luther Frye lived in the oldest house on Main Street, a little blue cottage with peeling paint and flower boxes in the front windows.

"If he's got flower boxes, that's a good sign," I said. "It takes a special soul to tend to a garden, even a little one."

"Don't get excited," Grace said. "Luther grows onions in his flower boxes."

"Oh."

On Luther's front porch was a garden gnome (a fake one, sadly) holding a sign that read: GO AWAY.

"I like that he's not subtle," I said as we made our way to the front door. "I appreciate a person who gets to the point."

Honestly, just the fact that Luther's house was accessible was a big win for me. And probably Grace, too. She'd said if there hadn't been a ramp to Luther's, she'd gladly carry me on her back. Like Luke carries Yoda in Star Wars. This seemed much safer.

"Be on your guard," Grace said as I raised my hand to knock on the door. "Luther's an apple flinger."

My hand froze midair. "A what?"

"He orders Arkansas Black apples with his groceries, every week. Those aren't good in pies. They aren't good fried. They're too hard to eat. You know what they're good for? Throwing at people you don't like. Same thing Nester Tuberose uses in her apple cannon."

"Geez, what's an apple cannon?" I asked. "I've never heard of her throwing apples at people in the cafe."

"Not there, she won't," Grace said. "That'd be bad for business. But you know that orchard her family owns? The one up on Grave Hill? There's a rumor that the apples on one of those trees tell people the future. If you bite into one of them, you'll see the sweetest someday moments you ever get to experience. People used to try to climb through the gates and steal the apples especially when times got hard. What's more encouraging when things get rough than knowing they'll get better, right?"

"Absolutely," I said. I had no intention of stealing apples from Nester. But I could understand the allure. I would love to catch a glimpse of my actual future.

"Do you really think she shoots them out of a cannon?" I asked.

"I dunno. There's some people I'd like to fling apples at. I wouldn't want to hurt anybody. But I'd like to pitch an apple sometimes. I'm not saying I don't get it. I'm just saying be cautious."

The door flung open.

And Luther Frye glared at us with such fury you'd think we'd rolled his yard with toilet paper. Tufts of thin white hair fluttered like chicken feathers atop his shiny head. "I ain't buying anything you kids are selling."

"Miss Rosie Snow is our librarian," I said quickly, so he wouldn't shut the door in our face. "She was supposed to call and tell you we were coming?"

"Hmm" was his only answer. "She might've left a message on my answering machine, I suppose. I ain't checked that thing in years." He squinted his eyes at Grace and cocked his head. "You bring me groceries sometimes." Then he looked at me. "And I go to church with you."

"You do!" I said brightly. "My mama loves your pet ferret. But she refuses to let me have one. One of life's great mysteries."

Gustav must have heard me talking about him because he leaped onto Luther's shoulder, fluffing his tail around the old man's wrinkly neck.

"Hmm," Luther said again. "Your mama's a nice lady. Your grandpa, too. We went to school together, me and Merlin. I was good at finding four-leaf clovers. And he was good at spottin' birds. But you know that already. What do y'all want?"

Grace cleared her throat. The high school marching band rounded the corner at exactly the moment she tried to talk. So she had to yell. "We're seeking the humming-bird and we wonder if you found it, too, years ago? I know you must be sick of people bugging you, asking for info. But we really, really need to crack that riddle."

"We're serious seekers," I said to him. "Please help us out? We just have a few questions. First one's easy: Is your real name Marvin Frye?"

"No," Luther said flatly, dashing my dreams with one simple word.

"Oh," I said, unable to hide the disappointment in my voice. "I guess you don't know him, either?"

Luther tucked his hands into the pocket of his overalls. He squinted his eyes at Grace. Then at me. I thought he'd shut the door in our faces again. But Gustav started chattering in his ear, like he was telling him a marvelous secret.

Or like he was having a ferret tantrum.

Or maybe just telling him not to be so hateful.

"Y'all promise you ain't little vandals?" Luther asked. "You ain't here to spray-paint my house or mess up my grass?"

We shook our heads. "No, sir."

"Why would we mess up grass?" Grace asked.

With a resigned sigh, Luther opened the door wide enough for us to move inside. "All right," he said. "Come in, if you're gonna. And I'll tell you about Marvin Frye."

I thought Luther's house would smell old and dusty, but I was most mistaken. His house was clean and simple, with a folded blanket on the couch and a fireplace that looked kind of lonely with no fire inside it. On the hearth, there was an old black-and-white picture of a young couple on their wedding day. An apple-scented candle flickered on top of his TV where *Wheel of Fortune* was paused.

Luther led us into his green-apple-colored kitchen. His table sat in front of a big window framing his garden. Spring sunshine had finally broken through the storm clouds, casting the whole room in a light I can only describe as memory-golden. When Luther sat down, the light even made him look more like a fancy painting than a grouchy old man.

Gustav jumped from his shoulder into Grace's lap.

"Hey, you," she said. Gustav chattered like they were friends.

"Last time I had a bunch of kids around my table," Luther said, "they was trying to steal my garden gnome. And I told 'em that I'd have given it to them if they'd asked. It's just that stealing somebody's private property is a big deal."

"Yes, it is!" Grace agreed. "My brother's always trying to steal my Dungeons and Dragons set. It's vintage! All original pieces. Do you have any snacks, sir?"

"Grace," I said under my breath.

"I'm starving," she whispered.

Luther seemed delighted, in his grumpy way. He bounded up out of his seat, disappeared briefly, and put a bowl of big red apple slices on the table. Grace raised her eyebrows at me like, *Told you so.*

"Now tell me something," Luther said. "If both of y'all

are seekers of this magical bird we got floating around, how you gonna decide who gets the wish?"

"We made a contract," I said. "And the two of us will just be happy for each other no matter what."

"Hm," he said. "That's what you think now."

"But we're not even going to get close to it if we can't crack the riddle," said Grace. "We heard it for the first time this week. And we have two big questions, specifically: What's the place where fear and wonder both collide and—"

"What are the missing words?" I finished for her. "I know it's been a long time, but we hope you remember them. Or some of them."

Maybe it was just my imagination, but the light in the room seemed to settle all around us, warming our shoulders like a fuzzy blanket, as Luther Frye sank into his chair. "I don't know if I can answer ye'r questions exactly," he said. "But I can tell you a thing or two."

Luther cleared his throat. "I first overheard the legend of the hummingbird when I was eleven years old. I heard it at Ruth's, a bar on the edge of town," he said.

"You went to a bar when you were eleven?" Grace asked.

He rolled his eyes. "I wasn't drinking in the bar," he clarified. "I was a kid! But me and my brother—Marvin—liked to go sit by Ruth's door every afternoon before the bar opened. She had a jukebox inside, see. And she'd crank it up for us to hear the music while she cleaned for the night's customers. We'd dance on the porch and sing into broomsticks and pretend it was a big concert. She didn't mind."

I nodded for him to continue.

"So we was listening to the jukebox—me and Marvin— but we also just happened to overhear Ruth talking to some stranger about a very unusual bird. The feathers had been flying all over the mountain, same as they are now. A blue moon was rising soon, according to the *Farmer's Almanac*."

"Same as now," I said.

Luther nodded. "This feller'd heard rumors about an old legend in the mountains. He'd come all the way from Bristol trying to find out if it was true, once he saw the signs in nature. He hoped a local like Ruth would help him crack the riddle. *The feathers are falling!* the Bristol man told her. *And the blue moon is rising!* And on and on . . . he was tossing out words like puzzle pieces. And the more me and Marvin put together, the more excited we got."

"I felt that way when Mr. Watson told the story!" I said. "Then what?"

"Well . . ." Luther said. "For some reason, Ruth wouldn't help him at all. Even though we had a hunch she knew all about the bird. The man must have, too. We heard that man holler, 'I'll find that bird if it's the last thing I do.' He was getting real, real hostile, see. But Ruth wouldn't have it. She was a tiny little lady, now. But she could stare a man down. Send 'im running for the hills."

Luther made a *hmm, hmm* sound, which I assumed was the closest he came to laughing.

"Then," he continued, "Ruth flung open the door and Marvin and I came tumbling down onto the hardwoods. 'Cause we'd been spying, you see."

"I get that," I said. "I love to eavesdrop. It's a terrible habit."

"But it's how you find the best stories," Luther confirmed. I'd always known this in my soul. "We told the same thing to Ruth: If somebody is talking about magic, we're gonna listen. I guess she liked the sound of that. Because she sat down there on the dusty hardwoods. And she told us the legend that changed our world. Changed everything . . .

"When bone-white feathers start to fall,
When the blue moon rises tall,
Where fear and wonder both collide,
That is where a creature hides."

Luther's grumpy exterior melted like candle wax as he spoke. His wrinkles seemed to soften. His eyes sparkled like tear-studded stars. There was a gentleness about him that made me want to hug him tight. I didn't. But I wanted to.

"We didn't know what the missing words meant," said Luther.

Grace sighed. "Neither do we."

"But," he said, "as soon as we knew the legend, we knew exactly where that bird would come shining. If there's any place in the world where fear and wonder both collide, it's the woods. Those dark, creepy-lookin' Piney Woods just north of here."

"I live there!"

"Mm-hmm." Luther nodded. "Then you know what I mean. Scary as heck."

I nodded out of politeness. But I really had no clue what he meant. The woods weren't scary at all to me. They were beautiful and deep, with twisty paths and furry evergreens. But I knew this was a time to listen, not argue.

"There's this poet I like," he said, "a feller named Wendell Berry. And he writes about how his soul feels settled when he's among the wild things. Woods can bring you that kind of peace: the peace of wild things. Woods can settle a person. Inspire them. The way branches criss-cross can be prettier than any stained-glass window you've ever seen. The sound of rain on the leaf-covered ground? Better than any church choir you'll ever hear."

Amen is what I said in my heart.

"There's hope in the woods. And there's always monsters, too."

"Real monsters?" Grace asked over a mouthful of apple.

"Depends on how you define a monster," Luther said.

"Woods are so dark that they'll test your courage. It's easy to think any place is haunted when you walk through it alone. Even if it's just a memory that haunts you."

Luther's sentence trailed off into silence. He cleared his throat. "So that's why Marvin and I went into the woods on the night of the blue moon. We were determined to find the bird, just like you girls, even if it meant walking into a place where we were terrified. And by golly, we did."

"So it really is real?" Even though I'd made a promise to Grace to always believe, the confirmation of this truth burned like hope inside my heart. "You saw it with your own eyes? You're not just telling us this because it's a good story?"

"Oh, it's real," he said sincerely. "Terrible things happen in this world. And exist in this world. But the absolute most wonderful things you can imagine—they also exist. The hummingbird is one of the wonderfuls."

"So do you remember where you found it in the woods?" Grace asked. "And what you said?"

With a trembling hand, he reached to rub his tired eyes. "I've forgotten so many things. I'm old as dirt, see. And it's been, what, sixty years since we saw that bird? I remember the moment like it happened a second ago. But . . . I don't remember *exactly* where I saw it. There was a sound, maybe, kind of a *shhhhh*. And the feathers were falling like snow, just like the legend says. The bright moon shone above us. It was Marvin the bird took a liking to. I watched it flutter right up to his nose. He glanced sideways at me. Say something, I told him! He didn't know what to do, so he belted out one of our favorite songs from Ruth's jukebox."

I grabbed my lucky purple pen and my notebook and flung it open to a clean sheet of paper. "Do you remember any words to the song?"

"I remember the whole thing," said Luther. "It was 'Blowin' in the Wind.' I reckon the bird likes folk music."

This was definitely not what I expected to hear. I glanced at Grace. She also looked confused.

"Yep," he said. "Those were the words that rose up in his soul. And that little thing appeared, no bigger than a baby fist. Bright as a star. Marvin was braver than me, always. He made his wish."

Golden silence filled the room. I let it surround us for a while. I liked imagining Luther as a little guy with a squirrel in his pocket, walking into the woods to touch the light of a magical bird. "What did you wish for, Mr. Frye?"

"You might as well call me Luther," he said. His mouth flattened in what I'd come to see as a Luther smile. "As for my wish . . . the bird has no power over life and death, as you know. Life and death aren't in its grasp, the riddle says. But there's still plenty to wish for beyond that which'd make life all the sweeter. Marvin always said he probably should have wished for money, see. For our family. We were dirt poor. But happy as we could be, so it didn't even cross his mind. My dad worked in the coal mines but never complained. We didn't even think of wishing him out. I should have, I know. But the bird will only grant the most honest wish of your heart. And Marvin and I already knew what we'd wish for, if the bird found us. And he kept his promise: He wished for a tree house."

"And you got it?" I asked. "It just appeared?"

"It was a wonder!" Luther said. "We'd dreamed of one for years, a place just for the two of us. We never fit in at school, see. We weren't athletic."

"Neither are we," Grace said, biting into an apple.

"Well, we weren't smart, either," said Luther. "I can tell you girls are bright, but not Marvin and me. We didn't have a place to belong, except with each other. We thought a tree house would feel like our own wonderful little kingdom, away from everybody, away from the whole world."

"Like Terabithia," I said.

Grace beamed. "I love that book."

"And sure enough," Luther continued, "the next day we found a unique trail in the woods—it shimmered somehow, all dreamlike and bright. A skeptic would say it was just the sun, the way it shone over a dewy path into the woods. But that trail sparkled in such a way we knew it had to be the work of the hummingbird. We followed that path and found enough wood to build a tree house ten stories tall."

"Whoa," Grace and I both said at the same time.

Luther took a swig of his coffee. "It was a beauty. You

could see clear to Knoxville from the rooftop. It was our kingdom deep in the woods. When we were boys, it was a castle and a clubhouse. And even when we were young men, it's where we'd go hang out after school. It's where we decided to go into service together."

Luther paused. The light shifted in the room. The sun sank deep into one of the storm clouds overhead. Golden light gave way to shadows. Even Luther's voice seemed to darken. "We went to boot camp at the same time, Marvin and me. Then we went to Vietnam. He left first. I followed a few weeks after. I was nervous about it all, not brave like my brother. He could tell I was worried. So on the day he left, he put his hand on my shoulder and said, 'Don't worry. We'll meet at the tree house when it's all over.'

"That's what he told me. 'You'll go home. And I'll go home. One of us will get there first, don't be scared. Just wait a while. The other will come home whistling down the path.'"

Any hint of a smile tugging at the corners of Luther's mouth faded away completely. His eyes turned stormy and sad.

"I'm still waiting," he said, his voice crackled.

The sunlight didn't seem golden at all now. If there was music and birdsong, I didn't hear it. All I heard was the painful quiet that surrounds the sadness of loss.

"I'm sorry," I whispered.

"Me too," Grace said.

Gustav climbed out of her lap in a furry, fluid motion, curling around Luther's neck in a hug.

"Wars are costly," Luther said. "Many people never came whistling down the path. Nobody knows what happened to Marvin. Not to this day. I realize he probably . . . passed away. I know that's true. But I used to imagine he had a whole other life somewhere. Thought maybe he was in Europe, 'cause we always wanted to go there together. I imagined him settling down. Maybe he found a pretty girl. Built a little house on the edge of the Black Forest. Maybe he can see the same stars I do. Maybe yellow leaves flutter down around his corner of the woods every year, and he remembers jumping in piles of them back when we were boys. Maybe he built a tree house with his son."

Luther pressed his mouth into a firm line. He pulled the handkerchief from his overalls and dabbed quickly at his eyes, before stuffing it back in his pocket. After a while, he said, "Thinking back on it now, I'm just grateful, ya know? For one day, in my many years of days, there was magic in the world and I did not miss it. Every kid deserves a day like that, full of summer-shining trails and good friends and fun. So I hope y'all find the hummingbird. I hope you have a memory like that to keep."

I didn't tell Luther Frye how high the stakes were for me now. I would have more than just a memory. My wish—if the bird chose me—would drastically change my life.

"Mr. Frye," Grace said as we headed toward the door. "You should hang out with us at school."

"Pass," he barked. "I hated school."

"You don't have to take tests and stuff," she said. "Miss Rosie Snow is always looking for Storykeepers, old people who come and hang out and tell us stories. Gustav would be an amazing therapy animal."

His shoulders softened a little. "This old person might be interested, then," he said. I could have sworn I heard the tiniest hint of lightness in his voice. "And Gustav loves to read. I just can't keep enough books around him, but golly he loves it. I'll consider it."

"Also," I said, pulling my backpack around to fish through the notebooks, "we'd like to make you an honorary member of the BlumeBird Society. That's what we're calling this whole wish-bird operation." I handed him a nectar ring. "The only rule is that we never stop looking for magic in the world."

Luther's cheek dimpled like a smile was hovering close by. It never quite showed up, but light slowly filled the room again: peaceful, warm, and golden.

"I'm sorry if we made you sad," I said. "That's definitely not why we came here."

"Remembering doesn't hurt as much as it used to. Missing him does. But remembering does not."

Luther said he didn't have much to share beyond that. And even though his story had been beautiful—and so helpful—I could feel the tiniest little zing of frustration deep inside. Something didn't feel right. Luther had found the hummingbird in the woods. That, he said, was where fear and wonder both collide.

But the woods had never, ever been a fearful place for me. Not even in the deepest corners. He'd told us the missing words were an old folk song. In my heart, I knew Luther wasn't lying.

Still, I felt uneasy. Because sometimes there's more than one truth. And real magic was always so tricky in a book. It's got to be even more of a trickster in real life.

Right before we left, Luther told us this: "Good luck, ladies. You're not the only ones looking, you know. I won't betray a trust, but one other kid came by asking me about the bird here recently. Just as determined as y'all to crack that riddle."

"Was it a girl named Madeline?" Grace asked. "Did she smell like bananas and flip her ponytail a lot?"

"Doesn't matter," he said. "Just wanted you to know . . . you're not the only seekers. You're not the only ones with a wish tucked deep in your soul."

CHAPTER 21
The Sleepover and the Secret

Jupiter was already waiting outside Luther's to take me home, so Grace and I didn't have time to debrief.

"This is so exciting, Olive!" Grace said. "We already know the song! Now we just have to find that spot in the woods! Meet me for breakfast tomorrow morning in the cafeteria so we can discuss?"

I nodded, but . . . I didn't know if I agreed with her about the song. It's not that I don't respect the music of the 1960s. Jupiter listens to it sometimes when he does yoga, and the lyrics are fire. But, first, I had a hard time believing the missing words that convince a magical creature to grant your deepest wish would be a folk song. Or any song. Especially a song that I'm pretty sure wasn't written or sung back in the '30s, when a mysterious girl named Twig Moody showed up in town telling wish-bird stories.

I wondered if it was possible for Luther to have forgotten the magic words. Memories take up lots of space in my brain and I'm only eleven. I can't imagine having a lifetime of memories crowded in there. Or maybe Luther's brother said different magic words or . . . something.

Also, I still had a hard time believing the woods were the place where fear and wonder both collide. I guess that was a harder point to argue, and Luther did make lots of good points about them. They've just never been fearful at all for me. Not even when I was little and Grandpa and I went searching for rememory birds in the shadow thickets. Woods are mysterious and mighty. They're wild and seem to have a mind of their own. But I was never afraid of them.

By the time I got to school the next day, I'd come to a conclusion: We had to talk to Nester Tuberose, too. Even if she pelted us with apples, we had to try. We needed to confirm the missing words and the magical place. Then in fifteen days, while the blue moon was shining, I would find the bird, make my wish, and dance on into the rest of my life.

"Hey," Uncle Dash said just as I'd started to roll away from the van and into the school.

I spun around. "Hey back."

He cocked his head at me and asked, "Where'd your jacket go? The glittery one?"

"Just didn't feel like wearing it today," I said. This was a semi-truth. I always feel like wearing glitter. It makes me feel like my best self. But I also realized it wasn't helping me blend in at Macklemore. If I stand out in any way there, I want it to be because I'm an awesome actress. Not because I'm a glitter lover.

"It's so you, though," said Uncle Dash.

"I'm all sorts of things," I told him, rolling Reba back and forth. I'd decided it was time to try my other chair and see if I liked it better for school. "Whole constellations. I'm still figuring it out."

"Everybody's still figuring it all out," he assured me as I spun around and headed into the building. I didn't need Hatch's or Ms. Pigeon's help now to get through the door, as long as one of them was there to hold it open. This morning, it was Hatch, who'd gone to school early with Coach Malone, like always.

"Hey, Olive," he said. "How's it going?"

His question left me stunned. I tried to think of the last time Hatch had asked me an open-ended question.

"Uhh . . . good!" I answered. "How's it going with you?"

"Fine," he said. He bowed low and dramatically like a butler as I wheeled through and into the cafeteria. This actually made me laugh. And it also made me wonder why my stepbrother was being so normal to me.

Grace Cho was halfway through her peanut butter banana toast when I found her.

"Don't panic," I said, trying to keep my voice low. The Maddies were only a table away. "But we have to find Nester Tuberose. I know she's reclusive. I know she'll pelt us with apples. But we gotta talk to her."

"What?" Grace asked over a mouthful of peanut butter. She passed me her second piece, which I promptly devoured. "Why? We already know the place and the words."

I shook my head. "I'm not so sure we do—"

And that's when the bell buzzed.

"Shoot," she said, glancing toward the table of Maddies. "It's not safe to talk about all this at school. We need a sleepover."

I nearly choked on my swig of chocolate milk. "A real sleepover?" I didn't even try to disguise the excitement in my voice.

Grace nodded. She was in business mode. "Want to ask your parents if we can do it at your house? My dad's helping me build a ramp so we can hang out at my house, too, but it's not done yet."

This was nearly too much kindness for my heart to hold. Grace wanted to have a sleepover with me *and* she wanted me to hang out at her house someday. This was all very legit friendship stuff!

"The BlumeBird Society needs to meet somewhere besides the library sometimes," Grace said. "Even though

I do love Edna. We need more time to figure this out. And we know somebody is spying on us, so your house is probably the safest place to really talk about it all."

"That's definitely true," I said. I remembered the sneaky eavesdropper in the theater. Then in the library, we knew somebody had been listening, too. Maybe that somebody was just Mrs. Fitch, the library ghost, but we couldn't take any chances.

"We have two weeks till the blue moon," Grace said. "So we have to talk bird stuff first. And then we can just watch movies or eat chips or whatever. Sleepover stuff. Want me to bring the snacks?"

"No," I assured her. "I'll take care of everything."

Friend, I'd never, ever had a sleepover before. I'd never been invited to one, either. But I vowed, deep inside, to make it the most awesome sleepover Grace Cho would ever attend.

The school day passed by turtle-paced, but then I called Mama and Jupiter from the office to get their approval. Then I turned to Uncle Dash for the absolute most important part of the plan: sleepover essentials.

"Sure," he said, "I'll take you to the market to get a few things."

I didn't elaborate and tell him my sleepover required way more than just a few things. But he caught on quick.

"I'm going to set up various Slumber Party Stations," I explained to him as I wheeled down the snack aisle. I tossed bags of chips and cookies into the cart he pushed behind me. "But I'm trying to keep it simple. I'm thinking manicures, mini library, movie with popcorn, and a chip buffet."

"Glad you're keeping it low-key," he said jokingly.

We left with a mighty haul of junk food, nail polish, magazines, and cookies. Hatch Malone was staring into the fridge when we unloaded our treasures into the kitchen.

"Thank goodness," he said. "I was so hungry."

"This is slumber party stuff," I informed him, slapping my arms down over the bags to protect my Oreos. "I'm about to do stations all over the house."

"Wait," he said, looking at me like he was seeing me for the first time. "You're having people over?"

"Why is that so surprising? You have people over all the time!"

"But girls are just so loud when they're all together," he said, shoving his hands deep in his hoodie pockets. "So squealy and weird."

"Your friends are weird, too! Plus, when a bunch of boys come over, the whole house smells like ketchup and sweat."

Hatch kept his face void of all emotion. "How about this?" he said. "I'll help you set up your slumber party stations for half your snacks."

"No," I countered immediately. "I'll give you a third. That's more than fair."

"Done," he said.

And really, I didn't know if it was more fun unpacking stuff or listening to Hatch grumble for the next hour while he helped me create a slumber party oasis. I organized the nail polish on the table (with newspaper underneath: a requirement from Mama) according to the colors of the rainbow. Then I used the prettiest bowls we had for cookies and a chip buffet.

Mama even let me light a candle after I promised I wouldn't accidentally burn the house to ashes. "I'm serious," she said. "We can't all fit in that yurt."

"What's this?" Hatch asked, opening the last shopping bag I'd brought from the market.

"Bunny slippers," I said. "Matching ones, for me and Grace. For after our pedicures."

"Girls are so weird," he whispered. But he settled the shoes carefully onto the ground, side by side in front of the couch. I had to admit: My stepbrother earned his junk food haul.

When Grace walked through the front door, duffel bag around her shoulder, she looked seriously stunned. Which made me smile so big it actually hurt my face.

"We can start with a BlumeBird Society Meeting in my bedroom," I said as she put down her bag by the door. "Maybe it'd be good to call Nester Tuberose and set up a meeting time?"

"Nester won't answer," said Grace. "I've written to her fifteen times in the last two years begging her to be my mentor. She also doesn't correspond. Or maybe I just freak her out a little. Anyway, she's going to be hard to get in touch with. Let's still talk about the bird, though." She cleared her throat and nodded behind me. I turned to see Hatch Malone, still in the kitchen, watching us while he munched on a bowl of chips.

"Hi!" Grace said to him. "We go to school together."

"I know." He nodded. Bowl in hand, he jogged upstairs. "Thanks for the junk food, Olive."

"Thanks for your help," I told him. "Really."

If there are historic days in family histories, that April afternoon would be one of ours. That would always be the day Hatch Malone and I came together over a chip buffet truce. I really couldn't have fixed it all if he hadn't helped.

"He's so quiet," Grace said when we heard his bedroom door close. "I love quiet people. They've always got so much going on in their heads and their hearts."

I had a feeling I could live in that house for seven lifetimes and still never, ever know what was going on in the mind of my stepbrother.

"So here's what we know," I said, rolling out a map on my bed between Grace and me. "Well . . . here's what we *think* we know. The feathers are flying. The blue moon is rising on May first, the same day as the May Day Festival. Same night of the play."

"And it's going to be somewhere in the Piney Woods," Grace added. "What were you going to say about that this morning?"

"So, I know Luther saw the bird in the woods. And the Everly sisters saw it in the woods. But something doesn't fit. It's like when you try to cram a puzzle piece in a place where it doesn't belong. The woods just aren't scary to me. I get that fear and wonder both collide in the woods for some people, but they've always just been a sanctuary for me."

"But there could be a place that's kinda scary, kinda beautiful, right? A place you just haven't seen?"

"There are whole words I've never seen," I said, holding up the map for a closer look. I don't know what I was hoping would happen. It's not like a map of the woods would give me all the answers. I could tell you where all kinds of bird species nested in the Piney Woods: sparrows, pigeons, rememory birds. But I had no clue where one little hummingbird might be hiding.

"What about the song?" Grace asked. "Did you find it?"

"Oh yeah," I said, transferring to my chair. I rolled to my dresser and put on a record I'd borrowed from Jupiter. The crackly sound of "Blowin' in the Wind" filled the room.

"It's fun to think of Luther singing this," I said. It's a fun song to hear, too. It's a song full of hope and an easy guitar sound and lines you want to shout when you hear them. "But 'Blowin' in the Wind' wasn't even released until the 1960s. So this can't be the magical words that came rising up inside the Everly girls back in the thirties."

Grace's shoulders slumped. "Oh," she said sadly.

"Don't lose hope," I told her. "Tell me the confusing part of the riddle again."

Grace cleared her throat and said, "When bone-white feathers start to fall, when the blue moon rises tall . . ."

"May first," I said. "Two weeks away. We know that."

She continued, "Where fear and wonder both collide, that is where the creature hides . . . in the woods, Olive!"

"That's what we don't know for sure," I said. "Keep going."

She groaned and continued:

"Life and death aren't in its grasp,
But if you're brave enough to ask,
There are still wishes,
Yours for keeping,
Find the bird and then,
Start listening!

The words you didn't know were missing
Will drift across your broken heart—"

"Shout those words into the dark!" I said, finishing the line. "We need to talk to Nester Tuberose, just to make sure we know the missing words. And really, we need the mystery third person, too. If they all remember it differently, then we'll go to three different places until we find the right spot. But we need to know which spots to go to."

"That makes sense," Grace said with a quick nod.

"Which brings me to one more thing I want to talk about," I said. "I don't really know how I'll even get in the woods, if that's where it's at. Jupiter made a third wheel that clips to my chair. That keeps me steady on some trails, if he or Uncle Dash or Grandpa Goad are there to help. But if it's deep in the woods? Down some rocky trail?"

"I'm working on that part," Grace said. "Don't worry."

And I had no doubt in my heart that she was, and would. It's like Grace doesn't even see a problem when she looks at a situation; she starts seeing pathways and puzzles and new ideas.

"You're great at figuring things out," I told her. "That's a cool skill to have. Is that how you got started building doghouses?"

Grace nodded. "I love dogs, for one. But I also love building things. Anything. I dream about skyscrapers at night. I dream I'm a giant, and I'm putting them together like LEGO sets." She turned an empty chip bag upside down to pour cheddar crumbs down her throat. "I love to create things. That's what I want to do with my life. And I don't want to do it when I'm old, like thirty or something. I want to do great things now. I know my doghouses seem silly, but they're very functional. And they're a starting place."

"I don't think it's silly at all!" I assured her. "They're so jazzy! Do you have any clients?"

"Not yet. Mom and Dad want me to focus on, and I quote, 'doing kid stuff.' But I want to do great stuff! I have so many ideas. So much I want to make. And if certain things worked out . . ." She fluttered her hands to let me know she was talking about the bird. As if I didn't know already. "If my custom doghouses became famous the world over, my parents would get why I spent so much time making them. They think it's just a phase, the doghouses. But, Olive, this is what I love."

"I get it," I said. "I feel that way about my writing sometimes. I would love to write a movie or a play or a poem that actually gets read by people. Someday."

"It doesn't have to be someday with the bird," Grace said. "It can be that day, right away. Something wonderful can really, truly happen. Wonderful is a wish away!"

The kitchen door slammed shut. Grace raised her eyebrows. "Who's that?"

"That's Hatch," I said. "He walks into the woods every night. My parents won't tell me why; they said I'm being nosy. I used to think maybe he was a vampire, but he's not. I don't know what he's looking for."

And then a terrible realization dawned on me, at exactly the same time Grace asked the question: "Olive, do you think, maybe, he's looking for the hummingbird, too?"

I let out a sharp burst of breath. *Bacon!* I'd been so obsessed with getting to Macklemore, and then so obsessed with finding the bird myself, that I hadn't really considered this. But it made perfect sense. I could think of a few times when Hatch seemed super interested in the hummingbird. And Hatch is so sneaky and fast. What if he'd been the one spying all along? Hatch is super smart! Super successful! Plus, he has Bouncers that could lift him into the treetops, if he needed to get there.

This was not good.

"I mean, what else is anybody doing in the woods right now but looking for magic?" Grace asked.

I flopped back into my pillows. "This could be a serious roadblock."

Grace flopped back on the pillow beside me. "Thank goodness for sleepovers."

We spent the rest of the night being very careful about what we said about the you-know-what. We also did each other's manicures, visited the chip buffet numerous times, and watched my favorite Reese Witherspoon movie of all time. Which was even better when I had a real friend to watch it with.

Hatch drifted through occasionally, sometimes shoving a handful of popcorn in his mouth. Sometimes he was quiet as a shadow. Was he spying on us? Or did he really just want more snacks?

What if Grace was right and every night Hatch went walking in the woods looking for the hummingbird? What if he knew something we didn't?

And what in the world did perfect Hatch Malone have to wish for?

CHAPTER 22
Macklemore, Awake

On the Monday after my first sleepover—twelve days until the bird's blue moon—two noteworthy occurrences happened bright and early. First, Felix crashed into my window, waking me up even before my alarm clock.

"I'm so sorry!" I told him after I'd zoomed back from the freezer in the kitchen. "I know I've not been a good friend lately. I just need to get a part in this play and find the hummingbird, in that order. And then we're back in action."

Felix's gaze was so honest and true that it broke my heart a little. He ate his fish stick slowly. And I realized, watching him, that he could fly to the lake and eat real fish whenever he wanted. He does that sometimes. But he likes being here with me. I'm not the kind of girl who abandons her friends, especially the feathered ones or the ones named Grace. Not that I have any others.

"I really am sorry," I told him sincerely. And he stretched out his wings, which I've always assumed is his way of hugging me. I love to watch a bird's wings open the way some people love a good sunset. For me, it's one of the little life miracles Mr. Watson loves to talk about in class. I kept my window open so Felix could see me, and I could see him, while I read over the rest of my lines. Feathers drifted in the wind, occasionally passing through my window like dandelion seeds.

One landed on my script.

One landed on the notebook where I keep all hummingbird research.

The other landed on the book of Emily Dickinson's poetry I'd checked out from the library. I shoved all three things in my backpack and rolled toward the van. This day's agenda was clear: The BlumeBird Society had to figure out where to find Nester Tuberose. I thought I was prepared for anything. Looking back, maybe Felix was trying to warn me change was on the wind again.

Because the next noteworthy occurrence happened as soon as I got to school.

I'd barely rolled Dolly in the door—I still preferred Dolly for school even though my glittery name was on the back—when Ms. Pigeon came running out of the office.

She pushed her way past a few students sleepy-zombie-walking toward the cafeteria for apple cakes. She was waving her arms around in big arcs above her head as if I couldn't see her.

"I think I can manage getting to class," I told her. "People watch for me when I move through the halls so I'm really not worried—"

"Oh, I know that," she said. "You do fine on your own. But the phone's for you."

"The office phone?"

She gave me a look like, *What other phone is there?* And then actually jolted with fear when I squealed out loud. I assumed it was the radio station calling me. Over the weekend, when I wasn't thinking about humming-birds, dead poets, or feather-flakes, I was trying to call in to win tickets to Dollywood on the Chirp 105, Wildwood's one and only radio station. Maybe Beef McGoo, the lead DJ, was calling me at school, to tell me I'd won.

Friend, it was not Beef.

The voice on the other end of that office phone was even better than I dreamed.

Finally, at last, Grandpa Goad was calling me.

"Darlin'!" he shouted when I said hello. "I just tried you at home, but your mama said you were at Macklemore. Hooray! Now, I got something important that can't wait—"

"Me too!" I shouted into the receiver. "I have a

thousand things to tell you and only six minutes until class starts! Uncle Dash wanted a biscuit from Big John's and it made me SO late. Here goes: I'm trying to find the hummingbird. Do you know about it? Do you know where it's at? There's a riddle that says it's in the place where fear and wonder both collide. And something about missing words. And—"

"Slow down a second," he said. "I know you're— hummingbird—woods—but remember the—"

"Oh shoot," I said, sighing as I held the phone out and shook it hard. LeConte Lodge is a place for serious hikers and birders up on the tip-top of Mount LeConte. And I'm pretty sure the phone is only there for emergencies. The connection was horrible. And I couldn't patch enough words together to know what in the world he was actually saying to me.

"You're breaking up!" I shouted. All the office workers spun around to make sure I was okay. I cupped my hand over the phone for some privacy. "Grandpa, try to move around maybe?"

"Remember—rememory birds. Remember their nests? You saw them—kid? Go see them. Go see—rememory and you'll—understand. Love y—"

The line went dead.

"Bacon," I said sadly as I handed Ms. Pigeon the phone to hang up for me. I thought a phone call from the Goad would make everything about the riddle crystal clear. But the connection to Mount LeConte was so scratchy that I could barely hear Grandpa at all. And why had he mentioned rememory birds? I had a much more important bird to track!

Time felt like it was slip-sliding away from me! The Madelines were probably getting ahead by now.

I pressed my face into my hands and groaned.

"You okay, Olive?" Ms. Pigeon asked softly.

I dropped my hands immediately, took a yoga breath, and nodded once. "Yes. I just needed a minute to collect myself. Now, I press on!"

The clock in the hallway tick-tocked extra loud when I rolled underneath it. With every tick and tock, I tried to map out my days:

Tomorrow, I had auditions. In a few hours, over lunch, I was meeting with Grace Cho in the library to brainstorm getting in touch with Nester Tuberose. We really needed her input.

In less than two weeks, the blue moon was rising over Wildwood. Then the hummingbird would fly again. And Grandpa wanted me to think about rememory birds?

"I guess Grandpa can't help me at all," I said to nobody but myself. "I guess I'm really on my own now."

Unless he knows the rememory birds could lead me to the hummingbird. What if Grandpa knew exactly what I was searching for but wanted to help me find it in a different way?

I didn't say anything to Grace about the phone call all through our morning class. The words were about to explode out of my soul by the time we found a private table in the library at lunchtime. Mostly private, anyway. I shivered, then giggled as Edna the llama breathed over my shoulder.

"Your breath smells like peanut butter," I said. "I mean it as a compliment."

"*My* breath?" Grace asked.

"Edna's!"

"Phew," Grace said. "Okay. Proofread my new letter to Nester." She sat across from me at our table in the library, the one near the wide window that looks out over the town of Wildwood. I felt like a princess in a tower up here. A princess in need of a very shiny hummingbird.

I reached to take the paper from her, but she held it for a second longer. "Wait a sec, what are you looking at?"

"A map of the Piney Woods," I told her, pushing the book toward her. "Grandpa tried to call this morning. He sounded so excited; I thought he was going to tell me something about the you-know-what. He knows that's what I'm looking for. But he told me to find the rememory birds."

Grace cocked her head at me. "Why would he do that?"

"I don't know," I admitted, flipping through the pages. "But he's brilliant. He knew why I was calling." I lowered my voice to a whisper: "Maybe if we go there, we'll find something that leads to the hummingbird."

Grace shrugged. "It's worth trying!"

I pointed to squiggly trees on the map. "I think he showed me the nests here, years ago. Near Bridal Veil Falls."

"Never heard of the birds or the falls," she said.

"The birds look very ordinary," I said. "Kind of like sparrows, but the beaks are blue. What makes them unique, though, is that they only live in the Appalachian Mountains. And they make their nests out of memories. They move together as a flock, so if you can find the place where they nest, and the light hits them just right, you can actually see memories floating through the air."

"Are you serious?" Grace asked. "That doesn't sound real! That's more like magic than science."

"Sometimes they feel like the same thing, I think. That's one of the first things he showed me, when I was learning how to look for birds, too. A finch is the first bird we went out to spot. Then he took me out to see a rememory bird's nest. I thought the map might help me remember where it was. But I'm not great with maps, honestly. I think I do better just feeling my way through a place."

"I'm not pointing this out to be a jerk," Grace said.

"But the fact that you can't remember where the renegade birds are—"

"Rememory birds," I corrected her. We both giggled.

"Right," she said. "What that means is that there are places in the woods you haven't seen. And don't remember at all. So, there is very likely a place where fear and wonder both collide in the woods. Just like Luther said."

"What place are you most afraid of?" I asked her.

"The dentist's office," she said honestly. "And also the county fair. I don't think it's very sanitary."

"Exactly," I said. "I'm way more afraid of being onstage than I am of going into the woods. Everybody is afraid of something different. How do you know where the hummingbird shows up if people fear so many different things?"

"There is no wonder at the dentist's office," Grace said. "Or the county fair. But I want to make sure I heard you right: You're afraid of a stage? You love theater!"

"With all my heart," I said, drawing an imaginary criss-cross over my chest. "But I get so nervous at the thought of actually doing a play in front of people. I think the nervousness is what makes me want to do it. If that makes sense. When I feel jittery like that inside, I imagine fireworks are happening inside my soul. Like my body is throwing a party for how brave I am. That probably sounds silly."

"It makes sense to me," she said. "So you're pretty nervous about auditions, then?"

"Terrified," I admitted. "And I'll be terrified about meeting Nester Tuberose once we do, too. Since you said she's an apple flinger."

"If we get to meet her," Grace said. "Any idea who the third person might be? The one who saw the bird back in 1963?"

"I have an idea," I admitted. "Remember when Luther said he and Merlin went to school together? They would have been our age, and that's around the time Grandpa became obsessed with birds. It would make a lot of sense."

"Want me to pull the yearbooks down again?" Grace asked.

I shook my head. "I can't have a conversation with him, anyway, while he's up on the mountain. Plus, why wouldn't he tell me if he found the wish-bird?"

"Does he have a golden freckle?" Grace asked.

"He's got lots of freckles, just like Mama. I would have noticed if he had a golden one, right?"

Edna must have sensed how nervous I was becoming. She rested her fuzzy head on my lap.

"I want to ask you a question," said Grace. "But I'm afraid it's prickly. That it will offend you, I mean."

"I'm definitely interested now," I said. And I smiled. "Go ahead. I won't get offended."

"So, I have an idea for how we could both go into the woods and look for the place where fear and wonder both collide. Miss Snow says she can borrow the janitor's golf cart for us tomorrow after school. She has connections. If I drive really slow, would it be okay for you to ride along? Or is that too dangerous with the bone stuff? I'm really not offended either way. I just want us to go together. But I also don't want you to think I'm overstepping."

"I don't," I said excitedly. "I think that's really cool of you! I'll have to ask Mama and Jupiter. They'll want to see it, and they'll give me some rules. I mean, I can't go on super tough trails. But I think they would be open to it."

"Cool!" Grace shouted. "Fingers crossed! Why don't you call and see if they'll meet us here after school? And we can show them the cart and see what they think?"

"Love it!" I held up my hand for a high five, and she high-fived me back.

Then a fluttery something drifted across the back of my neck.

I spun around. But this time, it wasn't a feather. It was intuition—my gut—telling me somebody was listening again. We'd set up in front of a short bookshelf. But somebody could still be hiding there!

"Hatch Malone." I growled his name.

"Is he here?" Grace asked. "Are you sure? It could also be one of the Maddies or Mrs. Fitch. I don't think Mrs. Fitch needs a hummingbird, though."

"I'm going to go check," I decided. "Confrontation is good for the soul."

"I'll work on my letter," she said.

I checked behind the short shelf first; no Hatch. Then I rolled quietly through the aisles until I heard the pop of footsteps on floorboards, just one row over. I stilled my wheels and listened more closely. The library was open during lunch, but only a few people usually ended up in here. According to Ms. Pigeon, Hatch was one of them. Even though I'd never seen him there. How convenient, though, if he was having lunch on this floor within earshot of a BlumeBird Society meeting.

The sound of a hardback book sliding into the shelf on the opposite side of me gave the eavesdropper away. I zoomed quietly around a dark row of Nancy Drew novels, spun around the corner, and shouted, "Gotcha!"

And accidentally clunked right into someone's shins. The culprit yelped.

"I'm sorry!" I shouted.

Ransom was standing over me with fearful eyes. "I didn't hurt you, did I?"

"No," I said. "Did I hurt you?!"

"I'll survive," he said. He rubbed his hand over his sore shin.

"I'm glad I ran into you, though," I said with a nervous laugh. I pulled Ransom's purple pen from behind my ear. "I remembered my writing utensils. But thanks for this. I think it was lucky. I wrote some fantastical things with it."

"Oh no, you keep it," he said. "I knew when I picked it up I was supposed to give it to somebody. Same with this"—he pointed to his shark tooth—"I'm just waiting to figure out who needs it."

"It's a really cool necklace," I said.

"Great!" Ransom started to take it off, and I panicked.

"Wait, you don't have to give it to me! I wasn't asking for it, I swear."

"I want to!" he said. "Seriously! It's like the universe just tosses cool and weird trinkets at me, and I'm supposed to give them away."

"I do love tacky beach junk," I admitted.

"Awesome," he said. "Want me to put it on you?"

I nodded and sat up, just a little.

Ransom leaned over and I felt his thumbs on the back of my neck when he hooked it in place. I really hoped I didn't have dandruff. "Cool! Maybe it will give you good luck tomorrow, when you audition."

"I hope so," I said. I hadn't had as much time as I wanted to prepare, thanks to the hummingbird. My insides felt as tangled as an old set of Christmas lights.

"Go for the lead," he said, pushing his hands into his pockets. "I've heard you read Emily's part. You're really good, Olive."

For a rare moment in my life, I was speechless. This kind of compliment, coming from Ransom McCallister, made me feel so floaty-happy-free on the inside.

"I'll try," I promised. He gave me a thumbs-up and walked away, down the aisle toward the checkout.

I sat alone for a few minutes, in a long, dark row of books. And I realized:

If I'd had bones like steel . . . it wouldn't have changed that moment.

Standing wouldn't have made it better. Neither would running or walking without a limp. It was one day, in a lifetime of days, and I got to feel the full bliss of it in the body I had. This super sweet guy had just given me his tacky shark-tooth necklace. A moment like that is worth remembering.

Moments like that will surely be even sweeter, once I find the hummingbird.

"Girls!" Miss Snow shouted. "Come quick! Look at this!"

I rolled around to meet Grace, who grabbed my handles and pushed me down the ramps, all the way to the first floor of the library. Miss Snow flung the door open. All three of us zoomed into a hallway full of little kids who were unusually quiet, staring at the ceiling.

At what used to be the ceiling, anyway.

The school hallways of Macklemore were blooming, wild as any garden I've ever seen. Bright flowers and twists of shiny ivy crisscrossed over the ceiling tiles. A vine full of white lilies snaked up the hallway as we watched. Dandelions burst out of the doorknobs. Clusters of moss and lacy-white flowers covered the classroom doors.

"Grace," I breathed.

At the same time, she gasped my name. "Olive."

The paper butterflies taped to the second-grade door began to flutter. At first, I figured that was on account of the air vents. Then the wings clattered as they burst away from the door, darting all around us. All around little kids who were laughing and squealing. I hoped they remembered this moment forever: what their names looked like on a wing, in flight, with bright light filtering through. I would remember it. I would never forget. A paper butterfly perched on my hand. I reached to touch the penciled name on its wing: *Hope*, but it fluttered fast away from me.

Our school principal, Mrs. Asbury, stood in the hall with a stunned look on her face. "What in the world is happening here?"

First Maddie ran up behind her. "I think it's a mold issue, Mrs. Asbury!"

"It's not mold," Grace said. "It's magic!"

Miss Snow winked at us and said, "And this is only the beginning."

That night over dinner, Mama and Jupiter made a rare exception: I was allowed to study my lines at the table, since auditions were the very next day. This was unfortunate timing, honestly. Macklemore Middle School was waking up; magic was literally blooming in the halls and fluttering off the walls. You'd think this would be reason enough for a few teachers to cancel homework. Maybe push the play out a week or two. But Mrs. Matheson insisted the theater must go on.

So there I was, at dinner, trying to memorize two different parts I wanted to try out for. And the play mattered as much to me as all the magical stuff, I had the taco-proof.

By which I mean: There were tacos on the table, and I was ignoring them just to study.

I read my lines, then covered them with my hand and tried to say them aloud.

Emily: [groans] The view's always the same from this window. I could close my eyes and tell you everything I see, and will see, for the rest of my life.

Bird of Joy [outside window]: Oh, really? Then tell me the pattern on my wings. [Hides wings behind back.]

Emily: Excuse me? [Glances around, trying to catch a better glimpse of bird.]

Bird of Joy: No peeking! Tell me the patterns of my wings! Ha, you can't! [Bird makes happy squawk sound and dances around.] Now, tell me the patterns of the stars in the sky. Or maybe describe the colors of the leaves when they're changing; fall to spring and back again. Tell me the pitch of the cricket-songs in summer. Tell me about the sound of snow when it falls.

Emily: Snow doesn't make a sound.

Bird of Joy: What about a heart when it breaks?

[Emily starts to speak, looks confused, stops.]

Bird of Joy: Does this view look different to a heart that's breaking? Tell me how. [Bird leans in more closely, serious look on face.] Tell me the pattern on my wings.

Emily: No offense, but I would rather tell you about sunsets or pyramids or boat rides through the hidden jungle. If I had wings, I could see those things. But I don't. Your wings don't help me much.

Bird of Joy: [chirps sweetly] That's where you're mistaken, Emily dearest. My wings are whatever I want them to be. So are yours.

I turned the page to keep reading until I heard Uncle Dash say, "What about you, Hatch? How's your day been?"

Moments like this are when my stepbrother changes. He sat up straight. He flashed the kind of cheesy grin usually reserved for cereal commercials. And, much like the superheroes he likes to read about, he transformed into Mr. Personality as he described his Monday.

First, he practiced guitar in the band room, he told us. Then he met with the Comic Book Club. And he wrote a book talk for Mr. Watson's class. Then he'd gotten a start on next week's homework and practiced some French. The French is just a fun new hobby.

"I want to learn to say *good morning* in four different languages," he said.

"Do you get to hang out with Olive very often?" Coach Mo asked.

I stopped reading and looked at Hatch's eyes. And he looked in mine. I waited to see what he'd say. And at first, I thought he'd say nothing.

"You've been quiet lately, bud," Coach Malone said, resting a hand on his son's shoulder. "Is everything okay?"

Hatch looked so uneasy, sick almost. And I wondered if it was because, just maybe, he realized I knew the truth . . . about all of it. He wasn't in a comic book club, for sure. That didn't exist. All the other stuff might be true, but the only thing I ever saw Hatch do at school was read his comic book all alone.

"Have you spent much time together?" Coach asked.

Hatch shifted in his seat.

"Hatch is so busy I barely see him," I told them. "But I know he'd help if I needed anything."

The conversation moved on after that. But the look in Hatch's eyes surprised me. It's funny how you can read people one way and be so sure—like *so* confident—you know all about them. When really, you don't know anything. You can't see anybody's heart; you only see what they want you to see. Or what you want to see, which can be even worse.

That night, what I saw in Hatch Malone's eyes was sheer sadness. I was sure of it. And when he tilted his head back down to read his comic book, I felt that sadness reach toward me.

I never thought I had anything in common with Hatch Malone.

But now I know I was wrong. We both have fragile places inside.

Everybody does.

Later that night, once the sun was down and the spring moon was shining, I settled into my desk to read Emily's poems. Felix likes them, too, so I always read them aloud. I'd come to the line I love about hope, how it's like feathers, when someone knocked softly on my door.

Next came the unmistakable voice of my stepbrother: "Can I come in?"

"Okay?" I said. The word came out like a question because I wondered if he was lost. Hatch had never been in my room before. Not even once.

He pushed the door open but stood firmly at the threshold, as if crossing over would spin him into some parallel girly universe from which he could never return. "Thanks for saying that at dinner. We both know I'm not really involved with anything at school, but thanks for pretending like I have a social life."

"I'm not a snitch," I said. "But why lie?"

"I don't want my dad to worry about me," he said. "I don't want him to know that it's hard since we moved. As long as he sees me participate every now and then in PE, I think he assumes everything else is okay, too."

"Your friends that come over sometimes, are they from your old school?"

"So far," he said. "And I don't really do clubs. I, like, sit alone in the library and play chess with Bon Jovi. Or read books. I really am trying to learn French."

"That sounds lonely," I told him.

"Oui," he said with a sigh.

"I have a question," I said, turning to fully face him. "And it might sound prickly. I'm not mad, though. I just want to know: Are you spying on us? Grace and me?"

Hatch sucked on his lip and looked away. That was the only answer I needed. It had been him! Before I could ask why, he shot back with this:

"Can I ask you a prickly question, Olive? Do you really think your wish is worth it?"

Hatch's question was more than prickly. It landed like a bee sting. "Excuse you?"

"Yes, I know you and Grace Cho are looking for the bird. And you're related to the great Merlin Goad. And she's the mega-talented Grace Cho, so of course you'll find it. But why not let somebody find it who needs it?"

The more he talked, the more frustrated he sounded. So I tried to keep my voice calm. "Why are you so mad at me right now? Anybody can look for the bird! And really, I think it's the bird that chooses."

"It doesn't matter," he fired back. "What I'm saying is that things are already great for you. You started school a week ago and you have friends. Your family loves you."

"They love you, too!"

"You have a pelican you feed fish sticks to!"

"You can feed Felix anytime!" I said. "Seriously, what's wrong?"

"I need this." Hatch said each word slowly, like a declaration. "This isn't about a play for me. I know that's what you're wishing for. You don't have to say it—you want the lead in the play. But I want something way, way more important. I wouldn't say it if it weren't true. I . . ."

Hatch pressed his palms hard against his eyes, like he was trying to push tears back into his soul. And a sudden, magical what-if came floating through my imagination like a stray feather on the wind. *What if I don't know anything about Hatch at all?*

I'd seen Hatch two ways: quiet or very, very cheesy and obnoxious, talking about how amazing he was. But looking at him now, I saw him differently. And I wondered if seeing people differently is sometimes the first step to really seeing them at all.

Here's what I mean: The sleeves of Hatch's blue hoodie are frayed because he's constantly rubbing the edges between his fingers, over and over. But what if he doesn't just do that out of habit? What if he's nervous about something? Or anxious about something? Maybe Hatch always wears that same hoodie because it's more of a safety blanket than a shirt.

Maybe the wish Hatch wants—more than any other wish—has been on his heart a long time. And maybe the weight of it is causing his heart to break. I've had enough fractures to know that bones heal. I don't know if broken hearts ever do.

Hatch's hands dropped slowly from his sad eyes. They were rimmed red now. He pulled his hoodie up over his hair, his sleeves down over his wrists.

"Is your wish the reason you walk in the woods at night?" I asked. I tried to make my voice sound gentle.

He didn't say, but his eyes lifted so fast I knew the answer was yes.

"Birthday rules apply to the wish," he said. "You can't tell anybody what you wish for. Ever."

"You can tell me if it's connected," I said. I didn't actually know if this was true, but it seemed to follow birthday logic. "You know what it's connected to for me."

"Maybe," he admitted. "Maybe what I want is in the woods. I don't really know where it's at." His voice broke over the last words. This wish meant a lot to him.

But so did mine!

My wish was actually much bigger than just the play. But I hoped it would happen that same night—so I could spin around the stage, dance like a lonely poet.

"I'm going to find it, Olive. I'll do whatever it takes. I'm sorry."

I didn't know if the look on his face was sadness or determination. Maybe it was a little of both.

He spun and walked out the door before I could say anything. My stepbrother had just made it clear: We were in a race to get to the hummingbird first. I should have been upset, fired up, and ready to roll out into the woods and find a magical creature before him.

So why was my heart hurting so much? Miss Snow had warned us other people had wishes and hopes as deep as the ones Grace and I shared. Maybe she warned us because it's so hard when your wish isn't the one that comes true— whether that person was Hatch, or Grace, or me.

I cleared my throat, trying to make the sinky feeling in my heart fade away.

"We're okay, though," I promised Felix. "We're getting so close. We'll find the place, then the song, then the bird. We have as good a shot at this as Hatch."

The wind howled outside my window, and I shivered.

CHAPTER 23
Becoming a Bird

On Tuesday after school, Foster Auditorium smelled like blooming jasmine. Probably because jasmine flowers were literally blooming cloudy white on thick vines surrounding the chandelier. I might have associated the smell of jasmines with how nervous I felt for the rest of my life had it not been for Dylan, who always had a way of making me laugh.

"I keep saying," Dylan said, sneezing between every word. "If the school board would just give theater like a third of the money they give the football team, we could at least patch the roof."

"Exactly, it's mold," First Maddie told us, hands on her hips from the stage. "My dad is the mayor and he's also a meteorologist. He knows things."

"Ooooh," said Dylan quietly to me. "A meteorologist."

And he smashed his hands against his cheeks in mock astonishment.

"Everybody calm down and get prepared," said Mrs. Matheson. "I don't care what's blooming in here. I don't care if the hummingbird floats into this room in the middle of class. Focus, friends! Auditions are here!" She clapped her hands together. "Commit to your craft! We have less than two weeks until we perform for the entire town of Wildwood. And you might only have a twenty-minute slot, but you will use that slot to shine. You understand? What's the holdup with the wings, Grace?"

"I'm working as fast as I can!" Grace said, tying a pair of gauzy blue butterfly wings to Second Maddie's back. "Costuming takes time!"

Grace moved to me next.

"I don't know if I should wear them," I said quietly. "I love them. And I'm trying out for a bird-part. But they might get stuck in my wheelchair and I want Mrs. Matheson to see that I can move around—"

"Oh, I thought of that already," Grace said. That day, she'd worn her hair up in a fluffy-pouf directly on top of her head. To that pouf, she'd affixed two googly eyes. It was a great look and made me miss my sequin jacket. "I made this pair of wings just for you," she said. "They won't catch on anything. But listen to me—you should read for Emily, too. Not just one of the birds. Read for both parts."

"What if I'm terrible at it?"

"What if you're great? Those are fireworks in your chest, not nerves. Remember?"

I was so lucky to have a friend like her. "Any word on Nester?" I asked as Grace tied the wings in place.

"Not yet. And we've got to get the riddle figured out. So my next plan is just to write something on a poster board and stand in front of the Ragged Apple Cafe with it until she responds."

"I like your commitment," I said, trying to sound optimistic. Really, I was terrified we'd missed our opportunity. Hatch and the Maddies also wanted to find the bird. What if they figured out the clues before we did? We had only eleven more days!

"You can't think about it now," Grace told me. "You have to focus on your lines."

"You're right," I said with a sigh. I should know my lines. I practiced all night. I said them to Felix that morning. Then again to Mama and Uncle Dash over breakfast. A final time when Jupiter dropped me at the front door. Logically, I knew I could be part of other plays in my lifetime. I could be in movies someday, maybe. I could be on Broadway with Dylan. But for that one space of a minute, while Grace was attaching fake wings to my chair, nothing felt more important than the Macklemore Middle School play.

"You're all set," Grace said. "Go be a butterfly with a dagger and a Judy Blume book."

242

"Thanks for making a pair just for me." I held out my fist. "You're superior."

She smiled, silver-sparkly, and bumped my fist with hers. Then we clapped twice and twirled. (My slumber party also included a secret handshake station.)

Mrs. Matheson called Dylan to the stage.

"Don't break a leg, Olive," Dylan said with a wink as he bounded past me and up the stairs. I assumed Dylan would try out for the Bird of Joy, too. Dylan radiates joy no matter where he's at. But when the spotlight found him, his smile faded. The sparkle in his eyes seemed to dim somehow, like his whole personality shifted. And then he read for the part of the Bird of Sorrow so convincingly I nearly cried.

Even without a spotlight, Dylan is the kind of person who shines. He didn't need the light, but he seemed to pull it toward him. I watched in awe as he let the stage completely transform him into someone else. He spoke some lines. He sang others even though the script didn't say to do that. He moved like he was dancing, so fluidly you'd think he was ready to fly every time he lifted his arms. When he finished, I applauded so hard it made my hands hurt.

Next, all the Maddies auditioned. Second and Third Maddie read for a few different parts. But First Maddie, ever the class celebrity, only read for Emily. She walked out onstage wearing a shiny white dress and wings made of chicken wire. She'd worn a full face of makeup today, which made her look even more perfect than usual. At first, I was a little frustrated when she read the part so well.

Then I hated that I had felt that way.

I recognized the little tug in my heart as jealousy. And I squashed that right back down. Mama and Jupiter have always told me that one person's talent does not take away from your talent. Everybody in the world deserves joy.

Deserves a moment in the spotlight.

It's just a little hard not to be jealous of someone, like First Maddie, whose whole life is a shiny spotlight. She's naturally awesome at everything.

There's a place for me, too, I told my heart.

And in less than two weeks, once I found the bird, I'd climb the stage steps and not even think about it. Just like everybody else. I wouldn't even need the stupid ramp. (Which hadn't been built.)

"Olive Martin?" Mrs. Matheson called out. She pivoted around to look at me, glasses balanced on the tip of her nose. "You want to read for anything, sweetie?"

"Yes! I'm reading for the Bird of Joy," I said. Grace glared at me—with her real eyes and her googly eyes. Before I could lose my nerve, I added, "And for Emily Dickinson."

First Maddie spun around from the front row, staring like she was seeing me for the very first time.

Grace beamed. Dylan pumped his arms in the air.

But Mrs. Matheson only said, "Oh. Interesting." She

didn't smile or wink at me, like she'd done on day one. She just watched as I rolled to the front of the auditorium.

I knew I couldn't go on the stage. There was no ramp. But I rolled to the front center of the room, eye level with everybody—why were there so many people?—and took a deep breath.

The spotlight found me even without the stage. At first, it was a shock to feel the light on my face. But my eyes adjusted quickly to the light. Behind the light, I saw Ransom McCallister giving me a thumbs-up. And a smile.

The flutters went wild inside me, like a bonafide butterfly jamboree was happening in my stomach . . . and then I forgot my lines.

Sweat beaded across my forehead. How was this happening?

I'd studied my lines all night. I'd studied for *days*. But it's like the words flew out of my brain!

I don't get nervous reading scripts, not like this. I get nervous about going to the doctor. I get nervous when I walk around. Or if I even think about the school cafeteria. But not about a script.

Then again, I'd never acted in front of so many people. And the thoughts of all of them seeing me fail was terrifying.

"When you're ready," Mrs. Matheson said.

I closed my eyes.

I didn't remember lines just

words that felt broken inside me
in pieces.

Broken,
the way Emily writes.
I remembered reading Emily's poems in my bed at night,
window wide open to hear the rain and the birds.

When I read the lines,
I thought:
Why do poets write something so beautiful just to
break it?

"Hope is the thing with feathers
That perches in the soul."
Emily wrote that. It's my favorite line she's got.
See like Emily, I told my heart.
Soar like the birds today.

"We know the secret of the sky," I finally said, remembering the words of the Bird of Joy. I lifted my head slowly, pretended I was watching the whole crowd through eagle eyes and not my own. I spread my arms, flexed my fingers like claws, and said, "And we know your secrets, too."

I unlocked Dolly's brakes, moving around, gliding, swooping my arms as the wheels rolled. I pretended to be as free as a bird, staying in character the whole time. Still, I noticed a funny look on Mrs. Matheson's face. Her mouth was open. Her eyebrows had floated up her forehead. Either she thought I was horrible or she was surprised that I wasn't. I'd picked a scene that called for dance on purpose. Mrs. Matheson had mentioned that I probably couldn't do those. And I wanted her to see that I actually could, even if my choreography looked a little different.

I paused at the end of my bird audition. Dylan smiled and gave me a double thumbs-up from the front row. First Maddie scowled.

"Now I'd like to audition for Emily," I said. This time, there was no hesitation. I moved into character even more easily than last time. I knew the rhythm of her words because I'd read her poems. Because her poems meant something to me. At this point, I even felt like I knew her heart a little bit.

That audition went even better than the first one until I got a little too close to the front row . . . and rolled over Dylan's toe. His eyes crossed. His face flamed bright red as he lifted his foot off the ground in total pain. I could tell he was trying to keep quiet, to not mess up my line. "Don't stop," he whispered to me.

But First Maddie saw it all and burst out laughing.

And when First Maddie laughs, everybody laughs. I pretended to laugh, too, so I wouldn't look stupid. My audition was over.

"I'm sorry," I said earnestly to Dylan.

"It's fine," he said, "I have nine other ones."

Mrs. Matheson patted my shoulder. "Great effort, Olive! You gotta be careful when you're rolling around up here, okay?"

I nodded, feeling like a scolded little kid.

I folded my script into my lap and rolled back to the middle aisle, where I sat on the end of a row.

"Let's try that dance with the Maddies and Dylan," Mrs. Matheson said, waving the girls up onstage. "Watch your toes, Dylan."

Melba Marcum plucked her banjo. Of course, the Madelines danced in perfect unison. They did everything that way. They made it all look so easy and super fun.

I'll do it, too, I reminded my heart. *I'll dance exactly like them soon.*

"Olive," Grace whispered, slipping into the seat beside me. "Are you crying?"

"Am I?!" I pressed my hands against my face. My cheeks were definitely wet.

So embarrassing!

They'd think I was crying because I was a baby, because I didn't think I'd get a part.

When that wasn't it. Honestly, I had no clue why I was teary. Maybe my heart was just tired. I wiped my tears away quickly and brushed my hair back.

"All right," Mrs. Matheson said. "I'll post the official

results on Thursday. Be ready for your first practice that same afternoon!"

"Good job out there, Olive!" Melba Marcum said. I hadn't even seen her slip up behind me. She looked a little bit like an angel standing over me with the lights shining down on her silvery hair. She carried her banjo to the side, instead of strapped to her back.

"I've never tried out for a part before," I said. "It didn't go perfect."

Grace, who was still sitting beside me, slipped her arm gently through mine. She didn't say a word. She didn't have to; just knowing she was there helped me feel a little better about it all.

"You looked like a bird in flight," Melba said. "Don't be so hard on yourself. I gotta run to play my banjo on Main Street. Crowds are still rolling in! But I wanted to let you two know something."

She lowered her voice. So we tried to lean in a little closer to listen. People in this school only lowered their voice to talk about one thing: the hummingbird.

"I've been giving banjo lessons to your good buddy Dylan," she said. "And he mentioned to me that you two would really like an audience with Nester Tuberose."

I jerked my head toward Grace. She was wide-eyed, her hand over her heart. "Really?" she breathed.

"That would be amazing!" I shouted. Then I hesitated.

This felt a little too good to be true. "She's impossible to get in touch with, though. Do you know her?"

"Ha!" Melba laughed. "Sure do. She's kin! You know my sister, Jessie, right? Plays the piano at church? We're Nester's favorite aunts. She's our oldest niece. I'd say we know her quite well."

"How old are you two, anyway?" Grace asked. And I jerked my head to look at her again. I adore Grace Cho but she seriously has no filter.

Melba winked. "I'll never tell. Jessie and I were sort of adopted into the family, technically. She's not that much younger than us, but she lets us boss her around. She's a busy lady, our Nester. But I spoke with her. And she said she could meet y'all at the Ragged Apple Cafe tomorrow afternoon. As long as you don't ask for any future-telling apples, she'll talk. And when Nester talks? Girls, you better be listening."

CHAPTER 24
The Mountain Ballerina

The next day after school, Uncle Dash accidentally bumped the van up on the curb outside the Ragged Apple Cafe. The only accessible space was occupied by a news van (which was super annoying). But there were no other spots, either. Main Street was as full as it had been for days.

"Slight issue," Grace said, running up to us on the sidewalk when Dash helped me transfer to Dolly.

"What's that?"

"The tables up top are full. There are spots down by the river, but I didn't know if—"

I glanced up at Dash, but he was looking at me, waiting to see what I wanted to do. Most of the time, there are plenty of tables on the street-level part of the Ragged Apple Cafe. But there's also an overflow down a few stairs, then down a little path, right beside the river. Sometimes, if I'm walking pretty well, Mama or Jupiter will hold on to me and let me walk it. But I was still feeling a little wobbly with my balance.

"I could carry you down there," Uncle Dash said. "Then come back and grab your chair. If you're not too embarrassed."

I looked at Grace. "Would it embarrass you?"

"Would what embarrass me?"

"If my uncle carried me?"

"Not even a little bit!"

I had no clue how many of my sixth-grade classmates might be down by the river this afternoon. The thought of them seeing me get carried like a baby was not ideal. But we had to talk to Nester, and she was only giving us today!

"Let's do this," I said, reaching out. Uncle Dash swooped me up into his strong arms, and we headed for the river.

It's a weird thing to be carried when you're eleven. And even though I'm little, I started thinking about how it's probably not easy. What if it's not something somebody can do for me forever? I can't expect it, at least. Someday there will be trails I just can't walk. Or buildings I can't enter. And it all makes me wonder how hard it will be to live alone.

And it made me think how nice it was going to be when the hummingbird gave me a golden kiss and I could leap down this trail in Bouncers if I wanted.

At the end of the path, the woods circled around a wide meadow full of picnic tables. String lights stretched from one of the small Oaks to a tiny tin-roof drink kiosk. *Shh*, begged the river as it rushed along on one side of us, and "Never!" sang the birds nesting in the tips of the maple trees. Waiters looked as if they were dancing, scurrying around one another with their trays of cookies, scoops of rainbow ice cream in dark chocolate cones, and candy apples, shiny-red as birthday balloons. In a chair near the kiosk, Melba Marcum picked her banjo. Her sister, Jessie, sat at a table nearby, clapping along.

"Nester's not here yet," Grace said, scanning the scene. "Or she's not out here, at least. I'm going to wait up top just to make sure we don't miss her. Gosh, I'm so nervous. I've wanted to meet her for a long time. Even before the bird stuff, she was my hero. She was the first entrepreneur in town. This is so huge, Olive. She's my version of Dolly Parton."

I knew Grace looked up to Nester Tuberose, but I had no idea her love rivaled my love for Dolly. "Good thinking," I said to her. "I'll watch for her down here. I'll do the finch whistle if she shows up here first."

Grace raced back up the stairs.

"Can we sit by the river?" I asked. Because a river sound is second to a banjo for my favorite sound in the world. I remember at church once when Pastor Mitra told us how peace feels like a river: sometimes a quiet calm.

Sometimes a wild rush of a feeling. The wild kind of peace is my favorite.

"It's pretty crowded, so I'll just wait in the van. I want you two to have some time together. Have Grace come and get me when—"

"You can sit with me," said my favorite wind chime–fairy voice at Macklemore Middle School. Uncle Dash and I looked behind us, where Rosie Snow sat at a table by herself. She was wearing huge sunglasses and a wide-brimmed hat. Her lips were candy-apple red.

Uncle Dash smoothed his hair. He cleared his throat. "I don't want to interrupt you."

"You aren't," she said, pulling out a chair for him. "Come on over."

I smiled up at him. This could be an interesting development! He nodded to me, then tripped over a chair trying to walk two feet to sit beside Rosie Snow. It's a good thing I had to focus on Nester Tuberose, or I would be eavesdropping on their whole conversation.

The rest of the tables were full of families, friends, and professional birders. I knew the birders by the binoculars they wore around their neck. They were studying maps the most carefully.

They were plotting their move.

It definitely wasn't just me and Grace or even Hatch looking for the bird now.

A very loud clearing of someone's throat caused me to look up.

Blocking the sun was a tall woman, with equally tall hair. She was chewing madly on a pencil. She had dark glasses and dangly earrings.

"Nester Tuberose," she said, extending her hand, which I shook. "You Grace?"

"I'm her best friend," I said. "Hold on just a second, ma'am."

I let out the finch whistle, which made Nester startle. But Grace came running.

"She looks awful excited," said Nester.

"You're her hero," I told her.

"Oh geez."

Grace threw her arms around the old woman's waist and squeezed tightly. "Ms. Tuberose," Grace said, stepping back. "I, too, am an entrepreneur. I want to build custom doghouses here in Macklemore. Your orchard is famous the world over, and I'm using it to model my own fancy business someday."

"Interesting," Nester said. She flung the chair back from our table, making it squeak along the paving stones. Then she plopped down in it. "Now, girls, I got a lot going on, but my aunt says it's important that I talk to you. And she has promised me that you won't ask for any future-telling apples."

"We're looking for the hummingbird," I said. "I was hoping you could help us. We're trying to find the missing words. And the place where fear and wonder both collide."

"We talked to Luther Frye," Grace said, scooting her seat even closer to Nester. "He says he remembers walking through the woods singing 'Blowin' in the Wind.' We just want to confirm that those were the magic words?"

Nester sighed. "He's a good man, Luther Frye. Ain't smiled since he lost his wife. Lost his brother first, years ago, and that took the wind from his sails, so to speak. Then he lost his wife and that's when he really changed. He didn't turn mean or hateful. But the sunshine left his soul. I'm glad he's talking about the bird again. That was a fun year. Maybe that memory will bring him some joy."

My sneaker was tapping out a frantic rhythm on the ground again. "So do you remember how you found it?" I asked. "Do you remember the wish you made?"

The look on Nester's face as she thought back reminded me so much of Luther. Her steely confidence slipped away. Her eyes looked brighter, but sadder, too. She rested her elbows on the table, let out a long breath, and said, "Yes, I remember."

And she told us her story.

"I grew up on the apple orchard over on the edge of the county," Nester said. Her voice reminded me of beautiful raspy things, like record players and old screen doors. "My folks were all apple people, as far back as I remember. One generation passed that orchard on to the next and that's what we did; we pruned and loved and cared for the trees. And there was one tree in particular, we call it the Forever Tree. Only my people know which one it is. And if a person bites from an apple on that tree, they see a little bit of their future.

"Whoa!" I declared. "Those are some jazzy apples."

"Jazzy for other people," Nester clarified. "My family only cares for the trees. We don't see the future when we bite into 'em. It remains a wild abyss for the Tuberose family. For most people, really. But some folks get a glimpse of their future. And that's not always a good thing."

"Why not?" Grace asked.

"Seeing the future can terrify people," Nester said solemnly. "Doesn't matter if people see something good or bad. They stop thinking about right now and focus on twenty years ahead of now. They waste all this good time. Today's where the living's at. Know what I mean?"

"Yes, ma'am," Grace and I both said. Though I wasn't sure I did. I was just trying to get to the bird-part.

"So anywho," Nester said, gnawing on her pencil, "The point is: I did *not* want to run an apple orchard. I wanted to be a ballerina. Dance made my heart the happiest. I danced constantly, every morning—right through those foggy fields. I remember the big, spidery shadows

257

of the apple trees leaning down on me while I spun and leaped. I'd never felt more alive than when I moved. I need to move, girls! And dancing is the opposite of sitting down on the ground and picking up apples all day. Or deciding who can come in the orchard and who can't, like it's some weird carnival attraction."

A waitress left a steaming basket of apple fritters in the center of our table, gooey white sugar-icing overflowing down the sides.

"On the house," Nester said, waving her arm like this was no big deal. Grace and I partook immediately.

"The tree situation is different now," she said. "Most people think it's only a legend. They don't go looking for the Forever Tree anymore. It's still there, though," she said with a wink.

"Is that why you wanted to find the bird?" I asked. "Did it have to do with your dancing?"

"It did indeed," she said. "When I was your age, things began happening. Strange things. Those white feathers started spinning on the wind, like a thousand little ballerinas on a stage. The almanac called for a blue moon rising. And the schoolhouse . . . well . . . it did what it's doing now."

"Who told you about the riddle?" Grace asked, over a mouthful of fritter.

"Jessie and Melba! They'd come to live on the farm several years before I was born. I loved them like sisters.

Called them my aunts. They were the ones who told me about the bird, when the feathers started falling here in the valley. On the night of the blue moon, we knew the bird would be out . . . somewhere . . . in the place where fear and wonder both collide." She smiled at the memory. "I told my dad what I was doing. Just flat out told him: *I do not want to raise apple trees. I will be a ballerina, in New York City; it is my calling. My livelihood!* And I was going to wish upon a bird to do exactly that."

"Was he upset?" Grace asked.

"No," she said. "He didn't seem to be, anyhow. He told me to be very, very careful what I wished for. *Wishes come straight from the stars*, he said. They ride on the backs of magical birds, like the hummingbird, to get to us. But they're so powerful. You have to word a wish very, very carefully. I thought of his words all night while I searched through the woods, deeper, deeper. I remember a soft *shhhh* of a sound and then I heard it—"

"Heard what?" I asked.

"My words. They were not some old folk song." She rolled her eyes. "They didn't make sense at all, not at first. But it's like they were burning in my throat and I had to say them: *I am a dancer anywhere, and everywhere I dance.*"

Grace scribbled this note down in her notebook.

"And then I touched the bird and . . ." Nester gulped. Her eyes watered, just like Luther's had. "I changed my wish, right at the last second. I didn't wish to be a ballerina in New York City. It's like when it came right down to it, when that bird was right in front of me, what I wished for changed. I wished to spend my life doing something that gave me tremendous joy." She shrugged. "I figured I'd still end up in NYC. Nothing gives me more joy than dancing."

"Did you go to New York?" I asked.

"Never," she said without a trace of bitterness. "I've never set foot in the Big Apple. I stayed here, tending to my apples. I guess New York never wanted me. First, the bus pulled out and left me. Years later, the plane had a glitch and couldn't leave the runway. I tried to drive myself, but my truck broke down. I always ended up right back here. Always back in the orchard. I think I was twenty years old when I finally tried to make it on my own. When I finally tried to . . . love it. I didn't have to try. I do love that orchard."

"But you didn't get to dance?" Grace said.

"I dance every day," Nester said, slapping her hand down on her thigh. "I dance anywhere I want. That's what I learned, from the hummingbird. I thought I had to move to a big city to be a dancer. But to be a dancer, girls, all you have to do is dance. Shall I prove it?"

Grace and I looked at each other. We weren't sure how to answer.

Nester flung the pencil on the table, and stood. "Aunt Melba!" she yelled out.

The banjo picking stopped.

"Yes, darlin'?"

"Play a dancing tune," Nester insisted.

Miss Melba winked and said, "Anywhere. Everywhere."

It made me feel especially special, and grateful, to know what those two words meant between such long-time friends. The song started slow and plucky, but soon it pinged around the woods with a quicker pace.

Nester Tuberose clutched her skirt in her hands and rose up to the tiptoes of her sneakers. Then the banjo went wild. And so did she. She kicked her legs, then clogged across the paving stones. She spun so fast she looked like a blooming flower. People applauded. They whistled.

Then, one by one, they got up and started dancing, too. That feeling I'd noticed in the air earlier in the week—the static—seemed to get thicker. It was a force that was pulling us all together, asking us to move, to grab a hand, to spin in a circle. Even Uncle Dash was dancing! Miss Snow spun beneath the arch of his arm, giddy with laughter. It was a joy to watch.

I glanced over at Melba Marcum in time to see her trade places with Dylan. I didn't even know he was there. But he sat in her seat, picking his own banjo, just the way she'd taught him. Melba took her sister's hand. Jessie, with her long white hair, laughed as she followed her out to the stones. They danced together slowly even though the music was fast, hand in hand. Their shadows stretched out long beside them.

Their shadows shocked me to my core.

I blinked. Then squished my eyes shut tight and opened them again.

For a split second, on the shadows of Melba Marcum and her sister, Jessie, I could have sworn I saw wings.

"The feathers are coming!" shouted a little girl at one of the distant tables.

People got up and ran for them. But not me and Grace. We watched Nester, Jessie, and Melba.

The Tuberose ladies danced in the feather-storm, arms stretched long. Even though their hair was gray and their bodies moved slowly, they reminded me of beautiful ballerinas in a music box. When Dylan finished playing, they all smiled at each other and took a deep bow.

"Good luck, girls," she said. "And do be careful. You don't need to be touched by the hummingbird to know it's all magic. Every moment of this life."

"Before you go," Grace said, "I'm going to be brave and bold and ask you a question: Will you be my mentor?"

"She's so talented," I said. "Absolutely brilliant."

Nester sighed. "I'll make you a deal. Get one client on your own. When you do that, I'll be your mentor. Go leave your information with the cashier up front—"

"Yes, ma'am!" Grace said. She pulled her business card out of her pocket and ran for the register.

"She's really the best," I said. "I'm not just saying it because she's my best friend."

Nester Tuberose studied my face carefully. "The word of a friend," she said, "is the only referral that really matters. Good luck on your search." She swayed her hips, snapped her fingers, and danced away from the table.

People clapped as Nester passed by. She bowed once, low, gracefully, before walking back up the stairs through a feather-storm of white.

CHAPTER 25
Deep in the Woods

For most of my life, Thursday's only claim to fame has been that it's the day before Friday. But this Thursday—today—would either change my life or break my heart.

First, I would find out if I got a part in the school play. The results of the audition would be posted on the theater door by the time I got to school.

Second, after school, I needed my parents to let me ride in a golf cart through the woods in search of a magical creature's hiding place. Or a clue to a magical creature's hiding place, at least. After meeting with Nester Tuberose, we weren't any closer to figuring out the missing words. But we could still follow Grandpa's lead and see what the rememory birds might reveal. *If* my parents said yes.

"Still thinking about it," Mama said just as I was about to ask again if I could do it. Jupiter told her she could make the final decision. But we were almost to school, and she still hadn't.

White feathers drifted down from the skies, slow and dreamy, when she drove into the parking lot.

"Okay," I said to Mama as she reached for the door latch. "Surely you know by now."

"Yes, if you're careful." She said the words as if they'd literally caused her pain. "And I mean *careful*. Grace has to drive slow, Olive. We're trying to give you some independence here, but it's not easy. Uncle Dash said he talked to Miss Snow about it. She said Grace is very trustworthy."

"He talked to Miss Snow a lot yesterday," I pointed out. A big smile stretched over Mama's face, mirroring my own. She felt the same as me about it: It was pretty wonderful to see Uncle Dash with a friend.

"We'll be the most careful anybody has ever been on a golf cart," I said. "Thank you!"

But she didn't get out of the car. She kept watching my face, studying me, reading me the way only she can.

"Is something else going on today?" she asked. Her eyes looked concerned but not panicky.

I nodded. "The cast list is being posted. This morning. It's probably on the door of the theater now. There's a part of me that doesn't even want to go in there."

Mama smiled. "Nerves aren't a bad thing. All they do is show you how much something matters. Aren't you dying to see?"

"Kind of yes," I said. "Kind of no."

"I don't have to tell you that every actress starts some-where, right? I bet even Reese Witherspoon was a tree once."

"I'll probably be lucky to even be a tree," I said, laughing nervously. "I don't think Mrs. Matheson really wants me in the play."

"I think she does. This is still new for everybody."

We watched students unload from buses and cars, strolling into the building. Somewhere inside, Grace was probably looking for me. Hatch was probably reading his comic book. Ransom McCallister was unlocking the theater. He'd probably already seen the list.

"Before you go," Mama began, the tone of her voice making me very suspicious. "There's something I want to talk to you about. The timing just hasn't felt right."

"Uh-oh," I said. "This sounds serious."

"Jupiter said you're looking for the hummingbird, with your friend Grace. What are you wishing for?"

The silence between us felt so heavy with words and thoughts and feelings. Based on the look in her eyes, she already knew what I wanted to wish for. I shifted in my seat.

"I can't tell you," I said. "Birthday rules apply." Maybe I should have explained to her that I wouldn't be any different once my wish come true. Just my bones! Really, it was a wish for both of us.

"Ah," said Mama. And I saw a certain sadness sweep

across her face. She stretched her fingers out over the steering wheel. "I just . . . I don't want you to feel like you have to live in a world where you wish part of yourself away. Maybe that's not what your wish is about. I hope it's not. Because all of you is wonderful."

I nodded slowly, staring down at my sparkly shoelaces. How did she know? How does my mama always know how to read me like a book? I plastered a happy smile on my face, something that might make her think this was no big deal and nothing she should worry about at all. This was a good kind of change. This was my wish—the right wish—even if she couldn't see it. "I know," I said. "I really do. Olive you."

"Olive you back," she said. Then she turned up my favorite Dolly Parton song to give me a little boost of courage before I rolled into the school.

She'll get it when she sees, I thought to myself as I traveled over the door bumps and toward the theater. Grandpa wouldn't let me down. The rememory birds would show us what to do.

Grace was pacing, arms full of wings, when I got to the doors of the auditorium. People were crowded around a single sheet of paper, a list of the play parts and our names.

"OLIVE!" Grace yelled. "HURRY! The names are on the door!"

"I'm a tree?" Second Maddie said, sounding distraught.

"I'm EMILY!" shouted First Maddie, raising her arms

and spinning in the hallway. That wasn't surprising. But I still felt a little zing of jealousy in my heart.

When I finally got to the front, I couldn't even see the list. It was too high up. But Ransom McCallister appeared out of nowhere, reaching around me, and snatched it off the door.

"Congrats, New Olive," he said with a sweet smile on his face. He passed me the list. My heart jolted.

And before I even read all the way down, my heart grew wings.

OLIVE MARTIN: BIRD OF JOY
   (UNDERSTUDY FOR: EMILY DICKINSON)

Grace leaned down and hugged me gently. Having a friend to celebrate made me even happier than getting a part in the play. Good news is still good even if you're alone. But it's great when somebody who loves you is there to share the joy-kabooms.

"Calm down, everybody," Mrs. Matheson called out from behind us. "Get to class and I'll see you all after school."

"My first real rehearsal," I said to Grace.

"I know," she said back. And we did our secret hand-shake and squealed.

"Girls," Mrs. Matheson said, "save the energy for the stage. We need all the miracles we can get."

School dragged on extra slow that day, because I couldn't wait for the afternoon. Grace was worried, understandably. We still didn't know the missing words. But as the day stretched on, hope filled my heart. First came play practice, and I had an actual part! Then we'd get to look for the rememory birds! And maybe they would put us on the right path.

I rolled into the auditorium feeling more confident than I ever had before. It felt a little bit like wearing a sequined jacket on the inside—like something so good was shining in me, and out of me. I was an actress! I was in the play, just like Dylan and First Maddie!

"This might be my best day ever," I told Grace while we waited for practice to start.

Friend, it was not.

I mentioned that it's awkward to try and talk to someone who is pushing me.

It's also awkward acting in a play when everyone is onstage but you. Still, I was determined to make it work.

"You're going to have to listen for cues, Olive," Mrs. Matheson said. "You can't watch them the whole time. And don't move around too much, or people will get distracted. I think what we'll do is put a cardboard tree around you down here. That way you can just perch."

For reasons I could not understand, Mrs. Matheson was absolutely determined to make a tree of me.

I nodded, trying to listen to what she was telling me

without getting hurt or offended. Still, if she had anything to criticize about the play, my name was always involved.

"Olive, look at the audience even when you are talking," she directed.

"You're a bird, Olive. Not a person." (I had no clue what that one meant.)

"Olive, maybe we should have First Maddie come down here to you for a few scenes. Would that help you understand how to project your voice if you could see First Maddie?" (Maybe? Maybe not? I was up for trying whatever she wanted, so I said okay.)

"Olive, you don't need to try to dance down here like the birds onstage are dancing. Just flutter your arms a little. Like that, yes! Flutter!"

I had not expected my first play rehearsal to be confetti-amazingness. But I also hadn't expected it to be this. My first thought was, *How hard is it to make a ramp?* All the other birds flocked together, playing off one another's expressions. I couldn't even see anybody.

"You'll have more practice before the big play," Grace said, helping me out of my wings. "Don't stress about that. Stress about the bird." She leaned low and whispered, "The Maddies are already running into the woods, too."

"Rats!" I said. "What if they find its hiding place first?"

"Not happening," Grace assured me. We left the auditorium side by side. "Plus, they don't have access to a golf cart."

Miss Rosie Snow was waiting for us outside the double doors. Standing beside her was my beloved uncle. They were turned toward each other, talking and laughing.

"Oh, he's all dressed up," I said. "Those are his church jeans—the only ones without holes! I think he's legit trying to date Miss Snow."

"I legit don't think she minds," Grace said as Miss Snow laughed at something Uncle Dash said, then reached to touch his arm.

I cleared my throat.

"Hey, friends!" Miss Snow said. "I didn't even see you there. Come on and let me show you the cart so you can get started on this big adventure. Have a good practice?"

"I bet you did great," Uncle Dash added quickly, falling in step beside me.

"It didn't feel great," I said. "But there's always hope, I guess."

"Behold," Miss Snow said with a flourish of her arm. She opened one of the side doors of the school. "Le cart!" I rolled down the ramp beside Grace, toward our afternoon chariot. The cart was teal and shiny, with four seats and two plungers in the back.

"So, Olive," Uncle Dash said as he helped me transfer to the cart. "Grace will drive very, very slowly, right?"

"SO SLOW," Grace said, a little too loudly.

A smile tugged at the corners of my uncle's mouth. "Half an hour, okay? Stay on the flat paths. I'll wait right here."

"I'll wait with you," said Miss Snow.

Grace wiggled her eyebrows at me and I giggled.

Once Uncle Dash checked to make sure my seat belt was in place, Grace and I puttered toward the woods. I flattened the map open in my lap.

"BlumeBirds, away!" Grace said, nudging the gas.

I glanced back to see Uncle Dash and Miss Snow. They were leaning against the brick wall, facing each other, just talking. I'd never seen him smile like that. Maybe some people find church in a building. But I wondered if Uncle Dash had found it in a person.

I couldn't wait to remind him: Sometimes change is wonderful.

The afternoon was full of sunlight, breezy-warm and bright. White clouds floated overhead. White feathers floated through the wind.

We drove around the corner of the school, then underneath a canopy of maple trees. Their shadows fluttered across my face. There were lots of paths in the woods, twisting into deeper, darker places. But Grace and I stayed on the well-worn path to Bridal Veil Falls. There in the light, rolling along, I wondered if I'd ever felt happier, or more excited. Or more free.

Free in my body, right now exactly the way it is.

Then Grace smashed the brakes and I lurched forward.

"We still have a ways to go," I reminded her, poking the map.

"I know. But let's try Luther's words and see if anything happens," she said. She handed me a printed page with the lyrics from "Blowin' in the Wind."

"Grace," I said, laughing. "This won't work. It has to be the night of a blue moon rising."

"Well, let's practice, anyway," she said. "And maybe it'll decide to fly out and grant our wish early!"

And Grace belted out the song as loud as she could. At first it just made me laugh, so much I couldn't even sing along. Then I joined in and we were both laughing. Then Grace accidentally rolled off the golf cart.

Little moments like this
make me so excited
for the hummingbird to find me.

How sweet would it feel to fall,
just dive into the world,
roll into the green, rolling grass of it all
and not worry about anything that breaks?

Grace bounced up and jogged around to the front of the cart. She opened her arms wide and shouted the words of Nester Tuberose.

A mighty wind howled through the woods. The maple

trees fluttered again, shattering light and shadows over our faces. I closed my eyes and pretended that light was the hummingbird coming to find us. Why couldn't magic find us now? Maybe magic can find anybody, anywhere!

I opened one eye, hoping to see a little fistful of light coming toward us. But all I saw was Grace Cho, skinny arms stretched long. Even when she's not wearing wings, my best friend looks like she's capable of flying.

"Dang," she said, hopping back on the cart. "I guess we gotta play by the rules."

"Do you ever wonder if it's watching us, though?" I asked. "Maybe even right now?"

Just before Grace pushed the gas, a soft wind whispered through the trees and across the back of my neck. Twigs snapped along the path we'd just rolled down.

Someone—or something—had followed us into the woods.

CHAPTER 26
The Nest

There are people who believe the Piney Woods are full of monsters, ghosts, and magical creatures. Today, the woods for sure held my stepbrother.

Hatch Malone stood behind us, his hoodie as blue as the sky above. He had it zipped all the way to the neck, comic book shoved in his front pocket.

For the record, I was becoming very curious about his comic book obsession.

For a second, he just stared. So I stared. That got awkward.

"Um . . . hi?" I tried.

"I want to join the BlumeBird Society," he blurted out. "I think I have a lot to offer this mission. I've eavesdropped on everything, which I don't feel bad about. You two are really loud. To show you how serious I am about being a team player, I'm going to tell you my theory about the missing words. Which I'm pretty positive is the right theory."

"We're listening," I said with skepticism in my voice. How was I supposed to know if he seriously wanted to do this or if Hatch just wanted to throw us off track?

"The words are different for every person," he said. "Maybe you've put that together already. But I just heard y'all screaming out 'Blowin' in the Wind' so maybe you haven't. Your words won't be Luther's words. Or Nester's words. Or the words of the mysterious third person who found the bird. And there are probably other people in town who've found it, too. I bet all their words are different. I think you'll only know your words when you see the bird. The legend says it's the words that *you've* been missing."

I spun around to look at Grace Cho. She nodded thoughtfully. "That does make sense."

"You promise you aren't trying to throw us off?"

"Of course I'm not," Hatch said. "But I want to make sure I understand the rules. The deal is the bird picks who it picks, right? We'll all help one another find it. But no hard feelings if it picks me?"

This time, Grace looked back at me. Since Hatch was my stepbrother, I guess she was letting me decide. And even though I'd already told him he could join us, I still hesitated for a moment. My wish might have started out

276

as a flicker in my heart, but it was a full-blown fire now. Especially after today's play practice. I needed the hummingbird. Everything would change if that creature picked me. Could I really have zero hard feelings if it picked Hatch instead? I honestly didn't know if it was a good idea, letting him join the squad. But I couldn't just leave him in the woods either.

"That's right," I said. "Those are the rules."

Hatch nodded, once. Then reached to shake both of our hands. I fished through my backpack until I found another nectar ring and handed it to him.

"You're in," I said.

Hatch looked at the ring like it was a dead bug, shoved it in his hoodie, then climbed on the back of the cart.

"Can I drive?" I asked.

"Sure!" Grace said, running around to the passenger's side. And we meandered through the woods, steady and slow while shadows and sunlight painted the pathway.

We drove in silence all the way to Bridal Veil Falls, watching together, eyes peeled for a shiny glint of gold in the woods. But all we saw were twists of mountain laurel and trees freckled white by dogwood blooms. A cluster of butterflies darted around the cart. Grace squealed at their fluttery cuteness.

"See what I mean?" I said to her. Hatch leaned up close to listen. It was going to take a second, remembering he was part of the BlumeBirds now. I spoke louder so he could hear me over the motor. "The woods are like a magical sanctuary. They're not creepy."

"Not today," Grace clarified.

I finally nudged the golf cart's brakes to a stop under a canopy of maple trees.

"I think the nests were here," I said. "I remember they were close to the waterfall. But you have to wait for the sun to hit them at just the right angle."

"How do these lead you to the hummingbird?" Hatch asked.

"Not sure," I admitted. "But Grandpa knows I'm looking for it. And the only advice he gave me was to find the rememory birds. They weave memories into nests. So I wonder if there's a memory he wants me to see. A memory he knows is here? Maybe, if we do this, we can see where the hummingbird will be. That would be one of the greatest moments of your life, if you actually found it. That's a memory you'd hold on to."

"An actual memory?" Hatch asked, spinning around. "How do you weave a memory?"

"I remember asking Grandpa that. He said animals see emotions, thoughts, and memories in ways we can't. He said some memories are so special—or so tragic—they're too big to hold in a human heart. So they float up and out. Into the woods and over the hills. Have you ever gone out for a stroll or a roll and you feel happy all of a sudden? Or sad all of a sudden? Have you ever smelled the most random thing and it made you miss somebody?"

"Yeah," Hatch said, his voice a little hoarse.

"I have, too," said Grace softly.

I nodded. "You've probably walked right through a flying memory and not even realized it. Rememory birds see those and snatch them up to build nests. And when the light hits them just right, you'll see the memories shine."

We rested our heads against the seats and looked up into the trees, watching for the light to bend and reflect something so magical it was hard to describe. Maybe we waited twenty seconds. Maybe it was twenty minutes. Time stretches forever when you're hoping for miracles or magic to show up. But eventually, the sun stopped holding out and angled just right through the trees.

Hatch Malone gasped. (And Hatch never reacts to anything!)

"I see the nests!" Grace said.

"And I see . . . bubbles?" Hatch jumped out of the cart and ran to another tree to look up.

Bubbles on a bird's nest. That's how it looked at first. Memories curved in shiny domes over all the nests in the trees. As the sun pushed deeper into the thicket, the memories grew bigger, billowing until they popped off the nest and floated down over our faces.

Up close they reminded me of snow globes with whole worlds—moving worlds—happening right inside.

We saw two little girls dancing in an apple orchard.

Boys playing hopscotch in the shadow of a barn.

A football streaked across the surface of one memory. Somebody had imagined their most famous touchdown over and over, a thousand times. Maybe they still did.

The bubbles held family reunions and pouncing dogs. First kisses and Halloween parties. People danced and drove old cars. They got married and had babies.

"This one has a horse and buggy," Hatch shouted, running beside one past the cart. "That's the oldest I've seen!"

I watched him stop, squat down, and jump once, twice, then rocket up into a treetop with his Bouncers. "Hey, Olive," he shouted from a high-up branch, "did Jupiter live in London?"

"Jupiter has lived everywhere," I explained.

"I think I see him!" said Hatch. "He's catching an underground train headed for Hyde Park."

At first, just the fact that this place existed felt too magical to be real.

But after a while, it started to feel heavy. Because it's not just the joyful memories people roll over forever in their hearts and minds. It's the hard ones. It's the loss, the loneliness, and the letting go. Some bubbles were filled with war, and tearful goodbyes.

"This is it," Grace said. I looked in time to see a tear rolling down her face. "Fear and wonder definitely both collide in a place like this, right? Those feelings have to live wherever memories are."

"I guess so," I said. My heart thumped, wild and hopeful. "So that means if we come back here on the night of the blue moon, we'll find it. Right?"

The rememory bird nests seemed like a place a magical bird would hide. This had to be the place. So why didn't it feel right in my heart?

"Something still feels . . . off," I admitted.

But nobody was listening to me talk. Hatch was climbing higher in the trees. And Grace was walking across the thicket, following a memory as if she'd been hypnotized. I was about to call out to them, tell them we should probably head back.

But that's when a memory stole my attention. I watched it pull away from the tree overhead, then float slowly down in front of my face. The image played over and over like a scene in a movie:

A boy in the woods faced a blinding light. I could only see his back, and the back of the girl beside him, who had long hair and wore a billowy dress. He reached for her hand. She reached for his. Then the bright light refined to a tiny, fluttering dot between them, and flew at her.

The hummingbird. Somebody was remembering the hummingbird. Someone did find it, somewhere in the woods. This had to be what Grandpa wanted me to see!

"Grace!" I yelled. "Hatch! There's a hummingbird

memory here. They found it in the woods!" That was proof, wasn't it? The hummingbird had to be *here* somewhere. I pressed my hand over my heart, to smoosh that truth deep inside it: The bird would be here. I might find it. Everything really was about to change.

Grace climbed back in the cart, her face wet with tears. "This is a sacred place," she said, sniffing. "I'm so hungry right now. I get hungry when I'm sad. Where'd Hatch go?"

"I think he's up in the tr—" Before I could finish, Hatch walked beside the cart like he was in a daze, following a shiny bubble that held another kind of image: a white dog, with floppy ears, pounced through the bubble again, and again. He couldn't stop staring.

"Hatch?" I called out softly.

"I'll catch up with you later," he managed to mumble. The comic book tumbled out of his hoodie, thunking on the ground. He didn't even notice. He followed a fragile memory farther, and deeper, into the dark.

CHAPTER 27
Dance of the Martins

I've often wondered if carrying so many memories feels exhausting as a person gets older. Good memories are precious to hold on to, fun to look at again and again. But toting old memories around? That has to feel heavy after a while. Like hauling bulging luggage through an airport.

Here's what I know for sure: When memories are vivid enough to get snatched up and turned into a nest by a rememory bird, they're powerful. And seeing so many, all together, had tuckered me out. I didn't even live those memories, but I jumped in bed as soon as I got home and pressed my pillow over my eyes. I needed a brain break.

Grace felt better by the time we got back to the school. She was elated, actually, convinced we'd found the place where the hummingbird would be on the night of the blue moon. Where else would fear and wonder both collide but a thicket full of memories? A place that was beautiful and scary and wonderful and sad? I had to agree now—the nests were enchanting. But I still felt zero fear out there.

Whatever Hatch thought about the thicket, he kept to himself. He was quiet when he met up with us at school. But I had to admit, his theory about the missing words was spot-on. He said they were unique to an individual. That, just like the clue says, the words will drift across your broken heart.

When you see the bird—or when the bird sees you—that's when you know.

Hatch Malone: man of mystery, cracker of clues.

I wonder what my stepbrother's wish would be?

Then I remembered: I had Hatch's comic book.

I flung the pillow off my eyes and fished my stepbrother's most treasured possession out of my backpack. I meant to give it to him in the car, but I honestly forgot. Now I could see exactly what he read all the time.

I've wondered how a story can be so wonderful you want to read it over and over every day for a year. I've read lots of books more than once. But not every single day!

I settled back against the pillow and read the title aloud. *"The Adventures of Marvelo the Great and His Fine Dog, Hank."*

I planned to flip through the pages fast, just to get an idea of the story. Just because I'm curious and nosy and need to know. But I only got to page one before something surprised me. There was no Hank. There was no Marvelo.

Instead, notebook pages had been taped inside the pages of the comic. And they were full of Hatch's own drawings.

My stepbrother had his own story to tell: about a boy named Hatch, and his fine dog, Biscuit.

"Once upon a time," I whisper-read, "there lived a boy who wore a blue hoodie and bright shoes that bounced him into the galaxy. And that boy had a fine dog, a beautiful terrier with bright brown eyes, named Biscuit. Biscuit's ears were cloudy white, so floppy they flapped like wings and carried her all around the world. Always with Hatch. They were each other's truest friend."

I swallowed down a lump in my throat. Dog books always make me kinda sad. I read silently after that, pages full of adventures that Biscuit and Hatch had together. In the end, they battled a terrible villain who controlled the weather. As a tornado spun across the hills, Hatch kept fighting . . . and Biscuit ran away. Lost.

"Oh no," I whispered, flipping the page quickly.

Hatch the Great searched for the dog night and day. Finally, in the last scene, Biscuit came flying through the woods, back into her owner's arms.

When I finished the story, I hugged it against my heart like a teddy bear. And that's when I heard my stepbrother's unmistakable mellow voice say, "Hey."

My eyes opened wide. Hatch was standing in my bedroom doorway.

"You dropped it in the woods," I said nervously. "I was just going to give it back to you. But I'm so nosy. I'm sorry. It's a great story, though. You're really, really talented."

I offered the book to him. He stepped into the room slowly, glancing around like I'd booby-trapped the place with glitter. He tucked it, carefully, back into his hoodie. He didn't look upset, at least, which was nice. But what he said still shocked me a little.

"Want to watch a movie?"

"Let me make sure I understand," Mama said. "You want to watch a movie together? Here in the living room?"

"Is that okay?" I asked, my mouth full of popcorn.

Hatch had just crammed a bunch of popcorn in his mouth, too. He looked like a chipmunk.

Mama looked at Coach Malone, who was doing dishes. He must have given her a telepathic thumbs-up because she nodded slowly and walked away.

"We're doing homework while we watch," I declared.

"You are," Hatch said. "I'm not."

Then the credits for my favorite Reese Witherspoon movie began to play.

And Hatch said, "Actually, maybe I will do homework."

"Just give it a chance!" I said. "You can pick next."

"Cool," he said. And then he kept talking. *To me!* While the movie rolled and we talked, Mama kept the popcorn bowl refilled. Watching us a little bit suspiciously. I guess I couldn't blame her. Hatch and I had barely communicated until a few days ago.

Hanging out with him wasn't terrible, to be honest.

"This isn't awful," he said at the same time I thought it. But he was talking about the movie. "It's kind of funny . . ."

"I think so, too," I said excitedly. "What's your favorite movie?"

"The Goonies," he said.

"Great pick," I said. "Did you know you can see the director's van parked in one of the first scenes of *The Goonies*? I'll show you when we watch it."

"Sometimes," Hatch said with a laugh, "I think you like to read about movies more than you like to watch them."

"That's a little bit true," I said. "I like to read scripts and write scripts—as you know."

He nodded. "Oh, I know."

"I don't know everything I want to be someday," I said. "Maybe nobody ever really knows that. But I think I would be a good screenwriter. Or director. I just want to tell stories."

"Mr. Watson says everybody is a storyteller," Hatch

said. "No matter what kind of job you have or what you do, we all tell stories, whether we realize it or not."

"That makes sense," I said.

"So what would you change about this one?" he asked, leaning back on the couch. He tossed a grape in his mouth.

"Nothing," I said.

"If you *had* to pick something to change," he said. "What would it be?"

"It's going to sound kind of silly," I said. "And I don't mean for it to sound all 'woe is me.' I'm not saying it so you'll feel sorry for me, okay? But sometimes I wish you could see people who look different in the main roles. Different like me. People with disabilities, I mean. I think it'd would be cool to see somebody with *osteogenesis imperfecta* in a movie like this. I've seen one person with OI in a movie and the character was a villain. A really, really mean one."

"That stinks," Hatch said.

"It really does," I said. "I get that we're all heroes and villains deep down. So why not show both? What if a girl in a wheelchair starred in a romantic comedy? And her wheelchair is no big deal, just part of a story where she also gets to fall in love? Or what if it's some secret spy movie and she's got a cane that turns into a laser pointer that she uses to distract all the cats on the enemy's yacht?"

"You've thought about this a lot," Hatch said.

"There are actresses with disabilities," I said. "So why aren't they in movies more often?"

"Maybe you need to write the parts."

"I can't write a whole screenplay yet," I reminded him. "I don't have the life experience."

"You will, though," he said, like he had all the confidence in the world in this truth. "And you'll find a way onto that stage if you want to be there."

"You really think I could convince Jupiter and Mama and Mrs. Matheson to let me get on a stage?"

"I don't do theater, so I don't know about First Maddie's mom," he said. "But yeah, you can convince your parents. I mean, every day you show them you can do more and more without them always watching. That's got to be tough for you and them. But you keep finding a way."

I was pretty sure, almost positive, Hatch Malone was giving me an actual compliment. I said "thank you" kind of like a question because I wasn't sure.

Hatch opened his notebook, and at first I thought he was finally going to abandon the movie. But he said,

"Have you ever heard of Shirley Chisholm?"

I nodded. "First Black woman elected to Congress."

"Yeah," he said, kind of surprised that I knew. (People seem seriously surprised that I actually learned things in homeschool.)

"I just did a report about her for history class. So Shirley

Chisholm had a really great quote that my dad used to love and say to me over and over all the time. She said, 'If they don't give you a seat at the table, bring a folding chair.'"

"I'd have to bring a wheelchair," I said.

"Exactly." He smiled.

Or you could catch a bird, my heart reminded me.

Then falling would never be an issue again. I wouldn't need ramps to a stage or anywhere else I wanted to go. My parents wouldn't have to watch me scream through a broken bone. I could be ordinary-awesome then, blending in just enough—like a periwinkle crayon.

"I also get that Mrs. Matheson can't make some special adjustment for me," I said. "I mean, she can't build a ramp just for me. She has lots of other things going on."

"See, though," said Hatch. "It's not just for you. You don't think other people need a ramp? That's just basic etiquette. I think she just wants First Maddie to get a good role because she's her mom. But seriously, Olive—it doesn't matter if you're a tree or a dodo bird or a piece of grass. Someday you get to write a movie however you want, with all the people you want. Storytellers have a lot of power, ya know. You can write things better than they are."

"Or maybe just how they really are," I said. "A disabled girl can be weird and fun and cool and make mistakes. She doesn't have to be everybody's shining inspiration. But she can fall in love and have adventures and just live her life. Especially if all she needs is a freaking ramp."

"Yeah!" he said. "Exactly! And maybe a sidekick who wears Bouncers."

"Obviously."

He laughed. So did I. And then, so help me, I nearly hugged Hatch Malone. Mama told me once that Hatch needed lots of personal space. So I didn't. But just the fact that I could have is something.

"I thought you hated me for such a long time," Hatch said. "You've always been kinda . . . weird around me."

"I'm just weird in general," I assured him. "I thought you hated *me*. When you all first moved in, you told your dad you didn't want to be around me. Because I made you nervous."

"I was afraid to be around you," Hatch said. "Big difference. All I knew is that you were . . . fragile. And I'm kind of like a grizzly bear at a tea party, just super clumsy and bouncy, and I was afraid I'd hurt you accidentally. And I never want to hurt anybody. Never ever."

"I don't, either," I said. "Sorry I didn't make you feel welcome."

"It's no big deal, Olive." He started fiddling with the threads of his hoodie again. I thought about the time he asked me about my bones: Why did they break? Why were they like that?

I'd appreciated Hatch's genuine curiosity.

So I decided to ask him a question straight up, too. I made sure my voice was gentle like Mama's when I did it:

291

"Why do you always do that with your sleeves?"

His hands stopped fidgeting. "I like how it feels," he said. "And . . . I have to do it. I can't explain why. It's weird."

I shrugged. "Everybody's weird."

"Yeah, but this is my mega weirdness. I can't stand the way certain things feel against my skin. Fabrics or fibers or whatever. I think about it until it makes me sick. But then some things are the total opposite, like this hoodie. Or the blanket on my bed. If I hold those things against me, I feel . . . peaceful. I feel safe. I'm taking medicine now that helps me think about all that a little less. But I used to spend whole days obsessed with whatever piece of clothing was touching me. All that was going so much better when Biscuit was here."

He flinched when he said her name. Like he hadn't meant to bring her up.

"That was your dog," I said gently.

He nodded. "When we were packing up the car to come here, it was storming outside. This huge boom of thunder clapped overhead and she ran out the door and . . ." He looked down at his Bouncers. His chin trembled. "I can't find her. I've looked ever since. I watch the roads and the woods every time I get in a car. She was my best friend, seriously. All dogs are good dogs. But she was the best dog. She was the most magical creature I've ever been around. No hummingbird can hold a candle to her. I imagine her all the time, out there somewhere making her way home to me."

"Hatch," I said. "I know we can't tell each other our wishes. Not exactly. But does your wish possibly have something to do with her?"

Hatch didn't answer. But his big eyes filled up with tears before he looked away. I wondered if he was remembering the feel of her in his arms. The weight of her on his heart. If the hummingbird had enough power to take that loss away, or to bring her back home, that was some incredible magic, indeed.

In a week, the blue moon was rising. The hummingbird was coming. Hatch was determined to find it, to bring back his dog.

An uneasy what-if floated through my mind just then. But I shoved it back down and changed the subject. I wanted the bird, too. I needed it. And I would find it.

Later that night, I rolled into the kitchen to find Mama, Coach Malone, and Jupiter all playing cards around the kitchen table.

"Hey, fam," I said. "Where's Uncle Dash?"

"At the movies with Rosie Snow," Jupiter said, tossing a card down on the table. "I think he's made a new friend."

I had a feeling they were more than just friends, which made me feel squealy on the inside.

"How's the search going?" Mama asked.

"I think we're close!" I said. "Grace thinks we found the spot. Hatch cracked the missing words. As Coach Mo likes to say, 'Teamwork makes the dream work.'"

Coach Malone gave me a thumbs-up. He's constantly sharing cheesy quotes, and he loves it when we remember them.

"Uncle Dash said you did great on the golf cart," Mama said.

I nodded and nearly laughed. Truly, I think Uncle Dash was paying more attention to Miss Snow than the cart. But it's always nice knowing he's there.

Jupiter reached out and patted my arm. "Thanks for being so careful and taking this slow."

"Definitely," I said, rolling up underneath the table. "And while we're on that topic—of how careful I've been, and how good I'm doing—I wanted to discuss something."

"Olive." Mama said my name flatly.

"Hear me out!" I said. "All I was wondering is if one of you could help me up onstage for play rehearsals tomorrow. And then, if it works, help me up there again on the night of the play. I'll just sit in my wheelchair. I really want Mrs. Matheson to see how much better I do when I can interact with the other birds."

"We could have one wheelchair up there for you," Mama said. "So you could back up behind something when you're

294

not in a scene. Roll out when you are. Then, when you're done, we can help you walk down."

"Yes!" I said. This was a milestone moment, but I wasn't sure if she realized it. Instead of immediately reminding me to be careful, or telling me the reasons it wasn't smart, Mama was looking at the situation with a Grace Cho point of view.

"I think that's smart," said Jupiter. "I have a yoga class in the morning. What's your schedule, Misty?"

It's so weird when I actually hear someone say my mama's name. Sometimes I forget she has a name other than Mama.

"I could meet Olive at school," she said. "I could help you walk up there."

"This went so much better than I predicted," I said.

"Just wait for your mom to get there," Jupiter said. "Don't try to climb the stairs on your own, okay?"

"I promise," I said excitedly. "You have no idea how that's going to change things! Now the only part I can't really do is dance. She said she feels much more comfortable if I sit still while the other birds dance. Especially after I almost broke Dylan's toe. Nester Tuberose says she's a dancer; anywhere and everywhere she dances. Alas, I am not."

"Wrong," said Jupiter, flinging his hand of cards down on the table.

"Ha," said Coach Malone, leaning over to look. "I win!" And he threw his cards down, too.

"You can't dance there, maybe," Jupiter said, and he jumped up and jogged to the record player. "But at the cottage in the woods, we'll dance anytime we want."

Jupiter blew the dust off an old record, then gently positioned the needle to crackle against it. "Eleanor," a song by my favorite band, the Avett Brothers, played through the speakers, echoing all through the kitchen. Jupiter pretend to sing it while he made his way toward me, shuffling, swaying.

"Shall we, my love?" Jupiter asked, bowing in front of my wheelchair.

I locked the brakes. He helped me stand up, very carefully. And in our own way, our weird-wonderful Olive and Jupiter way, we danced.

My body is stiff sometimes.
I walk like my joints
are glued together.
I walk like the Tin Man in *The Wizard of Oz*.

I don't move
like a dancer.
But when my dad dances with me,
I feel like my bones are made of stardust
and I'm floating in his orbit and safe.
And one thousand percent loved.

Once when I was little,

I had to wear a cast that came above my belly button.
I couldn't sit up, but
Jupiter would fly me in his arms sometimes.
You're Supergirl, he'd say,
and we'd zoom through the air of the living room.
You're an astronaut, he'd say
as he taped plastic stars to my ceiling.
You're a writer, he'd say
when he brought me new notebooks in the hospital.
With my parents—with Jupiter and Mama—
I've always been a constellation of things.

"You're a great dancer," Jupiter said tonight
as the song echoed around the room.
"Anywhere and everywhere, you dance.
Don't ever forget that."
I knew I never would.

Mama and Coach Mo slow-danced beside us. Felix the
Pelican watched from outside, flapping his wings in time
with the music. Even Hatch Malone, who'd come to dig
through the fridge, was snapping his fingers and doing his
own funny dance. Just grooving back and forth. It was a
peaceful, perfectly, nearly summer night.

And the next day, it all shattered to pieces.

CHAPTER 28
Broken Birds

I rode to school early with Coach Malone and Hatch. Somehow, maybe because it was too early for him to argue, I also convinced Hatch to run lines with me in the car.

"You already know all this," Hatch said. "You knew both parts last night and you know it now. Relax, Olive. You've got this."

"You're right," I admitted. "I just like to be prepared."

I leaned back into the seat and smiled. Joy-kabooms: I knew my lines.

Grace was certain we knew where to go on the night of the blue moon.

I was pretty sure Mama and Jupiter would let me golf-cart out there to find it, even.

Hatch believed we'd know the missing words when we saw it.

This was all a better-than-good kind of day. My dreams were close enough to touch. I couldn't wait to hold them in my arms. I couldn't wait to feel magic in my bones.

The day started good, better than good.

But the wind is always changing.

The school was sunrise-quiet when Hatch and I rolled inside. I'd planned to go the gym and study for our second rehearsal, but Mr. Watson intercepted us when we were headed down the hall.

"Chicken miracles!" he shouted. "Come quick if you want to watch!"

We zoomed down the hallway so fast, you'd think the school was on fire. I rolled into the classroom, right up to the cardboard box, where Mr. Watson, Miss Snow, and Ms. Pigeon were already watching. Hatch leaned over my shoulder.

The eggs were all wobbly, jolting around under the light.

"I've seen chickens before," I whispered. "And I'm still so excited I can barely breathe."

I didn't move my gaze from the egg until it cracked and broke. Until a tiny beak poked through.

Mr. Watson was right; it was a miracle. For a second, it occurred to me that some broken things really were amazing, like eggs and poetry. And some broken things were awful, like bones and hearts.

"You two can stay in here until class if you want," said Mr. Watson.

"Hatch shoots hoops until the bell rings, but I'd love to study my lines. Thank you!"

Hatch started laughing. Really laughing. This was so shocking to see that I pinched myself to make sure I wasn't dreaming. "What's so funny?" I asked.

"Shoots hoops?" Hatch asked.

"That's what you do!"

"That's just a funny way to say it," he said, settling into his desk beside mine. "I'll run lines with you, Olive. It's fine. Sometimes I get bored shooting hoops."

Hatch and I settled into our desks, side by side. At first I thought I'd scooted into the wrong one because of a beautiful new journal situated on top.

"Somebody probably left it there," said Hatch, opening the front to look for a name. Then he smiled and passed it back to me.

The front page read:

The Poetry of Olive Martin.
Congratulations on your first play!
From Mr. Watson, Miss Snow, and Ms. Pigeon.

The inside was blank, ready to be filled up with poems that were mine. Not Emily's, but mine.

They day was going good. Better than good.

But the wind is always changing.

When it was finally time for theater, Ransom held the door open and I rolled toward the front, where Mama stood waiting.

"Thanks for doing this," I said to Mama as she helped me climb to the stage, one step at a time. "I didn't want to be the only bird on the ground."

"Don't go too fast," she said, her voice low so she wouldn't embarrass me. It was hard not to speed up, though. I knew not everybody was watching me. They were practicing lines out in the theater somewhere. But enough people were around that I wanted my walking to look as normal as possible. The play was only eight days away. We had a few practices left, then a dress rehearsal. I already knew my lines, but now I could really block my movement on the stage and prove to everybody—even to myself—what all I could do. I felt so victorious when I was onstage, with my friends. Mrs. Matheson sat in the audience looking up at us.

Nobody can stick this bird in a tree, is what I wanted to say. *I am born to fly*!

Mama helped me all the way to Reba, my stage wheel-chair. From the start, the scenes went better. Even my scenes with First Maddie went great. And my scenes with Dylan were so fun that I wanted to do them over and over. I thought I would get to do exactly that.

The problem, I guess, is that life doesn't always cooperate with what we want to do. Neither do miracles. Neither does magic. Neither does God, I guess. Because things can be better-than-good until, suddenly, they aren't.

Ten minutes before the bell rang, two random things happened almost at the same time: One was the best thing. And one was the worst. The chaos started when I dropped my pages. And I should have left them there—I knew my lines. I hadn't even used the script. But I was feeling confident, so happy there in the moment. Mama was talking to Coach Malone in the very back of the room, facing away from me. Nobody was really paying attention.

So I stood up and took two steps. Just two steps was all it would take for me to pick up the script. Then I'd get right back in my chair. That was the plan.

First thing, the best thing: The pages made a rushing *shh* sound as they fell, which reminded me of Bridal Veil Falls. But it reminded me of something else, too. Something Nester and Luther both said: They heard a *shh* sound in the place where they found the hummingbird.

They heard the waterfall.

Grace had been right all along—the hummingbird would be somewhere in the thicket. Somewhere near the falls!

Which brings me to the second thing, the worst thing:
I was so excited by this discovery that I didn't see Dylan
spinning across the stage. And he hadn't seen me take two
steps, arms stretched, to grab my fallen script.

He knocked into me, completely by accident.

"No!" he shouted as I lost my balance. I

stepped back and slipped on a piece of paper.
Then my left leg twisted behind me as I spiraled to
the floor. But before
I ever hit, I heard the sound.
The worst sound.

I heard the watery pop of my thigh bone,
which might be the same sound
my heart makes when it breaks.

CHAPTER 29
The Roar in Me

"Give her some space, everybody!" Mrs. Matheson shouted. "We're getting you help, sweetie. We're getting you—"

Mama pushed past her and leaned down over me. Her face was calm. Her eyes were bright, shining with tears. "It's okay, baby," she said. "We'll get through it."

Mama might have nightmares about me falling. I know she worries about this happening every time I do anything. But when it actually happens, she and Jupiter are my anchors. They're steady. They take care of me. They don't waver.

I, however, become a mess.
I couldn't even hear my mama because I
was
screaming.

"It's okay to cry!" someone shouted.
I know they were trying to make me feel better but
everybody crowded around watching
made me feel worse.

Mrs. Matheson told the other students to go have a
seat in the auditorium. She didn't even tell them to leave!
This was a terrible first performance on a real stage.

"I'm here!" yelled Coach Malone, running down the
aisle. He hopped onstage in a single leap—blue Bouncers
working overtime.

He kneeled down beside me and rested his hand on my
shoulder. "You are so brave," he said. And then, "You'll be
okay. Jupiter is meeting us at the hospital. Your mom and
I will be with you the whole time."

Hatch Malone stood over his dad's shoulder, looking
terrified. His eyes were rimmed red.

My fingers dug deep into the flesh of my thigh,
right over my femur,
the badly broken place,
the part of me jolting and throbbing with pain that felt
electric.
If you hold the broken places still,
they don't hurt as much.
(Eventually.)
When I wasn't screaming through my teeth,

When I wasn't biting my lip so hard
Blood pooled at the surface,
I heard people in the auditorium talking.
Talking,
Like this was a normal day.
talking, talking,
like it was all okay.

Hatch Malone kneeled down beside me.
He took my hand in his.
"You're brave," he said.
His words hit me like an arrow through the heart.
I didn't feel brave.
But I tried to be it.
EMTs scrambled into the auditorium and
down the aisle.

A Black woman in a short-sleeved uniform kneeled down beside me. Red roses and black vines were tattooed on her arms. "Hey there, Olive. We've never met but I've heard plenty about you. I'm Ransom McCallister's mom."

I sighed. *Bacon.*

Listen, I'm eleven, so I'm not allowed to cuss. But I kind of wanted to at this revelation. The only thing that might be worse than a broken leg in front of your whole theater troupe is this: when your crush's mom just happens to be the EMT who has to set your broken leg and see you scream like a baby through the process. I dug my nails into my palms hoping maybe I would wake up from this terrible dream.

But I didn't. I'd broken my leg, again.

This was my rotten reality.

And I knew this break would change everything.

"We need to straighten your leg, Olive," she said gently. "And then we'll load you onto a stretcher and get you to the hospital. This will all be over soon."

Bolts of icy fear
sizzled through my body because
I knew pain was coming.
My body remembers how much this hurts.

My hands shook like I was freezing
even though the stage was a warm place.
Breath scraped over my lungs
so shallow that I couldn't catch it;
Mama took my free hand in hers.
Hatch never let go.

"You're so brave," Hatch said again.

Hot tears gushed
out of my eyes.
"Ready?" the EMT asked.

I nodded and
squinched my eyes tightly shut.

When I break,
I try to hide inside myself. I pretend that I'm
in Narnia with Aslan.
I feel his mane in my hands;
I feel his roar inside my chest and it
becomes my roar.

I'm in Green Gables with Anne,
running through haunted woods,
fearless with my friend beside me.

Or I'm here,
in this perfect, magical town where all kinds of
miracles bloom.
I'm in the woods with Grace and Ransom and Hatch,
and we're running after the hummingbird.
No fear of falling,
no stupid bones breaking,
we feel streamers of sunlight in our hands
and we have wildflowers in our hair.

I imagine a world where I am wild
and nothing can hurt me.

"Roar like Aslan,"
Mama reminds me.

Ransom's mom slides her warm hand
under my knee.
Slowly, she begins to pull my leg straight.
The pain slithers,
stretches inside my leg,
and bites down hard.

I will be brave,
for Aslan
for Jupiter and Mama,
for myself, most of all.
But a wild scream—my roar—rips loose from my chest.

Hot tears
rushed down my face.
"I'm so embarrassed," I said
as I cried.

"You're a beast, Olive!" shouted Grace from the
auditorium.
"You got this! When you roar,
we'll roar with you!"
And then every sixth-grade student in the theater is yelling,

not at me,
but with me.
They were roaring,
while I was roaring.

I took their roar
and made it mine.

My friends were better than Narnia that day.
This isn't a play we're in. This is real life,
and it's really hard.
Here's how we survive:
Together, we roar.

Once I was finally loaded onto the stretcher, Hatch
turned my hand loose.

"Hey," I said, my voice groggy. "Make sure Dylan
knows none of that was his fault. He's amazing. It was an
accident. I'm not mad."

"I'll tell him," he said.

And then Ransom was there, writing something on my
wrist with a purple pen:

BRAVE

That word was all around me. Why couldn't I feel it?

"You'll be back in no time, New Olive."

I tried to smile, but I don't think it worked. My smile felt broken, too.

Grace ran along beside him. "We'll come see you as soon as we can. He's right—you'll be back before you know it!"

"Not on a stage," I said softly. My throat hurt from crying. "Birds don't fly broken."

"You do," Grace said. "You've got a best friend who can make you wings."

CHAPTER 30
The BlumeBird Promise

I spent three days in the Wildwood Hospital.

During surgery,
Dr. Kass attached a rod to
my left femur bone.

Then Chris the nurse,
Mama, and Jupiter helped me relearn how to scoot—
from the bed
to the potty chair
(so embarrassing)
back to the bed,
then to my wheelchair.
Over and over again.

Chris the nurse helped me balance on my good leg and use a walker, but only for bathroom purposes. A real bathroom is way better than a potty chair but also feels very slow when you gotta go, if you know what I mean.

One of the weirdest parts of breaking so much is healing. Because healing doesn't happen fast. Not as fast as I want it to, ever. It's like constantly reteaching your body what it's made to do. But forgets to do.

We don't always like each other,
    my body and me.

"Looks like you're going home Thursday," Mama said on the third night.

I smiled and said, "Great." I meant it, but my voice sounded as tired as I felt. Maybe my voice sounded a little defeated, too.

I lost so much when I broke my leg in the auditorium.

I lost my part in the play. I couldn't get up onstage now, for sure. And I didn't want to sit on the ground covered by a tree, completely stuck while I said my lines.

My search for the hummingbird was also over. The blue moon was rising in five days. I definitely wouldn't be ready to take a ride in a bumpy golf cart through the woods by then. My leg needed time to heal.

But maybe Grace would still be able to find the bird. Or Hatch. I hoped one of them did, truly. But I had been so excited about sharing this adventure with them.

Grandpa Goad says it's one of the hardest things in the world—learning to sit with sadness and disappointment. Now I knew what he meant. Because I knew the awesome life I'd imagined wasn't meant for me. I'll always be fragile. I'll always be broken, or waiting to break.

I stared at the ceiling, at the plastic stars Jupiter stuck there years ago, and watched them blur into shapeless colors. Thinking about my friends chasing the hummingbird without me made my heart feel even more fragile than my leg.

I heard a soft knock on the door, and Jupiter peeked inside. "Hatch and Grace are here. Okay to let them in?"

Let them in. The words hung in the air for a second. They were like birdsong, repeating over and over in my ears.

Should I let them in when I feel this bad? Let them in—let them see me—when I feel this stuck and broken?

"They really want to see you," Jupiter said as if he could read my mind.

"Okay," I said weakly. Jupiter smiled and pushed the door wide open. Grace shot into the room like a tiny rocket.

"Olive! I'm so sorry you're hurt!"

Hatch meandered in behind her, holding a stuffed unicorn with a purple ribbon around its neck.

"Hey," he said with a sheepish grin.

"Did you bring me a stuffy?" I asked.

"No," he said, and rolled his eyes. "This is from Ransom McCallister. I'm just the delivery guy."

For the first time in days, my heart fluttered with a little burst of joy. It was the most priceless and perfect unicorn I'd ever seen. I smiled when I tucked it up under my chin and gave it a squeeze.

"He won it in one of those claw games at Big John's," Hatch said. "It took him an hour—he wouldn't give up until he got the unicorn. He knew it was meant for you."

"When you're more mobile, we're all going there for pizza together," Grace said.

"Sounds fun," I admitted. And it happened again: the little flicker of happiness. Of hope.

The quiet stretched out between us, and Jupiter's words settled over my heart again: *Let them in.*

"So," I said, clearing my throat. "Did anybody feed Felix for me?"

Hatch nodded. "He's had plenty of fish sticks. He's just missing you."

"And I've got notes you can borrow and all the work you missed," said Grace, pulling up a chair to plop down beside me. "Everyone keeps asking about you. Even Mrs. Matheson. She can't find anybody to be the Bird of Joy. She's making Second Maddie do that, instead of the tree part."

I nodded and sighed. "At least I saved somebody else from their tree fate."

Hatch pulled a chair up beside Grace and plopped down. "Grace and I got two seats on the end of a row, so the three of us can all sit together."

"And then," Grace began. I steadied my heart, bracing for what would surely come next: her plan to leave and find the hummingbird.

But that's not what she said.

"I was thinking we can do our own version of the play at your house," she continued. "Dylan is all in. Even First Maddie said she'd be game. Some of the greatest actors in the world start on very small stages. That's the story you'll get to tell when you win your Academy Award someday— you started in your living room!"

Maybe it's because I was tired. Or surprised. Or because I'd had an ocean of emotions rolling through me over the past few days. But those little flickers of happiness melted into full-on joy. And thankfulness, too. They were more worried about me than they were about finding the hummingbird. They would give it up for me. And in that moment I knew: I would give it up for them, too. I realized then how fiercely I loved my friends. Yes, I was mad about my broken leg. Also, I wanted them to have every wonderful thing in the world.

Words ripped through me like fire. "If I go watch the play with y'all," I said, "you have to make me one big promise. If the feathers fall that night, and they will, and if the blue moon rises, and it will . . . you have to go find the bird. Go make your wish. I can't, but you have to do it. It's a BlumeBird Society promise: We keep looking for magic."

"Not without you," Grace said. "We look for magic together."

"The two of you can still go together," I said. "If you don't go make a wish that night, I will turn loose my unicorn on you." I held up my stuffy and pushed it into her face. "Both of you. Find the hummingbird and make your wishes, or you'll toot rainbows for the rest of your lives!"

They hesitated, glancing at each other.

"Please find it?" I said seriously. "And then tell me all about it."

Grace held out her pinkie. I locked it inside mine. "If there's magic," she said, "I'll find it."

"Same," said Hatch.

"And it'll find you two," I said, gulping my tears. "You two deserve it. I believe that with my whole heart."

Maybe that was the magic the hummingbird had wanted me to find all along: two new friends. Maybe they were the truest desire of my heart, my wish come true. And if so, that would have been more than enough. I thought the magic was over then.

Friend, it was just getting started.

CHAPTER 31
Homecoming

Jupiter and Mama drove me home on Thursday. Uncle Dash was waiting in the driveway with Dolly, my favorite chair, and he had the leg kicked out already, to keep my new leg-of-steel perfectly straight. He rolled me in to my bedroom, which Mama had cleaned for me.

If I had to find a bright side to breaking my leg it's gotta be this: Mama actually cleans my room for me.

"Felix is so excited to see you," said Uncle Dash. Before he'd even finished the sentence, Felix happy-crashed into my window.

My world was back to the way it was before I ever went to Macklemore. And that was fine! I didn't need anything besides my quirky birds and my books and my family. I wasn't missing out on anything.

That's what I tried to tell my heart.

But my heart kept disagreeing, just a little.

Mama and Jupiter helped me transfer to my bed. He held my leg steady while Mama helped me scoot. The sheets were comfy-cozy. They held me like a hug.

"Do you want to write a poem in your new journal?" Mama asked.

"Not tonight," I answered.

"Want to watch a movie with Hatch?" Jupiter asked. "Or invite Grace over? It's still early."

"I would rather just turn in for the night," I told them. I drifted off to sleep and wondered if Macklemore, and everything and every person I loved there, had only been a really awesome dream.

It was dark when the sound of my bedroom door opening woke me up.

"Are you a ghost?" I said, assuming my mama or dad would be the one to answer.

"No, ma'am," said a gravelly old voice that sent my heart soaring. "Just an old adventure seeker."

"Grandpa Goad!" I sat up and rubbed the crusty sleep out of my eyes. At first, all I could see was his silhouette in the door.

His small silhouette.

Grandpa Goad is four feet six inches tall.

He has a large rib cage, like me.

His arms are long, and his shin bones are bowed, just like mine. And if you know to look, and you lean in close, sometimes the whites of his eyes look barely blue.

Grandpa Goad has *osteogenesis imperfecta*, too, just the same as I do.

I reached my arms toward him as he walked into the room. He has a limp from arthritis in his right hip and knee, but he says he doesn't mind. He says it doesn't keep him from traveling the world or watching birds or loving his people, so who cares? If anything, he says, brittle bones slow him down. And he doesn't mind that, either. He likes taking the world in at his own pace.

"How's my girl?" he said, pulling a chair over beside my bed. He flicked on the lamp, and warm light flooded my bedroom.

"I'm good, I guess. I have a rod in both legs now. I'm like a superhero origin story." The truth, of course, is that I wasn't good at all. I'd set out to wish for magic in my bones. I'd ended up with another broken leg. Really, I was mad and frustrated and feeling super stuck.

"Honestly," I said, because my grandpa would want the real truth, "I'm a little down right now. I won't be down forever. But when it hurts, it's hard."

"It absolutely is," he said. And he leaned close to me. "And it's okay to say when it is. Sometimes life is gravy. Sometimes it's gravel. We get through all of it together. I've got rods in both legs, too, by the way."

"Go, team," I said weakly. He reached out to give me a fist bump, and I smiled.

"Did you find the warbler fleece?" I asked.

"I did," he said. The sound of his raspy old voice felt like a blanket for my soul. He cleared his throat. "My assistant had to leave early, so I thought I'd miss it. Had to climb the tree myself and wait for days. I'm not as young as I used to be. It's harder now, to sleep on branches. But I saw the bird and it was worth it. Did you know their wings reflect the last place they've been? And they can travel hundreds of miles a day. I saw beaches and mountains and redwood trees all on tiny wings. All in a tree."

I felt a sharp ache in my heart because his words reminded me of a line in the play. A line I wouldn't get to say.

"I have one more question for you," I said. "You probably know what it is. Were you the third person who found the hummingbird years ago? And if you were, why didn't you tell me about it?"

Grandpa's expression didn't change even though I'm sure he heard the hurt in my voice. I still couldn't believe he hadn't told me this one amazing, life-changing fact! Then I would have known from the start the bird was coming!

"Why didn't you tell me?" I asked again, my voice all gravelly with tears.

"I knew if the feathers ever fell when you could see

them—and I dearly hoped they would—you'd want to figure all that out by yourself. The discovery is part of what makes it all so magical. Maybe I should have told you. But hearing that legend, especially with friends, was such a joy to me when I was a kid. You're a smart girl, Olive. I knew you'd find your own way."

"You figured it all out, didn't you? You found the bird back in 1963?"

Grandpa held up his pointer finger like he was saying, "Wait a minute." I thought maybe he had to burp or something. But then he pulled off his glasses and pointed right beside his nose.

"Look closely," he said.

The tiniest little golden freckle had been hidden under his glasses all these years.

My voice felt very far away from me when I quoted the legend to him, "The bird will leave a golden kiss on the face of one who gets their wish."

He squeezed my hand. "Yes, I found the hummingbird."

"I knew it!" I yelled, for the first time in a week. Part of me was proud for figuring it out. But I was still frustrated, too. "I should have put it together even sooner. That's when you got obsessed with birds! Gosh, I can't wait to tell Grace. Spill the beans, sir. It's too late for me to find it, but this has been my whole life for two weeks. Well, almost my whole life. There's also been the play and Grace and Hatch and lots of stuff. Life stuff."

"The best stuff," Grandpa affirmed.

I sighed and smiled. "The very best stuff. But finding a magical bird is also big stuff! Tell me!"

He chuckled as he leaned back into the seat. "I was your age when I searched for it, along with a super smart, super competitive girl in my class named Elizabeth."

"Hold up," I said, reaching to take a sip of my water. "Like, Grandma Elizabeth?"

"Eventually," he said. "But obviously I didn't marry her when I was twelve. I didn't even have a crush on her. If anything, I was mad that she was searching for the hummingbird, too. Because she was so good at everything. I knew she'd probably find it first."

"I get that," I said. "That's how I felt when I knew Hatch was looking for it, too."

"Long story shorter," said Grandpa Goad, "we came upon the bird at the same time. It fluttered toward me, and all I could see was light. Light, and that little gold wish-bird hovering right in front of my face. And then the words came rising up inside me and they were nothing— absolutely nothing—like I expected: *Fame can't compare to the friend who walks beside you.*"

"You were going to wish to be famous?" I asked.

"Mm-hmm," he admitted. "A famous explorer. I wanted to see the world so badly. And I wanted to be known for it. But I changed and wished for a friend, instead. What's weird is that, when the words came rising up inside my soul, I realized how much I cared for Elizabeth. She was so smart and funny and fun to be around. I'd started liking her even more, the longer we searched for that little thing. We were best friends until the day we got married. And then, we became even better friends than best. A true friend is better than any adventure."

I pulled my unicorn close to my chest and hugged it tight. There was something I needed to say. Something I needed to get out of my heart. Birthday rules no longer applied, since I couldn't go looking for the bird, anyway.

"Can I be super brutally honest with you?" I asked. "I was going to wish for my bones to be normal."

He nodded.

"You're not disappointed?" I asked.

"Why would I be?"

"Because I love you exactly the way you are," I said, wiping a tear off my face. "And I know I should be happy the way I am. I am happy. Do you think God's mad at me for wanting anything else? Do you think he's teaching me a lesson?"

"No, no, no," Grandpa said, reaching over to wipe the tears off my face. "God's not like that, Olive. God loves you. If anybody ever tells you any different, they don't know God at all."

"Did you ever wish you didn't have it, though—the bone stuff? I know that's not what you were going to wish from the hummingbird. But did you ever think it?"

"Oh sure," he said, like it was no big deal. "Probably lots of times. Sometimes I don't care. It's my disability, it's one part of me, who cares? And other days, I have to think about it a lot. Or it hurts a lot. Or it just gets annoying. It's nothing to be ashamed of, trying to wish away the painful parts. I think everybody does it. Doesn't mean you don't like yourself as you are, or you're not grateful for your life."

"I'd started imagining my life without candy bones," I said. "Really believing it could happen. And I liked it."

"What did you see that you liked?"

"I saw myself on a stage," I said, blushing. "Not at school, but a big stage somewhere. Maybe on Broadway with Dylan. I saw myself writing screenplays. Maybe getting married someday when I'm old. Like, old, old."

"Olive," he said, propping his leg on his knee. "You can still do all that. Let me tell you a secret that changed my life—that has nothing to do with a wish-bird—there is *this much* you can't do."

Grandpa drew a teeny-tiny circle in the air.

"But there is this much," he said, "that you can do."

He stretched his arms out wide.

"Here's what's going to happen, kiddo: As you get

older, your world will get bigger. And bigger. And you'll realize, there's way more that you can do than you can't do. It just takes time for us to see it. Birds are born with wings. The rest of us have to find our wings as we go. And you will, Olive Miracle. You'll find them, and you'll fly."

CHAPTER 32

Where Fear and Wonder Both Collide

May first arrived two days later, right on schedule. Grace, who came over every afternoon while I did physical therapy, thought it would probably rain.

"Then the blue moon won't be visible," she said as she concentrated on picking off her green nail polish. She does that when she's anxious. "And the hummingbird won't come, but that's okay. We'll just watch the play together."

I couldn't tell if puzzling that thought out made her happy or sad or a little bit of both.

"It's coming," I said, "so do not forget your promise. You and Hatch have to go to the falls and find it."

There was no rain on May first. The sky was a soft,

springtime blue all through the day and afternoon. Hatch knocked on my door just as the day turned into gauzy-twilight.

He carried a backpack and a flashlight.

"Good luck," I told him. And I really meant it, despite my sadness.

"You're still going to the play, right?" Hatch asked. "You'll be there after I find the bird?"

"Yep," I said. "I'll be in the front row with Miss Snow and Uncle Dash. Whole family is going. I can't wait to hear your story. You will find it."

Hatch chewed on his bottom lip and looked down at his shoes. "I know I will. I'm sorry you can't come, too."

"No big deal," I said. This was a lie and we both knew it. This was the biggest deal of all. "Could you toss me that notebook on my desk before you leave?"

Hatch bounced into my room, retrieved the journal, and passed it to me. "Thank you," he said. "For helping me find it. I'll find you as soon as it's over."

I nodded and listened for the familiar sound of the screen door slapping shut. Felix squawked outside. One friend had left to find the bird.

I opened the book Mr. Watson, Miss Snow, and Ms. Pigeon had given me, a book they said was for my own poetry. Because I finally knew what I wanted to write. On an empty page, I pressed my pen to paper and poured out my heart:

Things that Break Easy:
Jelly Jars
and Tender Hearts
the bones beneath my skin.

Banjo strings
and window glass
(but sunlight still gets in).

Promises and cocoons do, too.
(The Butterfly still pushes through.)
The dark night breaks,
revealing day.

Some breaks remain,
some mend and heal,
some help us fly away.

And some help us find our way, I realized.
This journey wasn't ending the way I'd hoped. But it was
ending with two friends I never saw coming. And that was
a pretty big miracle, too.

"I'm wearing the sparkly Macklemore jacket," I said
to Mama when she walked in the room to help me get
dressed. "It's exhausting, trying not to shine."

"That's my girl," she said with a wink.

My whole family, even Grandpa Goad, crowded into the van with me. Uncle Dash had modified the family van to actually have a wheelchair lift, which was way easier than transferring back and forth with a broken leg. Main Street was thick with crowds, people holding flashlights and binoculars. String lights dotted the trees, and waiters pushed pie carts along the sidewalks.

"Happy May Day!" Pastor Mitra was shouting to passing cars from in front of the church. She was handing out red balloons for free. "Good luck finding the hummingbird!"

Grandpa Goad looped an arm around my shoulders. "Don't forget," he said. "There's a whole big world out there for you."

"I won't forget," I promised him.

When the van circled into the Macklemore parking lot, I saw Grace Cho standing on the sidewalk. She had a backpack over her shoulders, too. She was going for the bird just like she promised.

We did our secret handshake. Then she leaned over and gave me a gentle hug.

"Don't make this weird and sad," I told her. "Just go get it. I can't wait to hear the story!"

"And be careful out there," Mama said from behind me. "I don't know about all these kids running through the woods."

"Oh, it's fine," said Coach Malone. "The town is

treating it like Halloween. Cops all over the woods to make sure kids are safe. Earlier the Ragged Apple Cafe cart was even selling little golden, fake-freckle tattoos you can put on your face. Pretend the hummingbird granted your wish."

"One of you won't have to pretend," I said to Grace.

"BlumeBirds forever," she told me. And then she spun around and scampered off into the woods. I watched until the light of her flashlight was as tiny as a firefly-tail. Just like that, my friends were off to find the hummingbird. I pressed my hand over my broken heart and said a little prayer that this would be the most magical night of their lives. I was genuinely hopeful for them both.

Which is why I didn't pay much attention to how hard the trees were trembling.

Or how loudly the birds were singing.

Change was on the wind.

We weren't even to the auditorium entrance when Mrs. Matheson came running toward me. "Thank goodness you're here, Olive! Thank goodness! I need you in the play! Any chance that can happen?"

"Alas," I said, waving my hands around my kicked-out leg, "this bird can't fly tonight."

"I don't need you to be a bird," she said, her voice hovering on the edge of a frantic scream. "I need you to be Emily."

My mouth fell open. "Do what?"

"First Maddie has mono!" She said this as if it was an actual national emergency. "Nobody else knows the part! I hoped the other Maddies might know the lines. But shocker, they do not."

She rolled her eyes and growled a little. "Grace Cho built a ramp onto the main stage last week, so you can get up there, if it's okay with your parents." Finally, she looked up at Mama and Jupiter. "Emily's onstage the whole time. She wouldn't have to move. Just say the part."

Mama leaned down. "Olive, if you want to do the part, Jupiter or I could push you up there. As long as you're not zooming around, I think it's fine. You decide."

"Seriously?" I looked up at her. "I thought you would never let me do anything ever, ever again, including going back to Macklemore. I wasn't careful. I broke my leg!"

"You were very careful," said Jupiter. "You always are. It's biology and it stinks sometimes. Want to do the play? It's your choice."

"If you don't do it, I'm canceling," said Mrs. Matheson. "There's no way around it."

I glanced over at Grandpa Goad, who smiled at me. "A whole big world," he said softly. He was so right: There's a whole big world for me, and maybe it starts right here.

Being Emily Dickinson in the school play had been my dream for weeks now. But I hadn't imagined being Emily like this: broken, in my chair with my leg kicked out, very obviously not sporting a golden freckle on my face courtesy of the hummingbird. I didn't want people to see me as weak. They definitely would, if I went up there like this.

"Hey." Grandpa Goad leaned down. "Don't do it if you don't wanna. But don't skip it just because you're afraid. Why not try?"

A new and shimmering kind of joy was already stretching its wings inside me. I pressed my hands against my chest so I could feel my heart, so I could remember this moment was real.

"Okay," I said, my voice full of a confidence I didn't even recognize. "I'll do it. I'll be Emily."

Mrs. Matheson let out a very dramatic gasp-sigh and ran back in the auditorium.

"Are you okay with not moving around much?" Mama asked, pushing me inside.

"Fine with it," I said, smiling up at her. "I've got my voice. That's all I need."

Dylan helped me fasten the most beautiful wings I'd ever seen to the back of my wheelchair.

"Grace made them today," he said. "Just in case First Maddie didn't show up. These are a little bit personalized."

From far away, the wings looked gauzy-white with

squiggle patterns. But up close, those patterns were very detailed: butterflies with daggers and books, tiny hearts, and little pieces of pizza.

"Want any stage makeup?" Dylan asked as he finished donning his bird gear. "Emily's look is subtle, but we could do something special if you want—"

"Glitter?" I asked. "Just a little?"

"Always glitter," he said. He painted a subtle, starry sheen of golden sparkles on my cheekbones, then his. The theater became a chorus of voices as people took their seats. Melba was tuning her banjo. Ransom tested the spotlight.

"It's okay to be nervous," Dylan said in a whisper. "When you're nervous about something, that means it matters. That's a good thing."

"Thank you," I whispered back. My voice was a little shaky.

I heard a last rumble from the crowd before the room went silent. The lights blinked backstage.

"Here we go," Dylan said, taking my hands in his. He squeezed them very gently. "I got your back up there, Emily. If you forget your lines, or need anything, I'm your bird. Let me know."

I nodded. I was too excited to actually even speak. Jupiter pushed me from the backstage area up the new ramp Grace had constructed that day. From there, he pushed me out to center stage.

"Good luck, my shining star," he whispered before he darted backstage again.

The curtain rose. My breath caught.

Even though the room was dark, I could see the outlines of so many people. The room was full. And I'd never felt more vulnerable in my life. My big plan had been to walk out here, to be in a play like a normal person.

Whatever *normal* meant.

Normal is overrated, is what Grandpa Goad says. In that moment, I understood what he meant. Because there was nowhere else I wanted to be besides exactly where I was.

"Ready?" Mrs. Matheson whispered from the edge of the stage. "When the light shines on you, go."

I took a deep breath to steady my soul. I closed my eyes as Olive.

Then the spotlight flickered on.

And I opened my eyes center stage, alone in the light, as Emily Dickinson.

On the first line, my nerves made my words rattle, just a little. But I steadied my breathing, like Jupiter had taught me, and eased into the scene. The longer I talked, the more I forgot about everybody else in the room. Everybody except my birds.

Dylan had people actually sniffling in the audience as the Bird of Sorrow. Madeline, who was just thrilled to be upgraded from a tree, was definitely in character for the

Bird of Joy. Sets changed around me. Lights dimmed, then shone again.

Just before the final act, Dylan slipped up behind me and stuck the finale wings on the back of my wheelchair. They were enormous, tip-to-tip, glittery gold on the edges. I angled my chair just barely, in just the way I knew they would catch the light and make people gasp. I wanted to show off what Grace had done.

And I wanted to show what I could do. My moment had come, and it was nothing like I expected. It was better.

"Hope," I said out into the darkness, out into the ears of every person listening. "Is the thing with feathers that perches in the soul. Sometimes when you find your words, you find your wings."

The lights dimmed a final time. The room fell so quiet I could hear my breaths.

I wondered: Had I done okay? Had I forgotten anything? Had Hatch or Grace found the hummingbird?!

The lights came on for the curtain call, and the rest of the Macklemore players gathered all around me. The applause was louder than a river rushing. It was a roar of its own, and I knew I would never experience anything else like it.

On either side of me, my friends took a deep bow. I couldn't do that, but I nodded my head, then looked up—up to where my parents, uncle, and grandpa were watching me, cheering. Up to the balcony, where people applauded and waved. And higher up than that, to the tip-top of the auditorium where pink flowers bloomed wild on the roof.

"Well?" asked Dylan. "What'd you think?"

"I was terrified," I said. "And I loved it."

And then, it happened.

A feeling like fire roared up through my bones, my heart, my vocal cords. Words formed on my tongue as proud and strong as any truth I'd ever spoken.

"My bones are fragile," I said. "But I am not."

"What?" said Dylan. His voice sounded muffled, and far away. The room faded, darkening all around me, all except for Ransom's spotlight. Suddenly, it was as if everybody had disappeared from Foster Auditorium except me. The noise lowered to a gentle hum. And the spotlight shrank to a tiny pinpoint far away from me. Shiny as a fallen star, smaller than a baby's fist.

In the light, I could barely make out the blur of tiny, fluttering wings.

The hummingbird was there. And it had come for me.

CHAPTER 33

The Magical What-Ifs

What if fairy tales are all
half-truths?
What if there's room for every princess to dance?
What if the girl in the ball gown
is rotten at the core,
but the witch in the woods,
leads a most enchanted life?

What if
the poisoned apple is safe once it's baked in a pie?
What if the story you think you know
doesn't end the way you think it does?

Living in the woods has taught me there are different kinds of darkness. There's a dark room, for example,

where the light goes out but you still feel hemmed in and safe. And then there's a dark forest, when the absence of light makes it all seem so much bigger.

That's how I felt in the auditorium with the bird, like I was part of a hidden world so much bigger, with so much more in it, than I'd ever realized. The hummingbird had come to the place where fear and wonder both collided for *me*. Maybe everybody's fearful place is different. And maybe wherever we're afraid, wonder still finds us. I know it found me. The blue moon shone through the tall windows in the auditorium.

And the bird fluttered closer, tiny but blinding in its radiant light.
I ran through the legend in my mind.
Shout those words into the dark!
Fragile, fragile, fragile.
I shook my head,
nope. Those were not my missing words.
That was only a small part
of the truth of me.
"My bones are fragile," I said aloud,
looking into the blinding golden light of a small creature.
A strong creature.
"But I am not."

The bird hummed, moving faster, darting up the stage, pausing in front of my face.

I could make out two dark eyes,
and the teal-gold plumage on its back and tail feather,
that's how close magic came to me!
Glitter fell from the edges of its wings like sifted
sugar.
I said my missing words one more time, just because I
could:

"My bones are fragile, but
I am not."

The bird edged closer to my face.
It was time to make my wish.
And yet . . .
All I could think about was Grandpa Goad, and what
he said
about experiences I would have someday in
this exact body I'm in:
the one with big scars (from surgeries)
and also small ones
(from trying to shave my legs, awkward),
In this body with twists,
that looks different from all the Maddies,
this body that's mine.

I felt some really wonderful things inside of it tonight.
I've already felt so much.

I remembered
long drives with Jupiter with the wind in our hair
and reading books with my mama and
fishing trips with Uncle Dash.

I remembered making wings
with Grace Cho backstage and laughing
with Hatch Malone
and the time
Ransom McCallister
locked a shark-tooth necklace around my neck.

I could wish away the hurting part. For today. But something would probably hurt again in the future. I don't think anybody gets to walk through the world without getting broken somehow. My bones would always heal.

Then I pictured Hatch Malone, out in the woods calling for his lost dog, waiting for his little best friend to come home again.

Broken bones eventually heal. I'm not sure if broken hearts ever do.

"My bones are fragile," I mumbled to myself. "But I am not."

I reached toward the hummingbird, and it flittered toward me, touching the tip of my nose with its gold sparkly beak.

I closed my eyes.

And I made my wish.

CHAPTER 34
Two Wishes

"Olive! Olive Martin!"

Everything in my imagination spiraled back to normal. I was onstage at Macklemore Middle School again. Emily's wings were still around my shoulders. The audience was on their feet, applauding, because they'd loved the play. They gave us a standing ovation!

I was still in my wheelchair. I was still just me. Like I'd always been.

But different.

"Did it work?" I asked.

"Did what work?" asked Dylan, leaning down so he could hear me. "Nice touch, by the way! Love the little golden freckle! Way to celebrate the hummingbird!"

All I could do was blink. He didn't even think it was real!

"I need to find Hatch," I said.

Dylan rolled me gently backstage and pulled my wings away. Jupiter was there waiting for me, holding a bundle of tulips. Mama, Uncle Dash, and Grandpa Goad all reached down to hug me. I'd made them proud, and that was a great feeling. But I had to find my friends!

"I need to find Hatch," I said to Jupiter. "And Grace. I need to know if they found the—"

"Olive!" Grace shouted, running down the aisle. "You were amazing!"

She had no golden freckle. And she didn't look like she'd been in the woods very long.

"Wait, why are you here?!" I asked. "You didn't go look for the bird?"

"I thought about it," she said, not looking the least bit sad or perplexed. "But on the way, Luther Frye asked me if I'd build one of my weird doghouses for Gustav. And you know what that means? I got a client. Which means Nester Tuberose will mentor me. I realized I don't really have to wish for a thriving doghouse empire. I'll just make it happen."

Grace looked truly happy, excited even. So I wasn't let down by that. The hummingbird had shown her something, too, just in a different way.

"That's great!" I said.

"I know!" she shouted.

"Let's continue this outside," said Jupiter. "It's getting a little crowded back here."

Jupiter pushed me toward the van while I glanced all

around for Hatch. The trees were trembling. The full springtime moon shone down all around us. But my step-brother still hadn't shown up. "Hold on just a sec," Grace said suddenly, leaning down close to my face as Jupiter pushed me along. "Is that a—"

"OLIVE!" Hatch Malone shouted my name. Grace and I turned our heads in time to see Hatch run out of the woods. Jupiter had paused to talk to another parent at this point, and I was grateful. Grace was in my face, looking at my new freckle. Hatch was skidding to a stop in front of my chair. He leaned down, breathless, and looked me in the eye.

"I . . . found . . . the . . . bird."

On the tip of his nose was a golden dot, like a tiny drop of paint. A permanent wishing freckle. "I'm so glad," I told him. "That's what I wanted. I wanted you to find it!"

"I wished for you," he said.

I pulled back quickly and narrowed my eyes. "What?!"

"I wished for you to get the lead in the play. To remember every line and love every second and see what you're capable of. Because you wanted the play so much."

"Hatch!" I yelped. I pointed to the golden freckle on my nose. "*I* saw the hummingbird. And I wished for you. I wished for . . ."

A sudden high-pitched, happy bark echoed through the woods. We turned our heads at the same time to see a fuzzy white dog pouncing down the path.

And directly into Hatch Malone's arms.

Biscuit was home, her little black nose covered in golden freckles.

They held each other for the longest time. Hatch barely moved. He didn't even mess with his hoodie sleeves. He wasn't afraid. He was still. He was smiling. And big teardrops were rolling down his face, sinking into her fur.

"Olive," he said, "meet Biscuit."

The dog climbed gently onto my lap, balancing on my good leg. Biscuit was so little. She wouldn't hurt me. She tucked in softly against me, like she was so happy to finally be home.

As the blue moon glittered on the surface of the river, the town of Wildwood gathered at the cafe for a dance. Melba played her banjo. Her sister, Jessie, jammed on a keyboard. Somebody brought a fiddle. Pretty much everybody danced, including Luther Frye. I watched Gustav's tail keep rhythm as the two of them shuffled around together.

Uncle Dash and Miss Snow couldn't keep their eyes off each other. Biscuit settled in Hatch's lap, listening to his stories about the days she'd missed.

Grace and I sat at a table, watching all the fun, sharing a basket of apple fritters. That's when I felt a tap on my shoulder.

"Can I get an autograph?" asked Ransom McCallister.

I pulled the purple pen from behind my ear. "You may, sir!"

"Sign my hand," he said. "I want to say I got your autograph before you became super famous. I was going to ask to sign your cast, but you don't have one."

"It's a brace," I said. "There's a rod against the bone. Keeps it steady. It's like a cast on the inside. Wanna sign my hand, too?"

He laughed and said, "Sure."

He leaned down low and took my hand in his. The ink tickled when he scribbled.

"Wait a sec!" I said, noticing a golden freckle on his cheek. "Did you see the bird?"

His eyes flicked up to meet mine. "This? It's one of those fake tattoos. But if I had, that's what I would have asked it." He glanced back down at my hand. And so did I. He hadn't written his name. He'd written three words:

Dance with me?

My heart did a somersault, flip-flop, jumping-jack kaboom.

"I wish," I said, smiling up at him. "I can't have fun on the dance floor right now. But if I could, I'd dance with you."

"What if I get to twirl you just one time," he said, "that way I can say I got the first dance?"

I glanced at Grace, who was smiling and blushing.

Hatch rolled his eyes beside her and fed a fritter to Biscuit.

"Okay," I said. "Let's try this. Let's twirl."

There on the edge of the peaceful-wild river,
under the light of a bright May moon,
Ransom McCallister held out his hand for mine.
I took it and

gently,
so gently,
He twirled me
once,
then twice,
just enough to say:
We danced.

I felt constellations
dancing with Ransom.
I felt constellations with his hand in mine:

Friend, here's what I know:
I am fragile.

And I'm also:
fearless,
funny,
smart,

vivacious,
lucky, and loved, with a
heart like a lion.

That night, that moment, felt like my birthday and a
holiday
wrapped up inside a night sky. But it was a normal day.
And it was normal feelings inside my body.

It's my body feeling all of this. Exactly as it is.
My body was capable of all this
magic.

Listen,
if God or the hummingbird ever decided to knit my
bones
perfect someday, I probably wouldn't complain.
But I also like my body
and my life exactly as it is.

My body is
made of stardust and lace and dreams and constellations.
My bones are fragile. But I am not.

AUTHOR'S NOTE

Every story challenges me in a different way. But this one turned my heart inside out. Because this is the first time I've written about a character who shares my disability.

Like Olive Martin, the protagonist of *Hummingbird*, I was born with a brittle bone disease called *osteogenesis imperfecta* (OI). OI means my bones break very easily. Like Olive, I used a wheelchair or walker throughout middle and elementary school. In most childhood photos, I'm wearing a cast. And like Olive, the word *fragile* is one I've heard used to describe myself—and my body—for as long as I can remember.

Here's the thing, though: At first, Olive's OI wasn't really a part of her story. I knew she had OI, like me. But it was almost an afterthought. I focused on the magic in her world, the friendships, and the adventure she was having . . . but there was something about her heart I couldn't quite figure out. So I searched deeper into mine.

During middle school, my self-esteem got extra wobbly because of how I felt inside my body. I think this is when I first realized how different my body looked from my friends' bodies. They grew taller, but I stayed extra short. Their legs were straight, while mine were bowed and scarred from surgeries. I didn't like being different. Sometimes, I hated being fragile.

I'm fully aware shaky self-esteem is not, and maybe has never been, an obstacle for every reader who also has OI. I believe a person's experience with disability is as unique as that individual's heart or fingerprints.

That's why my initial instinct was to write about a girl who'd fully accepted her OI. But that's not real for me. There are days I don't think much about my bones. And there are days I feel like my disability informs everything I do and every decision I make. Olive still has magic and friendship and adventure in her world. She also has a disability she thinks about, *has* to think about, sometimes a lot. And when her what-ifs turned into a wish most people wouldn't understand . . . her heart made more sense to me.

Treatment for *osteogensis imperfecta* is always progressing. When I was treated for fractures as a kid in the '80s, rods were installed against my femur bones (and later removed) to help fractures heal. Because I wanted to write from the truest place I knew, Olive's fracture is treated the same way. However, a more standard procedure now involves having a rod drilled directly through the center of the bone. (I have one of those now, too, and it's a pretty great upgrade!) There are also incredible new medications for OI now. While there's still no cure, science is always finding ways to make the quality of life even better for those of us who have brittle bones. If you'd like to learn more about OI, check out some of the great resources on www.oif.org.

After reading this story, I know readers might ask, "Would you wish your OI away if you could?"

The answer is complicated.

Sometimes, it's maybe.

Maybe yes when I'm in pain.

Yes when I feel left out.

But overall? Probably not. Because I've realized life is big and blazing bright, full of a thousand experiences. Some of them are hard—like broken bones and broken hearts and sad goodbyes—but some are amazing. All the love parts are so amazing.

I think we all have fragile places. If there's anything that birds—even teeny, little hummingbirds—can teach us, it's that fragile creatures still get to fly. It's true for Olive, for you, and for me. We're all made of stardust. Olive reminded me of that as I wrote her story, and I'm so thankful.

ACKNOWLEDGMENTS

I would like to extend baskets and bouquets of joy-ka-booms, pie sticks, and my heart-deep gratitude to the following people:

* **My incredible agent, Suzie Townsend.** She loved Olive's story from the first idea-sparks. I can't believe we get to work together. I'm also grateful to Joanna Volpe, Dani Segelbaum, Miranda Stinson, Veronica Grijalva, Victoria Hendersen, Pouya Shahbaziaian, Katherine Curtis—and the rest of the New Leaf squad—for helping my stories fly.

* **Mallory Kass, my editor–soul mate.** She walked through the forest of deep-hard questions with me for this book, always holding a flashlight steady on the path ahead. Her storytelling savvy has made me a better writer. Her friendship means the world to me.

* **My kind and talented friends at Scholastic.** From the beginning, they've been so supportive of this story,

of every story, and of me. Their talent is boundless. Thank you Ellie Berger, Lori Benton, David Levithan, Emily Heddleson, Lizette Serrano, Lauren Donovan, Paul Gagne, Janell Harris, Rachel Feld, Chris Stengel, Jody Corbett, and the superstar sales team who made me feel like family from the way-back beginning. If I'd found a wish-bird as a kid, I would have asked it to make me a Scholastic author.

* **Tracy van Straaten, brilliant publicity wizard.** Thanks for your expert advice before Olive flew.

* **John Watson, leader of the third-(not sixth)-grade adventurers.** I've thanked some of my favorite teachers in other books, but I feel like I should give more lines here to the real Mr. John Watson. Every day, after lunch, he dimmed the classroom lights and read novels aloud. He told us to listen, or rest, or both—just to enjoy the story. Books have always been a source of joy for me. But that's when I realized how restful they could be, too. Mr Watson was also the first teacher who told me I could be a writer someday. And have I told you about the time Mr. Watson carried me on, and off, the school bus (and loaded my wheelchair) so I could go on a field trip while my parents were working? He's an exceptional human. And on that note:

* **Nancy Smith.** Olive and I both had aides at school who helped us out through the day. Olive and Ms. Pigeon don't really click. But Nancy Smith was a

school aide who helped me—she was (and is!) funny, warm, hilarious, and a pro at helping me feel independent even as she was helping me navigate the world. I'm grateful for her light.

* **Teachers and librarians.** My heart feels heavy—in an amazing way (like, a-bag-of-candy-at-Halloween way)—when I think of teachers and librarians who've championed my stories over the years. *Hummingbird* was largely written during 2020, when the world felt fractured and sideways. School visits became virtual. Students had to distance and wear their superhero masks. What never changed, even in all that weirdness, were teachers and librarians: steady, constant, always giving young readers a safe space to be their most authentic selves. You are the magic-makers. It's an honor to be a tiny part of your classrooms.

* **Booksellers.** My candy-bag heart is also full of love for booksellers who've created community hubs and hope spots when we need both more than ever. Thanks for believing my books deserve a spot on your shelves, and thanks for sharing them with your young readers.

* **My imaginary campfire guests.** Many artists inspired and helped shape this story through their beautiful work including: Emily Dickinson, Dolly Parton, the Avett Brothers, Emmylou Harris, Silas House, Brandi Carlile, Gillian Welch, Kacey Musgraves, Jason

Isbell, Rick Bragg, Jeff Zentner, Judy Blume, and Tyler Childers. I wish I could hang out with all of them, all together, at an apple-cider bonfire in my backyard and say thank you. (I think Emily's ghost would be the life of the party.)

* **And, finally, I can't end this without thanking my family.** My parents learned about OI when there was no internet to google info. There was no small-town support group. No social media for crowdsourcing. And yet, even though I had a childhood with a bunch of broken bones, they also made my childhood amazing: full of willow-tree picnics and books and road trips with a wheelchair rattling in the trunk. My parents had an uncanny way of making me feel loved and brave. They still do. Jim and Elaine Lloyd, you're my heroes, now and always. Chase and Bridgett are my best friends, in addition to being my siblings. I'm grateful for the family they've added to our orbit.

* **Justin Long is the love story I thought was too good to be true.** He stole my heart and never even flinched when I told him about my disability. "I'm strong," he assured me once, when I was worried about all the what-ifs. "I can carry you if you ever want me to." He has carried me—in his arms, and his heart—many times since then. I can't believe we get to do life together.

Thank you, reader, for giving your imagination to this story.

Thank you, God, for a life full of so much magic, so much wonder, and so much hope. Hummingbird hope. The kind that's wild and fluttery, and fits perfect when it perches in my soul.